THE
GEMDARK
DYNASTY

COUNTERPART

ELLA
PYNE

COUNTERPART

THE GEMDARK DYNASTY
BOOK ONE

ELLA PYNE

CHAPTER 1

When Leda Locarno was ten years old she realised she was a person who things *happened* to.

Her foster mother had sent her out to pick berries for breakfast. She'd gone without complaint.

Her sister had shouted that she'd brought back the wrong kind. Leda had taken the vicious kick to her stomach with a repressed grunt.

Her foster father had laughed, knocked her basket of berries to the floor and sent her to her room. Leda had backed out of the kitchen, her head bowed.

When the door to her bedroom closed, Leda lowered herself shakily on to her bed and realised that she'd said nothing, not one word, the whole day. There she sat, eyes on the floor, as lifeless then as she would be when the time came for her ceremony.

That was the turning point, the moment that clarity hit her.

Leda's hands had curled into fists. She couldn't live the rest of her short life that way. She was humiliated, she was afraid, and she was so incredibly lonely.

No more.

The next morning was the first time she ever stole money. Leda remembered it as clear as day, even a decade later, watching the gold coin fall out of her foster father's pocket, the clink of it hitting the floor, the feel of it beneath her foot as she kicked it under the table to collect later. Her young mind had been certain of her reasoning. If she didn't escape she would die, and so she would need somewhere to escape to. If Leda wanted to evade her real father and mother and find somewhere to live out her life in anonymity and freedom, she'd better start pilfering coins young.

The gods knew she'd never be able to earn them herself.

Her foot slipped against stone and twenty-year-old Leda barely stifled a squeak, clenching her leg muscles to keep from falling down the chimney. She was about halfway up, her back pressed to one side, her feet jammed against the other. Her right leg shook alarmingly and she closed her eyes, bracing her hands on the wall either side of her and praying that her leg wouldn't choose now of all times to fail her.

She had hand- and footholds below that she could return to, ones that she'd painstakingly carved into the brick over the past few years, but time was running out. The older Leda got, the more likely it became that she and her sister Azaria would be chosen for their ceremony, and her life would end. Her progress at carving holds into the inside of the chimney had been excruciatingly slow over the past couple of years. This year, she had to finish it. There was still five feet to get done before she'd be able to lift herself out of the top and on to the palace roof.

When Leda had first discovered the chimney, years ago, she'd tried to climb straight to the top. She'd fallen, the space too large and her body too weak to hoist herself up all the way without holds. Her tailbone had been so badly bruised she hadn't been able to walk for a week.

With a sigh, Leda manoeuvred herself into position to climb back down, lingering out of sight of the room below as she listened for signs that anyone was there.

All was quiet.

Leda carefully avoided the grate as she dropped to the floor, and dusted off her hands. The armoury stood empty and cool before her.

Her father, the King, kept every fireplace in the palace burning all year round, even in the swelteringly hot summer, to ward off evil spirits. Leda had discovered years ago that there were two men in the palace stubborn enough to ignore that rule. Milos, the armourer, and his brother, Levi, the royal librarian. They were both old and cantankerous enough to refuse to have their fires burning lest their sleep be affected by the heat.

Leda was not allowed anywhere near the library, but the armoury? Oh, she came here all the time—the one perk of being the Counterpart of a princess obsessed with weaponry.

Leda tried vainly to shake the soot from her long, billowing skirts and moved further into the room. An array of fastidiously shined swords lined the wall, and she paused to observe them.

A shrill whistling next to Leda's right ear was followed by a clatter as the projectile hit the wall next to the window, a foot from her head. Leda dove in the opposite direction with such force that she slammed both palms on to the stone floor.

"Did you just shoot an arrow at me?"

Leda's half-sister, Azaria, frowned at her from the doorway, bow still slightly raised. "I called your name. You weren't listening."

3

"No shooting inside!" The hulking form of the armourer, Milos, hurried into the room, holding a half-eaten baguette in one hand. He pointed it accusingly at them before realising who he was talking to.

He executed a short bow. "Princess," he grumbled at Azaria.

Azaria did not feel the need to apologise to either of them, instead striding across the room and digging her arrow out of the wall.

Azaria was generally thought to be mesmerisingly beautiful, the most radiant princess anyone in court had ever seen. If their sycophantic compliments were to be believed, she was blessed by the gods themselves.

She had thick dark hair and startlingly pale blue eyes set in a face that looked as though it had been dreamed up by the court painter. There was something about her, though, a frostiness in her demeanour, that made people hold themselves back from her, if only for a second.

Azaria laid her bow and arrows down on Milos's desk. "Put these away.'"

Milos picked up the quiver with a long-suffering sigh and shoved the bow at Leda. "Hang this on the hook over there. It's labelled 'bow'."

Azaria scoffed as Leda turned towards the wall. "How is that supposed to help her? She can't read."

Leda's step faltered as she headed for the label that read 'bow'. She could slap herself for being so stupid.

Her sister was theoretically correct, she was not permitted to know how to read or write as a Counterpart. That hadn't prevented their foster mother, Fayne, from teaching her in secret.

Milos grunted in acknowledgement but had stopped paying attention to either of them. His enormous head, slick with sweat, was tilted slightly as he frowned at the surface of the table by the window. On it lay the half-eaten slab of bread he'd abandoned.

A few minutes earlier a fat silver coin had glistened on the desk, and now it was gone. He looked at Azaria with a blend of suspicion and fear that had him saying nothing.

Leda forced her fingers to release from around her skirt, the silver burning a moral hole through her pocket. She swallowed, battling to keep her face straight. The guilt ate her alive sometimes.

It didn't matter, Milos wasn't even looking at her. He didn't suspect.

No one ever really noticed her.

Leda was the definition of nondescript, with brown hair curling halfway down her back, and pale skin that teetered on the verge of sallow due to all the time she spent indoors. She had a face full of features that were pleasant in her view, but completely unmemorable. The fact that she wore brown wool dresses that looked like they had been cut from the same fabric as the hessian sacks of chainmail in the corner did her no favours either. Most of the time, people's gazes passed through her as though she were a ghost.

Leda staggered to the side, pulled roughly from her thoughts by a blow to her right leg. She whirled around with an incredulous expression. Azaria was watching her thigh with suspicion, the hand she'd used to hit it still outstretched.

"You're leaning to one side," Azaria said crisply. "You need to exercise it, or it will never recover its strength. You should take more walks."

Leda had long ago stopped marvelling at the gall of her sister, but now and again it was hard to bite her tongue.

"I'll take that under advisement." She shook out her leg, and pain shot up her spine like lightning. Fantastic.

"Where have you been, anyway?" Leda asked. She'd lost Azaria as soon as they'd arrived at the palace that morning.

"I went to see the royal tutor," Azaria said. "I solved a complex equation he shared with me last summer. He said it took him months to complete but I had it finished in a week. I wanted to discuss the process I used."

How thrilling that must have been for him.

Leda was glad that Azaria wasn't looking at her as she mentioned the royal tutor, a brilliant young man hailed through all of the Five Kingdoms as one of their foremost scholars. From the glimpses Leda had managed to get of him over the past couple of years he was unfairly handsome for someone so intellectually gifted.

She'd never spoken to him, she wasn't allowed.

Azaria, thankfully, hadn't noticed Leda disappearing into her own thoughts.

"Our trunks have arrived from Leatherfell. Come with me to fetch them."

Azaria would do none of the heavy lifting, of course, but she would want to order everybody around. Dutifully, Leda followed her out of the armoury, down five staircases and through the imposing entrance hall out on to the steps.

The hulking, glittering form of the palace cast a shadow over the squat little city at their feet.

The palace was a spectacular, audacious masterpiece of white marble, with elaborate sloped golden roofs. Thousands of stained-glass windows glittered as the sun began to set. It was almost too much for the eyes to take in, somehow hideous and beautiful all at once.

Leda hated it.

Gemdark, capital of Viridiana, was considered the most magnificent city in all of the Five Kingdoms that their father ruled. In the distance Leda could see the buildings glimmering with wealth in the sunlight. The houses and shops stretched out from the centre like spokes on a wheel, nestled between verdant forests on either side. In the very heart of the city towered the Temple of the Gods, even grander and uglier than the palace itself.

From the golden entrance gates of the palace to the bottom of the steps a number of horse-drawn carriages stood parked, trunks of varying shapes and sizes littered around them. Harried-looking servants flitted in between, trying to make sense of which trunks belonged to which royal child in the commotion.

Ahead of Leda, Azaria refused the hand of the footman who was attempting to help her down the steps towards the drive. She turned back to Leda and pointed at a silver-embossed trunk by the nearest carriage. "Leda, bring that one in."

Oh, for the sake of the gods. "The servants are bringing them up."

"I don't trust them with it. Take it upstairs."

So many curse words Leda could use. So many consequences for saying them.

Leda stifled the urge and shaped her face into something resembling a smile. "As you wish."

She and Azaria had been together nearly every day for twenty years, they shared a father and therefore half of his tyrannical, awful blood. Yet she still had no idea what was going through that girl's head most of the time.

There were so many trunks that Leda was feeling very sorry for the servants as she grabbed the one Azaria had pointed out.

Six royal children were due at the palace with their Counterparts that summer. Those Counterparts had the unfortunate distinction of being children of the King's mistresses, assigned to a royal child at birth. They lived with them, grew up with them, and were sacrificed by them to appease the gods.

One pair was already at the palace, and had been since last year. Now, they all awaited this summer's ceremony, to watch that royal child slaughter their Counterpart and see which pair would have the dubious honour of taking their place next year.

There was a commotion around one of the carriages and Leda looked down to see Princess Elina and her own Counterpart Sofie at the bottom of the steps, greeting their brothers and sisters. Sofie wore the same dress as Leda, long, plain wool that covered her from neck to ankle. Her dark blonde hair was pulled into a neat twist at the crown of her head. Her almond-shaped eyes perfectly matched Princess Elina's, despite their different mothers. She appeared as calm and reserved as always, her hands clasped in front of her.

Princess Elina was tall, sharp and strikingly beautiful in a deep purple gown with gold threading. A small tiara of silver sat on her head, her dark hair entwined around it. Her skin was a rich umber colour, gleaming in the sun. She seemed ethereally perfect, but when you looked closer parts of who she really was shined through, the dirt under the fingernails of a keen botanist, the pendant of the gods hanging from a pious neck. It was tarnished from how often she touched it in prayer.

Elina was smiling, showing none of her teeth, as Azaria walked towards them.

Azaria cut across their brother Prince Caspari as though he weren't even there, forcing him to stumble. He cast her a nasty look but said nothing. He was four years her junior and nursed a healthy fear of her, as they all should.

"Elina," Azaria said coldly. Sofie shrank back into the shadows.

Sensing danger, Leda picked up the trunk and dragged it over to their little gathering.

She couldn't bear to make eye contact with Sofie, and she hated herself for it.

"Princess Azaria. How lovely to see you back at the palace again," Elina said, though it was evident from her expression she did not mean that at all. Caspari snorted audibly as he passed them into the entrance hall, his jewel-encrusted doublet glimmering ostentatiously. Leda looked around for his Counterpart, Eber, but he appeared to have escaped at the first opportunity. Good for him.

Azaria frowned at Elina. 'That is untrue," she said bluntly. "You dislike my presence immensely."

Elina closed her eyes and took a long time to open them again. "You can't even *pretend* to be polite, can you? How our father would ever let a savage brat like you represent him in battle is beyond me."

Azaria tilted her head to one side. "He would because I outmatch you in every way. I will succeed in the task he sets me. I am less confident that you will."

An ugly flush had formed on Elina's cheeks. She leaned forward to poke a finger into Azaria's chest. "Now you listen to me, Azaria—"

"No!" Leda cried, but it was too late. The moment Elina's finger made contact with Azaria's chest it was grabbed, twisted and yanked so forcefully that with a strangled scream Elina was flying down the steps. She landed on the gravel at the bottom with a sickening crunch.

Everyone froze. Leda chanced a glance at Sofie, who was white as a sheet. Azaria rolled her eyes and stepped through the double doors into the palace, leaving Leda to deal with the aftermath of her actions. This was not unusual.

"*MONSTER!*" Elina's pride seemed to be more injured than anything else. "Sofie, help me up!"

9

Leda felt a sick sensation in her stomach as Sofie hauled Elina to her feet, stooping to brush the gravel from her dress.

Well aware of how unpleasant Elina could be when she was in a rage, Leda used the commotion to her advantage. She grabbed the handle of Azaria's trunk, yanking it into the entrance hall. It made a horrible grating noise against the floor.

Luckily, the hall was empty.

Having no other way to find out, Leda had measured her father's wealth and influence by taking notice of his palace and its grounds when she visited every summer. The year he had conquered Slofray was when he'd had the palace roofs wrapped in gold. Other years had seen intricate statues popping up in the corridors and elaborate diamond crowns appearing on the heads of his wives. His wealth now was almost unimaginable.

The palace was a sumptuously decorated spectacle that never failed to turn her stomach. It was also uncomfortably warm, the air dry and hot, every fireplace roaring.

Leda let out a long breath, pulling her hair off her neck as the sweat set in. She would be sticky and uncomfortable for the next few months and the thick, modest dresses that comprised her wardrobe would become the bane of her life. When she escaped she would never wear one of these stupid things ever again.

Signs of the King's obsession with patterns were everywhere in front of Leda, from the concentric shapes in the marble flooring to the duplicate statues framing every step of the red-carpeted staircase. It swept grandly upward and split in two directions at the far wall, which was comprised of one enormous painting.

Leda couldn't help but look at the familiar image as she

made her way up the steps, uncaring of the marks she was leaving on the carpet as she dragged the trunk.

The oil painting was easily twice her height and framed in gold, depicting the King sitting on his throne precisely in the centre. To his left and right stood his four queens. Behind them, his eight mistresses, including Leda's mother, whose likeness she studiously avoided. Placed around the King's feet at exact intervals were the twelve royal children of him and his wives, and each of their Counterparts, the products of his mistresses.

Leda came to a stop in front of her own face, sickly pale and weak-chinned in a way she really hoped she wasn't in real life. Her painted image stared adoringly at her father in a way she had never done. Azaria, positioned above her as always in the row of royal children, was magnificent. She looked fierce, like a character from a fairy tale brought to life. She held a spear in one hand and bow strung with an arrow in the other.

They all looked so happy.

It was a lie, a heinous one, and she wanted to tear the canvas apart with her bare hands.

CHAPTER 2

*L*eda's thoughts were interrupted by a series of echoing barks below her, and she whipped around. A pack of four dogs, squat, flat-faced and perfectly groomed, were sprinting through the hall below. Some said they were the only creatures in the world that the King loved.

Leda could believe that, he'd always tolerated the dogs' presence more than any of his children.

With a high-pitched bark the dog straggling at the back of the pack broke away and shot up the steps towards her. Leda cursed loudly.

"Oh gods, no! Creoste, get off!" She let the trunk fall from her grip and seized the bannister to give herself some leverage as she twisted around. Creoste, who was composed predominately of teeth, muscle and ropey saliva, had his jaw locked around the hem of her skirt and was yanking with all his might. "Get away, you little rat!"

At a certain point in her life she would have been ashamed of the kick she aimed at the dog with her slippered foot. She would never ordinarily hurt an animal. The first time Azaria had brought home a turkey she'd killed, Leda had spent twenty minutes trying to revive it while her foster father, Dalev, had laughed. The following hour she'd spent sobbing.

Creoste, however, was a special case. He had nursed a vicious hatred for her since he'd been a puppy and she'd accidentally stepped on his tail when trying to sneak out of a banquet. While the other dogs ignored Leda, he never missed an opportunity to sink his teeth into her. He must have inherited his master the King's disdain for her.

Leda had learned a few years ago that violence needed to be met with violence if she wanted a chance at getting away from him. Many ripped dresses, victims of his teeth, still hung sadly in her wardrobe until she could find time to mend them.

"Yes, wait—no!"

He had released Leda's skirt with a tearing sound that made her wince as she whirled to face him, only to feel him bite into the skin of her calf. Tears sprang to her eyes as she attempted to prise him off her. She fought the urge to cry out; it was best not to draw attention to herself in the public areas of the palace.

"Creoste!"

A shrill whistle and a clinking sound made Leda and the dog freeze in a ridiculous tableau. She had one foot in the air, trying to keep her balance, and Creoste had only his two back paws on the ground. She and the dog both looked down at the bottom of the staircase, where a man stood, half shrouded in shadow.

He was tall and dark-haired, dressed in exquisitely tailored black and white.

Leda's heart jumped into her throat, and a burst of adrenaline that made no sense ripped through her. She couldn't make him out clearly in the gloomy corridor he was emerging from, but she needed precious little detail to recognise Pyrrhus Selhurst, the royal tutor.

She didn't need to see him clearly to know that his eyes were so dark it was hard to distinguish the pupils from the iris, or that he had classically handsome features. His forehead showed no lines, unsurprising as she'd never seen him with any expression other than impassiveness.

This was not a man who emoted.

At that moment he moved into the light and stared up at her, true to form, without a hint of what he was thinking on his face.

He radiated a hypnotic sort of power. Everything about him screamed confidence and aristocratic breeding, and with the reluctant attraction that invariably welled up whenever Leda saw him there was always that subtle stab of jealousy.

He drew the eye in whichever room he entered, though he seemed most at home at the edge of a crowd. He looked four or five years older than her, but wiser by decades. Her father sought his opinion on everything, over and above some of his most experienced advisors, and had even appointed him the palace historian. Leda was less than invisible by comparison.

"Come here!" Pyrrhus snapped, and Creoste, the little traitor, let her go immediately. Panting as though he'd run a great distance, his tongue nearly on the floor, the dog trotted down the steps to sit obediently at Pyrrhus's feet.

Leda's skirt had been ripped to mid-thigh, most of her left leg now exposed. She felt a bead of blood slide down her calf but forced herself not to look down. Pyrrhus's gaze was squarely on her face and didn't drop so much as an inch towards her bare leg. He stayed neutral as her lips lifted in a tremulous smile.

They'd never spoken before. Not once. Leda couldn't

believe this was their first real interaction, how utterly humiliating. She prayed he wouldn't notice that her cheeks seemed to be on fire.

"Thank you," she called down to him, folding her skirt to cover her leg. She tried to appear demure, and it did not work.

As Pyrrhus moved further into the light her eyes passed over his hair, thick, dark and perfectly styled, not a single strand out of place. His skin was pale, as though he spent most of his time indoors, poring over books.

She'd heard incredible tales of his intellect. He was said to be a prodigy who had finished university years early and travelled all of the Five Kingdoms to progress his studies. He was fluent in multiple languages, had written two books, and was considered a master at chess. And as a Counterpart she was expressly not permitted to speak with him, lest he inadvertently educate her. It had made her want to seek him out even more over the two years he'd been at the palace, but she had held herself back.

Leda had experienced quite enough rejection in her life already.

Pyrrhus hadn't said anything else, so with a nod Leda turned around and picked up the trunk at her feet. A bitter taste welled in her mouth as she heaved it around the corner and up the second set of stairs, both legs now smarting.

For all her grudging attraction, she never enjoyed seeing Pyrrhus. She didn't think it was healthy to be drawn to someone for whom she felt so much jealousy. He'd accomplished so much in his life, only a few years older than her, and surpassed her at everything.

There was also the fact that, when Leda really studied him, as she had taken the time to do at countless balls and dinners and parties over the last two years, she felt she could detect something radiating from him. A sense of lone-liness, perhaps. A lack of belonging, like that which she felt every single day.

But that was foolish; she didn't know the man, had never spoken to him until today. Of course she would project her own thoughts and insecurities on to the tempting blank slate that he provided.

Besides, when she escaped she'd never see him again, so that would put paid to all her complicated feelings, and she wouldn't need to study them further. She would live her simple, happy life alone in a little house by the beach. She would make and sell dresses and not think about the fact that she'd never uncovered the secrets of the mysteriously compelling royal tutor.

By the time Leda arrived in Azaria's rooms on the fifth floor bearing the trunk, red faced and cursing under her breath, her sister had settled herself in. The heavily embroidered curtains in the sitting room had been thrown wide, stained-glass windows open to reveal the river gushing through the rolling lawn behind the palace. A fire crackled in the hearth.

The air was hot and hazy, the water outside a bright, shimmering blue. Birds sang as they perched on verdant trees without a care in the world. Leda cast them a nasty look before moving to Azaria.

Her sister was sitting on one of the over-stuffed settees, her back ramrod straight, surveying the room with a look of distaste. Gold-framed mirrors hung from each wall so they could see a thousand versions of themselves from every angle, priceless paintings crowding the spaces between. Every surface in the room, whether the mahogany dining table or marble mantelpiece, was cluttered with an array of expensive knick-knacks. It was a relentless assault on the senses.

The King's expansion throughout the lands had brought him so much treasure the palace staff had run out of places to put it, and so it was now stuffed into the rooms of his children.

Azaria watched Leda bend over double, trying to get her breath back, with a raised brow.

Leda's vision swam before her eyes and she considered when she'd need her next dose of hibcus. Her right leg was starting to throb. She could probably wait an hour or so, but no longer.

"They put another statue in my room. On a plinth," Azaria said.

Curious, Leda peered into Azaria's bedroom. She emerged with a smirk. "You'll need to do some acrobatics to get to bed tonight. Was the third chaise longue really necessary?"

Azaria made a frustrated sound, gliding over to the dining table laden with pastries and small cakes. She plucked a miniature lattice pie from the stack and popped it into her mouth. She swallowed with a grimace as Leda considered the upcoming nightmare that would be unpacking Azaria's things in these stuffed-to-bursting rooms.

"The decadence is becoming distasteful," Azaria announced. Leda snorted at the dramatic statement, watching as Azaria left for her bedroom, her dress sweeping across the marble floor.

"You're not wrong about that," Leda muttered to the now empty room, grabbing a bowl of grapes from the dining table and tucking it under her arm as she opened the door to her own room.

It was her favourite place in this hideous palace. The

door opened to reveal a tightly wound spiral staircase, which she climbed in small, dizzying circles until it turned her out into her bedroom.

It was a small, simple room, with a bed, wardrobe, dressing table and slightly battered armchair in the corner. A window sat in the wall above her bed, the glass so far out that she could squeeze herself on to the windowsill and look out at the sweeping view of the grounds and forest behind the palace. When she'd told her brother Eber about her fondness for this view a few years ago, he'd pilfered some pillows for her to put on the sill to sit on. They were faded and dusty by now, but still comfortable.

A fluffy rug sat on the stone floor at the top of the staircase, and she kicked off her shoes to curl her toes in it. Two years ago she'd managed to grab it from a pile of items about to be discarded from Prince Caspari's collection when he was having new furniture delivered to his rooms. No one had noticed it missing and it made her bedroom much cosier.

Thankfully the wound Creoste had inflicted on her was shallow, and she was able to bandage it up quickly and neatly.

Over the next hour Leda unpacked for both Azaria and herself with little issue, though she did manage to knock over a ceramic swan in the princess's room. She turned the chipped side to face the wall and hurried out.

She was barely ten steps down the corridor when the shadows to her right shifted.

"Leda."

"Sofie!" Leda jumped a foot in the air, a hand flying to her heart as Princess Elina's Counterpart, two years her junior, stepped out of a shadowy alcove. She'd clearly been waiting for her.

Sofie looked as dreadful as she had a couple of hours ago, her face grey and eyes red-rimmed.

It was no surprise to see her that way. They all knew what was coming for them, eventually, and Sofie's time was approaching.

It was all part of the King's design, his appeasement of the gods. When a royal child killed their Counterpart, they proved their loyalty to their father and to the gods. They were then ready to lead his next invasion.

Leda had no idea how far her father's lands stretched, though she had heard they were vast. She'd never been permitted to look at a map, lest it give her ideas. Trying to build a picture of the kingdoms in her mind, she'd attempted to steal geography books from the library of the village, Leatherfell, where she'd spent most of her childhood with Azaria and their foster parents. She'd been unsuccessful, however. Those kinds of books were kept under lock and key.

Panic held Leda in a tight grip. Sofie probably thought that, as the oldest remaining Counterpart, Leda would be able to offer her some comfort or wisdom about what was about to happen that night. She would be wrong, Leda had nothing to give.

Sofie looked up and down the corridor to confirm they were alone before drawing Leda into a hug. Unused to physical contact, Leda was stiff as a board, though she managed to bring herself to pat Sofie's back once.

"Shh. It's alright, it's alright." Leda had to fight the insane urge to rip herself away and sprint in the opposite direction. There was a reason she'd kept her siblings at arm's length for all these years. It was horribly selfish, but she couldn't live with herself any other way. Losing someone she loved would break her. Therefore, she couldn't let herself love any of them. They were all doomed to die, and she was too if she couldn't find a way to escape.

Sofie's fear and panic were contagious, and Leda took a deep breath to steady herself.

"It's *tonight*. How is that possible?" Sofie sobbed into her shoulder. Her body sagged and Leda found herself holding most of her weight up. It was taxing, the hibcus she took had made her progressively weaker, but she managed not to show the strain despite her leg threatening to buckle.

"I'm sorry. I'm so sorry." Leda placed a trembling hand on the back of her sister's head and tried to blink back her own tears. Her falling apart would do nothing to help Sofie.

"She's going to kill me."

"I know."

"She's going to enjoy it."

Leda swallowed over the lump in her throat. "She won't."

Elina and Sofie fought like any siblings, but Leda had always sensed how much they cared for each other, deep down. She pulled away and grabbed Sofie by her shoulders. She'd lost so much weight over the past year, her bones dug into Leda's fingers. "Is there anywhere you can go?"

She would offer her chimney, but it wasn't ready, wouldn't be for months. Sofie didn't have that kind of time.

Guilt flooded Leda; if only she'd known that the King would swap Azaria and Elina's ceremonies, she'd have been able to warn Sofie and direct her to the chimney so she could carve the final grooves into it over the past year. She'd tried to get word to her, but had been dragged out of the palace by the guards with Azaria before she'd had a chance, sent home in disgrace last year.

"It's not a question of where I can go; it's how I could ever get out. It's impossible. I've tried, Leda, countless times over the past year. There are guards on every exit; I'm watched constantly. They have spies in the city and soldiers patrolling the hills. The dogs have our scents. I've been pulled back every time I so much as looked at a door." Sofie pulled aside the collar of her dress to reveal fresh red welts across her shoulder. "Father doesn't tolerate escape attempts."

Leda pressed her bloodless lips together. She knew the severity of the punishment for trying to escape, but seeing the results in front of her made more dread well up in her. How naive had she been for thinking she'd be able to escape herself? The idea that she would be able to save herself or any of her Counterpart brothers and sisters was laughable.

"We'll find a way to get you out; we can cause a distraction. We'll hide you somewhere and get you out in the commotion," Leda said, knowing that if they succeeded she was signing her own death warrant. Even if her father didn't discover her role in Sofie's escape, having lost one Counterpart they would make sure there was a guard no more than six feet away from Leda for the entirety of the next year. She'd never get to her chimney. She'd never get away.

That didn't matter, though, when Sofie stood sobbing before her. Leda would find another way out, she had a year until her ceremony. Sofie had mere hours. In this, Leda couldn't be selfish.

"There's nothing for me out there," Sofie whispered brokenly. "I have no education, no skills. We've been raised like cattle for slaughter, Leda. I wouldn't make it one day out there on my own."

"Don't be ridiculous, you'd adapt—"

"There is no way out for me," Sofie said, clutching Leda's hands in hers. When she withdrew, Leda felt cold metal in her left hand. Flipping it over, she opened her palm to see two glimmering sapphire earrings.

Absolutely not.

"Sofie—"

"They were Princess Zuna's; I found them in her old rooms. No one will ever notice they're missing and maybe you'll be able to trade them for safe passage if you manage to get out," Sofie whispered.

Leda thought of all the coins hidden away in her room and grimaced.

"Listen to me." Sofie looked at her and she was struck by the fact that, though Sofie was a year younger, she'd gained wisdom in the last year that Leda lacked. "Don't let them do this to you, too. Promise me you'll escape. I don't care what the consequences are for Azaria or anyone else, you just need to find a way out. Do whatever it takes; you have to be brave."

There was a clink of metal at the end of the corridor. One of the patrolling guards had rounded the corner and was making his way towards them, eyes fixed on Sofie.

Sofie pressed a wet kiss to Leda's cheek. She forced herself not to flinch.

"Forget about me; just escape. Promise me," Sofie whispered in her ear before withdrawing.

"No—"

"Leda, please!"

"I ... I promise."

Sofie squeezed her hand a final time, and then was gone. The guard passed Leda and followed her sister all the way down the corridor.

CHAPTER 3

*L*eda wandered the halls of the palace for a long time before returning to Azaria's rooms. She'd paced each corridor on every floor, considering the windows and doors of every room. She searched for hard-to-find hiding places and unguarded exit points. As always, she found nothing.

A guard stood at every external door carrying a spear a foot taller than she was. All of the windows on the ground floor were locked shut. Those on the higher floors were too far off the ground to be easily climbed from. And even if someone managed it, the King's dogs roamed the grounds. Creoste would sniff Sofie out the moment she set foot outside. Leda had always suspected that their father had his dogs trained to scent his Counterpart children, so Sofie's confirmation did not surprise her.

Fighting the urge to rub her aching leg after all the walking, Leda flung herself down on the settee.

"Where have you been?" Azaria demanded from the doorway to her bedroom.

She looked like something out of a painting, her hair coiffed into an elaborate bun at the top of her head, lips painted red. Her gown was deep crimson with voluminous ruffles that somehow complemented her slim frame. Leda wondered how the ruffles had been created with such structure; she would have to try to teach herself how with the next dress she made.

Azaria paused in the act of pulling on a pair of white, elbow-length gloves when she saw Leda's state of dress.

"You're not ready yet?" Azaria snapped. "The ceremony is in fifteen minutes!"

"I only need five," Leda said shortly, glad that Azaria had not pressed her on where she'd been. She gave the maids who had entered to fuss with Azaria's skirts a wide berth to reach her room. Once upstairs, she pulled a comb roughly through her curly brown hair and braided it to one side. Mouth full of hairpins, she glared at her reflection in her small, rusted mirror.

With a huff Leda ripped her only ballgown off its hanger. It was lilac, strapless and drawn in at the waist. Her mother had given it to her when she was fifteen, and it now sat tight across her chest and back. She hadn't been given anything new since, nor was she allowed to wear anything as appealing as Azaria's dresses, so that ruled out anything she made herself.

When Leda pulled the dress on, it just looked indecent, crushing her breasts up until she was sure she could rest her chin on them. With a grimace she grabbed a white shawl from her wardrobe, wrapping it around her shoulders.

It didn't exactly look good, but it felt better.

It was all redundant anyway, it didn't matter what Leda wore. No one looked at the Counterparts. She knew this, and yet found herself powdering her cheeks and painting her lips a deeper pink. She also added dark powder in precise measures around her eyelashes with a brush she'd purloined from Azaria. It was a risk; the colours would either disguise the redness in her eyes or make her tears more obvious to everyone when black streaks began to appear.

Leda gave up when her hands started shaking so badly she could barely hold the brush. Yet again, she was preparing to watch one of her siblings die. It had happened five times before and it never ever got easier. If Azaria hadn't acted up last year, it would be Leda's head on the chopping block tonight. Remorse ate at her until her insides felt empty.

When Leda went back downstairs, her skirts pulled up carefully to avoid tripping, Azaria was waiting by the door with an impatient expression.

"Well?" Azaria said abruptly, causing Leda to freeze. She didn't want a confrontation, but judging by Azaria's tone she was spoiling for one.

Azaria had never reacted particularly well to the ceremonies, but it wasn't because of the death and gore. She couldn't care less about that, she just didn't want to have to see her mother, and that was always part of the process.

There was a painful silence.

"How do I look?" Azaria asked, running her hands along the bodice of her dress. 'Am I not stunning?'

Leda wasn't entirely sure Azaria had any appreciation for beauty, certainly not her own. It was wasted on her.

"Your mother won't approve of that neckline." It made Leda's look modest.

Azaria's lips tipped up in the ghost of a smirk that matched Leda's.

"Royal children aren't supposed to wear jewels to the ceremony," Leda pointed out, opening the door and getting out of Azaria's way as she strode past her.

"Exactly." Azaria left a cloud of perfume and hair pomade behind her, said jewellery clinking loudly as she moved. "No one will expect it, everyone will notice. I shall draw the focus tonight."

So she meant to show the court that she was back, that she shined brighter than her brothers and sisters and that this time, she would not be passed over by her father. That was just great.

Leda fought the urge to stamp on the back of Azaria's silly ruffled dress.

"Yes, I'm sure everyone's attention will be riveted on you when Elina brings the axe out," Leda muttered, closing the door with a snap and following in Azaria's wake.

Azaria slowed her pace so that she could walk next to Leda, the click of their heels echoing in the empty hallway.

"Don't wear that when it's our turn." There was nothing malicious or cruel in Azaria's expression, but still Leda felt her stomach clench at the blasé words. "It's a calamity of a dress."

That was perhaps too harsh, the dress was old but Leda had kept it in relatively good condition. She'd treated the fabric to make it resilient, re-stitched it to make it more flattering and had dropped the hem as she grew taller.

Even so.

"Don't worry, I won't wear it." Leda wouldn't be wearing this dress ever again, she would make her escape as soon as her chimney was complete and it would rot in this palace for the rest of eternity. That was if she didn't take it with her to use as kindling for a fire to warm her as she travelled through the forest. That was all it was good for.

They stayed silent after that, save for the rustling of their skirts as they joined the flow of people making their way to the throne room. The corridors bustled with the activity of sumptuously dressed royals and nobles, servants darting through the stream.

The atmosphere was hushed, though the whispers of

the crowd sounded excited. Some of them had travelled far for this spectacle, from all across the Five Kingdoms.

The air tasted of sickening anticipation, and it turned Leda's stomach. These people were looking forward to their barbaric yearly show. They were pampered, bored and bloodthirsty, and she hated every single one of them.

Drawing up before the throne room, each attendee stopped and bowed to the statue in the middle of the corridor. It depicted four faceless gods clustered in a circle, looking down at them with blank judgemental gazes despite the fact that there were no features where their faces should be.

Leda's curtsey was the slightest twitch of her knees, anything but reverent.

The throne room was lit by five huge chandeliers dangling from the ceiling. The light bounced off the marble floor, which had been polished so well that it seemed to emanate its own glow. The King reclined on his throne at the far end of the room, framed by enormous windows. The crown gleamed on his steel-grey hair. In his lap was curled one of his favourite dogs, and he scratched behind its ears and muttered to it with a genuine smile on his face that was rare to see.

He sat higher than everyone on a dais, with solid gold steps leading to it. His three closest advisors stood in formation to his right, his three splendidly dressed wives on the left. They were all standing precise distances apart, as if someone had measured between them with a ruler and advised where they should go. Leda wouldn't put it past her father to insist on it. She knew that if anyone else stepped up on to the dais, creating an odd number of people surrounding him, someone would be ordered to leave to re-establish the balance.

Hundreds of royals and nobles and politicians and

diplomats squeezed into the room, forming a loose semi-circle before the King. They gave a wide berth to the axe sitting on a plinth at the centre of the room. Its handle was intricately carved, the wood so dark it absorbed the light, with large jewels set into it so that it glittered threateningly. Its blade was perfectly curved, sharp and lethal.

Leda looked away, her stomach turning. That object was stained with the blood of her siblings. The image of it haunted her nightmares.

The King's mistresses were clustered over to one side of the room. Leda saw her mother's dark hair ripple as she threw her head back in laughter at a joke one of her companions had made.

Azaria seemed disinclined to look at her own mother, Queen Celandine. Instead, she beckoned Leda over to the small platform that had been erected between the plinth bearing the axe and the King's dais. There, the other royal children not participating in the ceremony had already gathered. Azaria was the oldest still at the palace, the youngest was Princess Gabriell, just two years old and sitting wide-eyed in a plush cot. Between them stood Princes Caspari, Elov and Fessler. Princess Annagret, the second youngest at four years old, was sitting next to Gabriell's cot, one chubby hand wound around a bar. Her Counterpart, Mira, gurgled from the step beneath her.

On that step beneath the royals were the other Counter-parts. Leda took her place in front of Azaria with what she hoped was good grace, her neck prickling as she turned her back on her father and faced the room. Eber, Markus and Ami lined up beside her, each one steadfastly avoiding eye contact. The King did not like to see his children interacting. He preferred them to be symmetrical dolls, dressed up and arranged in a formation he found appealing.

The blare of a trumpet sounded, quieting the crowd. As

one, the Counterparts dropped to their knees, facing away from their royal children, towards the courtiers. The wood of the platform was hard on Leda's knees and she shifted slightly, trying to ease the pressure. She was thankful that her dress provided at least some padding.

Leda looked sullenly out into the restless crowd, and the slightest inconsequential movement at the corner of her eye caught her attention.

Pyrrhus stood on a step between two pillars at the far side of the room, a little above the sea of people. His arms were crossed and his expression completely blank in contrast to the shining, excited faces of those around him. He was focused on the King, and she wished she knew what he was thinking. Did he revere her father like the others? Or did he see the evil beneath?

Next to Pyrrhus stood his assistant, Thorodin, red-haired and the same age as Leda. He taught the younger children of the palace while Pyrrhus undertook his research, carried out his historian duties and occasionally lectured the older children.

Thorodin leaned nonchalantly against one of the pillars, one ankle crossed over the other. He turned briefly to mutter to Ambrose, the royal physician, who completed the tableau. The three of them were a study in contradictions, Pyrrhus with his black tailcoat and dark trousers, the only contrast a splash of white linen at his throat where his shirt was visible. Ambrose wore a long, buttoned coat of shimmering silver, which looked odd against his light blonde hair. He was an attractive man in his mid-twenties but he looked somehow otherworldly, as though he didn't belong. Thorodin had dressed similarly to Pyrrhus, and had slicked his shock of red hair back tightly against his head. He was listening to the other two speak with a frown.

As if sensing Leda's appraisal, Pyrrhus's eyes flicked up

to meet hers, and she jerked her head away, pretending to scan the faces beneath him. From the corner of her eye, she saw him incline his head in a nod to Azaria. Turning slightly, she caught Azaria dipping her chin imperiously towards him in response.

Leda swayed a little, digging her fingernails into her hands to shock herself into staying upright. She could not faint here, or show the remotest sign of weakness. The wolves in this court would eat her alive.

The King raised a hand and silence fell over the chattering crowd. All of his children straightened up under his gaze, their vulnerable backs still facing him. The King's armour clanked ostentatiously as he got to his feet. He hadn't ridden out to battle in decades. He'd gone completely to seed, yet still insisted on wearing that stupid armour.

"Welcome, my subjects!" he boomed, voice reaching every corner of the room. "At the end of last year's summer sojourn, I chose my favoured royal child to keep with me, here, at the palace, for a year. That child will now go on to conquer lands in my name, having completed their final task—the severing of connections to those weaker than themselves, the ultimate show of loyalty to their one true King and to the gods. Their proof that they will not quail in battle, and that they will forge onward, never beholden to their emotions. This evening, my daughter Princess Elina will sever her ties to her Counterpart Sofielina. She will cast her body into the Blainchill River so that the gods may always protect and bestow luck upon her in all her endeavours."

There was a murmur and rustling as Elina and Sofie emerged from the crowd.

Sofie was a state, her hair bedraggled in a ponytail down her back, face stark white against the gold of her dress. Her hands were visibly shaking, bound in metal cuffs attached to a chain, which ended in Elina's grip.

Leda was surprised to see that Elina looked almost as terrible as Sofie. She had expected to see her preening for the crowd, revelling in their father's undivided attention. Elina was comfortable in public; she excelled at singing, dancing, and entertaining. Leda had expected to see her puffed up with excitement.

Instead, Elina looked small and unsure. Her eyes were red beneath the dark makeup around them. Her hands gripped Sofie's chains loosely. The metal looked as if it might run through her fingertips on to the floor at any moment. She appeared to be fixated on the ceremonial axe just ahead of her, and she stopped so suddenly Sofie nearly staggered into her back.

"Child," the King said, settling back on to his throne with a chilling smile. "Commence."

A round of thunderous applause greeted this word. Leda let the edges of her shawl drop past her hands to conceal their trembling. She couldn't bear to watch, but she also couldn't let Sofie be alone. She made herself look up and into the eyes of her younger half-sister, fighting the urge to wail and run away. But Leda could still see the guards with their spears guarding each entrance. None of them would get further than ten feet.

Sofie was doing a much better job than Leda at concealing her shaking. She looked at each of her Counterpart siblings in turn, ignoring the royal children, before turning to the King.

"Your ... Your Majesty," she said in a high, carrying voice, dropping to her knees at Elina's feet. "I ... Sofielina Locarno, hereby relinquish my life to the royal child. I am ready to ... to play my part in the advancement of my family ... providing good luck for its conquests forevermore. I ... I pray that the gods will accept Elina's sacrifice." Her voice caught on the last word.

Tears streamed down Elina's face. It seemed she'd had a better relationship with her Counterpart than Leda had suspected. Leda knew that Azaria wouldn't cry when their time came; she would bear it with her usual stoicism. Any sadness she might feel would be quickly and completely buried.

"F ... Father ..." Elina's trembling voice could just be made out over the sudden flourish of trumpets as she turned to the King. His expression didn't flicker at her pleading look. He waved a negligent hand as though telling her to get on with it. He was growing bored. He'd sat through so many of these ceremonies before, after all.

Leda felt a wave of sickness sweep over her as she watched Elina pick up the axe, wincing as her hand dipped sharply under its weight. She looked like a little girl, reaching up to wield the weapon above the head of her sister. Her next whimper was audible. Behind Leda, Prince Elov sank unnoticed to the floor, his face a sickly green.

During the five ceremonies that Leda had witnessed, some of the royal children cried and begged not to be made to do it. But the King persisted, threatening to kill both children in horrific ways if one refused to hurt the other. On the opposite end of the spectrum there were those who hacked their Counterpart to pieces with hatred etched into every line of their face. The King enjoyed those the most.

Leda thought about the stone-faced Azaria standing behind her and couldn't repress a shudder at the thought of how gruesome her own death would be.

Elina still held the axe aloft, arms shaking under the weight of it as she stared at Sofie, who had bowed her head. So this was how it would be, like the slaughter of an animal. Sofie swept her hair over one shoulder to expose her neck and leaned over the block of silver at the base of the plinth on which the axe had stood. Her neck fit perfectly into the groove on the surface.

"NOW!" the King bellowed.

The crowd roared and the axe seemed to fall in slow motion, its own weight giving it the power required to drive it through Sofie's neck with a sickening crunch.

Tasting blood in her mouth, Leda released her lip from between her teeth. Silent tears streamed down her face as she looked away from the rapidly spreading pool of crimson. Amongst the crowd's jeers she could detect a loud sobbing from the corner where the mistresses stood. They had turned as one away from the crowd and formed a protective circle around Sofie's mother.

Leda heard the gruesome sound of Sofie's body crumpling on the ground, and the ear-splitting clang of the axe as it fell to the marble floor. It was then that Princess Elina fainted, eyes rolling into the back of her head as she crashed to the stone with an almighty thud.

The servants didn't quite reach her fast enough. By the time they had picked her up the puddle of Sofie's blood had turned her fingertips and the edge of her gown scarlet. It was even smeared on her cheek as they lifted her.

The King grinned at the sight as he got to his feet.

Leda couldn't help but turn to look through the baying crowd at Pyrrhus. She needed to find someone, anyone, who might think that this spectacle was as awful and wrong as she did.

Pyrrhus was utterly still, fixated on the scene Leda couldn't bear to look at. As the King stepped over Sofie's body he made a small movement, as if he were about to step forward, but stopped himself. Thorodin was also transfixed on the blood with a horrified expression, but Ambrose ignored it completely, instead staring up at the frescoed ceiling.

Six Counterparts dead. And Leda was next.

Leda took a small intake of breath through her teeth as she looked up and directly into Pyrrhus's eyes. He must have sensed her watching him. Leda wondered if there was a trace of pity in his expression, or perhaps he didn't care at all and was intellectually curious to see her response to her sister's death. Tears continued to stream down her face and she broke the connection, turning away in shame.

Even if he were inclined to, there was nothing he could do to help them. No one could.

Leda was destined to die one year from today in this very room. Next year Pyrrhus would watch her blood spread across the floor and, like everyone else, would do nothing to stop it.

"Leda? Leda, get up!" Azaria's hiss broke through the haze surrounding Leda as she fought the pull to faint.

She got to her feet, helped by Azaria's hand dragging her up by the fabric at the back of her dress. Her knees protested painfully at the movement, but her sister's freakish strength helped. The feast would be beginning in the banquet hall at any moment. It would only take a moment to walk there, but to Leda the journey felt like miles.

"I'll be there in a moment," she said to Azaria, who was too preoccupied with keeping anyone from touching her as the crowds passed them to do more than nod irritably.

Leda fought her way through the people to the edge of the throne room, slipping into a smaller side corridor that led to the ambassador's waiting rooms.

Alone at last in the dark, she leaned against the cool stone wall. Every inch of her body hurt, the beginnings of hibcus withdrawal coupling with her dire mental state. It sent her to her knees on the cold floor with a whimper of pain.

"Ow, ow, ow ...," she groaned, clutching at her stomach as it spasmed. Rifling through the pockets she'd sewn into her dress, she let out a sigh of relief as her hand closed around the familiar leather pouch. The glittering dark powder fell on to the palm of her shaking hand and she wasted no time in sprinkling it on her tongue.

It transformed her instantly, soothing her frantically beating heart and calming the cramps in her stomach. She felt even weaker, though, the drawback of this particular remedy, and struggled to get herself on her feet. The light looked strange to her, probably due to her pupils dilating. Taking a shuddering breath, she stepped back out into the throne room.

For some reason, though Thorodin and Ambrose were gone, Pyrrhus still stood exactly where he had been for the ceremony, arms crossed so tightly she wondered if he was cutting off his own circulation. He stared straight at her, as though he had been waiting for her to emerge.

Leda almost snorted at that thought, how ridiculous, he barely even knew who she was. They were two of only a few people left in the room now, though a flurry of servants was entering to clean up.

Refusing to meet his eye, Leda turned and made her way out of the main doors, picking up her pace to reach the banquet hall as quickly as possible.

CHAPTER 4

The banquet hall was similar in design to the throne room, so bright that Leda fought the urge to shield her eyes whenever she stepped inside. Light bounced off every surface, from the gilt walls to the crystal chandeliers to the mirrored ceiling. The King's table, where he ate alone at every meal, sat on a dais towards the back of the room under the largest chandelier. Though the plates on his table were piled high with gently steaming food, his seat was empty.

Close to the left wall was another table, draped in gold cloth, at which sat all three of the King's living wives. A fourth chair had been left empty, marking Queen Agnetta's absence following her death, as was custom. At the opposite end of the room was a larger table covered in silver cloth, at which sat the King's mistresses.

Leda saw her mother almost immediately, but kept her head down. She staggered to one of the small tables for two that encircled the King's dais. Most were already occupied with royal children and their Counterparts. All except Azaria looked as if the last thing they wanted to do was eat.

Leda sat down opposite Azaria and almost jumped back up again.

"Venison?" she said. The palace meals, gluttonous and overpowered with salt and spices, rarely tempted her appetite. She watched the juices ooze grotesquely from the rare haunch of meat and pushed her plate away, wrinkling the tablecloth and jostling Azaria's crockery. Azaria frowned, fork poised halfway up to her mouth.

"You need a stronger stomach," Azaria said, but she tossed a plain bread roll from her plate on to Leda's. "Don't be a weakling."

Picking despondently at the roll, Leda didn't feel the prickle of being watched for a few minutes. As if drawn by a magnetic force, she looked over Azaria's shoulder and straight into the cold blue eyes of her sister's mother. Queen Celandine wore an unreadable expression so similar to that of her daughter that Leda shuddered. But beneath their similar beauty there were small differences; where Azaria was detached and emotionless, Celandine burned with contempt.

"Your mother's staring at us."

Azaria straightened up so abruptly that Leda jumped. "Does she look angry?"

If Leda didn't know any better, she'd think Azaria was fearful. But that wasn't possible, Azaria hadn't shown herself capable of that emotion since they were children.

Leda shrugged, occupied with tearing her bread into tiny pieces. She had no appetite to speak of.

"I don't want to visit her," Azaria said, attacking her venison with new fervour.

"You have to; we all do. It's tradition." Leda could feel the presence of her own mother at the table behind her. She refused to turn and check if she was still there.

Leda's relationship with her mother was about as close

and loving as Azaria's was with hers; that is to say, not at all. Leda had only seen her a handful of times since she was born, she had been raised with Azaria by Fayne and Dalev away from the palace. It was customary, however, for the royal children and their Counterparts to visit their mothers following the ceremony each summer, one of the rare times the King allowed them to be together.

Leda's chair scraped against the floor as she got to her feet. The King wasn't in attendance at his feast, nor were his advisors; he'd clearly been called away on urgent business. That meant she didn't need to sit through the meal. She could retire to her room, sit in her window seat and cry for Sofie. Then, she would go and visit her mother.

"I'll see you later," she said to Azaria, who made no move to get up despite her empty plate.

"Mend my green satin dress before bed, will you?" Azaria said absently, watching her mother's reflection in the mirrored surface of the opposite wall. "The hem tore yesterday."

Leda nodded, declining to mention that Azaria had been the one to rip the dress herself in a sudden rage upon discovering it no longer fit across her shoulders.

By the time she arrived at her mother's rooms later that night, Leda was pale and wan. She paused by the door to check her reflection in a nearby mirror. Oh, but she looked awful, her face a papery grey and eyes swollen. She dabbed ineffectually at her cheeks with a handkerchief before stuffing it into her pocket. That would have to do, there was no way to disguise that she'd been crying. It wouldn't matter anyway, her mother would probably barely notice. Olora didn't like to make eye contact with the daughter she didn't know and hadn't raised, who spent every year contemplating her steadily approaching death.

The corridor leading to Olora's rooms was dim and gloomy. She lived with all of the other mistresses in the basement of the palace. There were no windows, and the torches in brackets on the walls left flickering shadows that never failed to make goosebumps appear on Leda's arms. She pulled her shawl tightly around herself and knocked on her mother's door.

Olora had been the King's favourite mistress for many years. Though his attention was diverted frequently by younger or prettier women, he'd returned to her with some regularity. As a result, her rooms were more expansive and comfortable than those of most other mistresses. Opening the door, Leda peeked in to see a neat little sitting room, illuminated by candles.

A second later the door was yanked out of her grip and pulled wide, revealing an irate nine-year-old girl.

"Ami." Leda straightened up and nodded at her little sister. She had grown a few inches over the past year, and was wearing her brown hair, silky straight where Leda's was violently curly, in a long plait down the centre of her back. She had a sweet face and a talent for charming those older than her, but she rarely bothered to apply that skill to Leda.

As soon as Ami had learned to talk she'd begun to see Leda as a rival for their mother's affection. Leda had refrained from telling her that their mother didn't have much affection to split between them in the first place.

"Go away," Ami said, attempting to close the door in her face. "It's *my* time with mother!"

There was a loud thud that rattled through Leda's body as she threw her hand against the door. With a none-too-gentle shove that had Ami staggering, she was inside the sitting room.

"Nice to see you too, Ami," she said, going to give her scowling sister a pat on the shoulder and thinking better of it. Ami stalked away.

Their brother Eber, Prince Caspari's sixteen-year-old Counterpart, lounged on the blue settee and watched them with thinly veiled amusement.

Eber had a habit of lounging wherever he went. He couldn't see a wall or a column without feeling the need to prop himself against it, as though the idea of holding his own weight up was tiresome.

He had Leda's blue eyes and the same nose, but while they resembled each other physically their characters couldn't be more different. He was extroverted where she was introverted, a musician who could play any instrument he touched after a negligible amount of practice.

Eber was energetic and fun where Leda was quiet and reserved. He knew his time was limited and had decided at a young age to enjoy all of it. In every room he entered, he somehow fit. Leda was sure that, if he'd been born a royal child, he would have been one of the Five Kingdoms' favourites.

He was forever getting in trouble, though never anything serious, a prank or two here and there, charming the kitchen servants into giving him extra food or sabotaging his brother's snow boots. It seemed unfair to Leda that Eber had inherited all the charisma, leaving none whatsoever for her and Ami.

And yet, Leda felt affection for him that she had ruthlessly tried to stamp down on since he'd been born. She'd always thought it would be cruel to let her siblings love her only to lose her.

She had resolved years ago that she couldn't ever be close with Eber, despite him being her favourite, and so she held herself back whenever he reached out. He probably thought she was cold and haughty, just like Azaria. She hated the thought.

Eber had noticed none of Leda's internal monologue and it showed, as he hauled himself off the settee and came over to envelop her in a hug. Leda stiffened and permitted herself to settle her chin on his shoulder, but only for a second. He was four years younger and yet already taller than her.

"I'm sorry, Leda," he said quietly into her hair, uncharacteristically serious. "About Sofie."

She pulled away from him abruptly and took a step back. "Me too. Where is mother?"

Eber rolled his eyes, taking his seat back on the settee and thudding his muddy boots one by one on to the coffee table. In fact, all of him seemed to be muddy. He looked like he'd spent the time between dinner and now wrangling animals in the pigpen. "Readying herself for us. She wants to see us one by one."

Ami had lost interest in them both. She'd found a poker and was stabbing it into the logs in the fireplace, watching sparks fly up the chimney.

"You're looking relaxed," Leda said, sinking on to the chair across from Eber. He had deep purple bags under his eyes, though they nearly disappeared when he grinned.

"Caspari's got a new set of throwing knives, said he wanted to practice his aim on me out in the woods. The longer mother takes to see us, the longer I'll be able to keep my skull intact. I'm happy to stay here all night if I can."

He didn't seem too concerned for someone whose brother would imminently be throwing deadly pieces of metal at his head. Then again, he was probably used to it. Prince Caspari was a renowned brute, and openly looked forward to the day he would kill his Counterpart. His bloodthirst was even worse than Azaria's; while she was clinical and detached, a gleam of excitement entered Caspari's eyes at the thought of someone else's pain. He truly was their father's son. Leda had no idea how Eber had remained sane all these years.

"Azaria got me in the arm with an arrow a couple of months ago," Leda said, moving her wrap aside to show the short red line along her forearm. Eber frowned and she shrugged. "She was aiming for one of Dalev's dogs; I was pulling it away." Somehow, Azaria's behaviour when it came to animals was even poorer than with humans.

Eber laughed as if comparing injuries inflicted by their siblings was a normal topic of conversation. "Do you remember a few years ago when Azaria and Caspari got into that fight by the river and tried to drown each other? How different our lives might have been if they'd succeeded."

Leda snorted. "You know father would have just drowned us too as part of mourning. Everything must be in *perfect balance*. We can't have excess Counterparts."

"Excess Counterparts?" Olora had appeared in the doorway to her bedroom, resplendently pretty in a light blue gown, her face sombre. Her dark hair was twisted into an intricate knot at the back of her head and her neck and ears glittered with jewels—gifts from the King for his favourite mistress, that she for some reason felt the need to show off to her children.

"Mother!" Ami was across the room in an instant, her face lit up, arms outstretched. Olora held her back with one hand.

"Stay back, Amifessler, do not dirty my dress with those fingers. Have you been mucking about in the fireplace?" Olora snapped.

Leda kept her face carefully blank. There was one person in this room who had spent considerable time mucking about in a fireplace, and it certainly wasn't Ami.

Olora looked down at her youngest daughter with a kind of disdain that made Leda want to go after her with the poker Ami had left on the rug.

Olora turned to Leda and smiled, but her eyes were pained when their gazes met. Her focus slid over to Eber, and her expression darkened further.

"Come, Ebercaspari."

If he objected to the use of his formal name he didn't show it. Instead he got to his feet with a practised carelessness and followed their mother into her room without another word. He left a trail of mud on the carpet behind him.

With a sigh, Leda made her way to the alcove where a large window might have been had this room been located anywhere else in the palace. A comfortable, padded seat scattered with a few cushions filled the nook, and she climbed up on to it, taking care not to bang her head on the candelabra set into the wall.

Ignoring Ami, she wrapped her arms around her knees and drew her legs in tight.

Watching Sofie's death had galvanised her. She couldn't save her sister, or any of those who had gone before her, but she needed to save herself and those who would come after. Leda would spend that night doing further work on her chimney, exhausting as it may be. She also needed to prepare herself; surviving on her own was not something she'd ever been taught. She'd picked up scraps of information that would keep her alive over the years, but to give herself the best chance she needed to learn from the experts.

Tomorrow she would find a way into the room that had always been forbidden to her, the library. It would hold all of the information she'd need to survive. She'd tried to get what she needed from the books she'd stolen from the village library in previous years, but they were frustratingly short and didn't cover what she needed.

This year, there would be no room for failure.

Guilt shredded Leda as she heard Ami playing by the fireplace. If she found a way out for herself, she needed to get the information to Ami, Eber, Markus and Mira. That would be exponentially difficult given the latter was three years old.

Leda had spent her life dreaming of living alone in her little beach paradise, but she could bear all their company, even Ami's, if it meant saving their lives.

"Follow me, Ledazaria."

Leda jumped as her mother appeared in the doorway. Eber slammed the door as he left, fists clenched and cheeks red, all good humour erased. Their mother was the only person Leda knew who could turn his mood dark that quickly.

Olora's bedroom was cosy despite its location, filled with bright rugs, wall hangings and paintings, embroidered cushions scattered about.

Leda stopped just inside the threshold, hoping to keep the conversation under five minutes. She'd been attached to her mother once when she was young, clinging to her skirts the way Ami did, begging not to be sent home with Azaria at the end of each summer.

Her mother had been unmoved, and as Leda reached her teens she had pulled herself back into check. This woman was technically her mother, she had given her life—however short it might be—but she was no more than that. She was no friend to Leda. She would not save her.

Leda curtseyed. "I'm pleased to see you," she lied, keeping her chin dipped towards the floor.

Olora's gaze swept over her, pausing at her red eyes. Thankfully, she did not comment.

"You have grown to an impressive height over the past year, my dear. If only you had inherited my facial features. Alas," Olora sighed. "Your figure is lovely, but could be improved if you practised some self-control and avoided the refreshments in Azaria's rooms."

Leda shifted her wrap around her. She wouldn't rise to her mother's bait. Olora was a woman who competed every day with three wives and seven other mistresses for the King's attention. She was bored and desperate for diversion. A screaming match with a resentful daughter would definitely provide that.

"Ledazaria, are you listening to me? Your hair is falling right out of this twist." Her mother reached forward to tuck the errant locks away and Leda jerked in surprise.

The room seemed to spin around her. She felt the energy vacate her body and staggered, grabbing the edge of Olora's desk.

"Leda!" Her mother's hand was tight around her arm, holding her upright. "What was that?"

"I ..." For a second Leda contemplated telling her mother everything: her injuries, the hibcus she was taking, its worsening side effects. The years of abuse she'd suffered at the hands of Dalev and the lies she'd used to cover it up. Then clarity descended. She must not be stupid. This woman would not help her.

"Nothing," Leda said, straightening up. "I must be tired."

Olora released her arm. "I've heard what they say about you, Leda," she said softly, a crease forming between her perfect brows. "They say that you're sickly and weak, that Azaria has drained the life from you and it's only a matter of time until you—"

"Until I what?" Leda said irritably.

"Fade away and die."

Leda had heard the whispers too, the courtiers had never been subtle about it.

"Thank you for sharing that with me, mother, very comforting. Let's hope it happens soon so I'm spared having my head cut off in front of my family, a roomful of nobles and the court jester."

Leda was out of the door before Olora could reply.

She'd lasted three minutes; that was longer than last year.

At the bottom of the staircase that would take her up towards Azaria's rooms, Leda stopped. A figure stood partway up, curiosity on his face as he took her in. As the candlelight brought his face into focus and he dipped his head to acknowledge her, she recognised him. Pyrrhus's assistant.

"Thorodin." Leda nodded at him. She didn't want to get closer and make her tear-stained face and swollen eyes more obvious. "Good evening."

"Ledazaria," he said. "My apologies for disturbing you."

The fact that he knew her name shocked her, so few had ever bothered to learn it.

Thorodin put one hand to his heart to convey the sincerity in his apology, and she gave him a small smile. He wore the same tailored coat and trousers as Pyrrhus, clearly trying to embody the classic, cerebral style of those native to Rivernesse. He didn't manage to pull it off with the same grace, though, the thick rings glinting on each finger of his hands dulling the effect.

Unlike Pyrrhus, Thorodin's emotions sat clear upon his face. His eyes gleamed with interest. He looked like a man who laughed. Leda didn't quite know what to do with that.

She noticed his breathlessness, the messiness of his hair and the sweat at his temples.

"Running from someone?" Leda asked.

This was the first time they'd spoken since he'd arrived at the palace a year ago, but he exuded that same warm air as Eber, making her feel as if they knew each other already. He seemed open, friendly even. She'd heard rumours about him, a particularly scandalous one about a dalliance between him and one of the King's mistresses, though that had apparently been quickly hushed up. Leda hoped it was true, even a hint of rebellion against her father inside the palace walls appealed to her.

Thorodin gave her a lopsided smile. "To be frank, a young lady seems to believe that if she chases me about the place I'll return her amorous intentions. She has pursued me in a determined way tonight; the events of the ceremony must have ignited her passion."

Bile rose in Leda's throat. She couldn't imagine how watching death would put anyone in a romantic mood. The image of Sofie's body flashed in her mind and would not go away.

They were silent for a moment, sizing each other up. Perhaps Leda didn't like him so much after all.

"It's dusty down here. Not healthy for a young lady," Thorodin said with a smile. Leda felt the urge to comment on his condescension but stifled it. "Please do allow me to escort you back to your rooms."

Leda nodded, perfectly demure, and followed him. For someone who had only been at the palace for a year he seemed to know it well. She stayed a step or two behind him the whole way back to Azaria's rooms, noting that he led her the entire way. He knew the route by heart.

"I've never seen a ceremony before," he said as they rounded the corner just outside her rooms. "It was as exhilarating as they say. The lengths your father is willing to go to in order to keep the people of this kingdom safe and prosperous. His sacrifice is incomprehensible; I'm in awe of him."

"Most people are," Leda said dully.

So Thorodin was just another one of the King's fawning subjects, blindly believing the lie he fed the world that he gave up his children for their benefit. They never caught on to the fact that he did very well out of his bargain with the gods. And those who did notice and dared to speak their minds quickly found themselves sentenced to death in public squares.

Her father did not tolerate rebellion.

When Thorodin left her, she was glad to see the back of him.

CHAPTER 5

The next morning Leda lay awake in bed, staring at the ceiling. Arms crossed over her stomach, she watched the sunrise bathe the stone in orange and then yellow.

She needed to see to her hand, which she'd scratched while digging away at her chimney in darkness the previous night. She needed to get up and perform her daily chores for Azaria. She needed to put her grief over Sofie and terror for herself into a box and bury it deep within her mind.

Above all that, she needed to find a way to survive outside of this palace and make the long journey to Saint-Trevale without being detected, and that meant finding a way into the library she was expressly banned from. Today, she would make it happen.

With a sigh, Leda sat up and swung her legs over the side of her bed.

Something shifted at the corner of her eye and she let out a hoarse shriek. Her hand moved without conscious thought, flinging her pillow at the intruder.

"Scary," Eber said, smirking down at the projectile that had landed on his lap. He hadn't even thrown his hands up in defence, that was how little of a threat she posed. "Azaria can skewer a squirrel with a knife from ten feet away but it's really you we should fear." He tossed the pillow on to the foot of her bed.

Leda put a hand over her hammering heart and glowered at him. "How long have you been here, Eber? You scared the life out of me!"

"About ten minutes; you were awake when I came in." He grinned, one leg tossed casually over the other as he reclined in her chair. "You'd make a terrible spy, sister. I could have come in singing opera accompanied by a full orchestra and you wouldn't have noticed. I don't know what it was about the ceiling that was so interesting; I was hesitant to interrupt."

He looked bright and bushy-tailed this morning, all signs of his displeasure after his meeting with their mother gone.

"Ha ha," Leda said with little grace. She hated when he was in one of his effervescent moods, treating her like a normal sister he could tease. "Why are you here, Eber?"

"How was your discussion with mother?"

Leda's lips thinned as she got up and went to her wardrobe, pulling a worn brocade robe on over her nightdress and tying the sash with a flourish.

"No different from any other year," she said grimly. "She complained about my lack of beauty and said I'd be the next to die. She seemed even less upset about it than last year."

"So warm and loving, our mother," Eber said with a snort that held no humour. "She told me she preferred me when I was a child who didn't have the vocabulary to talk back to her."

Leda couldn't fight the smirk that emerged. "I preferred you that way too." She moved to her mirror and ran a brush through her hair.

"Was that a joke? From Ledazaria herself?" Eber recoiled with exaggerated alarm. "I thought they'd removed your sense of humour at birth."

That wiped the smile off Leda's face. She wished she could confide in him about her terror and her guilt, and her worry that she wouldn't be able to save anyone. But to put that burden on a sixteen-year-old would be too much.

"I can't afford a sense of humour, you know that," she said quietly, meeting his eyes in the mirror's reflection over her shoulder. "What is there in my life that's funny right now?"

He was years younger than her, but at that moment he looked at her like she was a stupid toddler attempting to eat rocks. Which she had once seen him do.

"Gods, look at you, so strait-laced and dour you might as well be from Rivernesse."

She didn't rise to the bait.

"So that's it, you're just giving up?" Eber got to his feet. "Sofie's gone and you're next and you're fine with that?"

How could he think that was possible?

"Of course not!" Leda said hotly, whirling round to face him properly. "I've spent *years* trying to find a way out, Eber! My village is as remote as it can be, in the mountains. Even if I had managed to escape, it would have been a race as to what would get me first, wolves or exposure. And if I managed to survive the trek to the nearest populated area there are dogs in Leatherfell that can track my scent. It's quite literally their only purpose. They'd have found me in an *instant*."

Eber looked about as annoyed as he did when a musician in the King's orchestra was playing out of tune, but she ploughed on.

"And here ... here? It's even worse! Guards patrolling the corridors, standing by every exit—even the servant's ones—

patrolling the grounds. I have a plan of escape but it's mad and unhinged and probably won't even work, and I can't tell you a word of it until I know it might." If he knew about the chimney he'd have tried to help, and if he was caught in the armoury he would be tortured and it would be her fault. She couldn't take that risk.

"Sorry, I didn't mean to have an outburst," Leda said, sitting back down on her bed to take the weight off her smarting right leg. She looked up in shock to see that Eber's hand had come down, once, in a firm pat on her shoulder.

"I know it feels hopeless," he said softly. "But what we just saw with Sofie ... I can't watch that next year with you in her place."

"You won't have a choice," Leda said softly. "I didn't."

"At least ... at least this one was clean." Eber nearly choked on the words. "When Agon killed Erdil, I couldn't stop having nightmares about it for months."

Their brother Prince Agon was twenty-seven years of age now. He'd been young and brutal when he had hacked his Counterpart into so many pieces they'd had to load them all into a bucket to cast him into the Blainchill River.

Leda tensed as the images she'd tried ruthlessly to suppress came roaring back to her. Thank the gods Agon was out ruling over Saint-Trevale on behalf of their father. The longer he stayed away from the palace the better.

"Not that Elias and Mat's ceremony was any better."

That one had involved Prince Elias chasing his Counterpart the length and breadth of the throne room, cackling maniacally all the while. He had now been dispatched to rule over Rivernesse, and a nastier, stupider ruler they'd never known.

Leda said nothing in response. What could she say? She didn't know if Azaria would kill her cleanly, or if she would make a show of it. There was no way to predict.

Eber looked at her for a long moment, face scrunched into a frown, before sighing. "I should go, Caspari will be wondering where I am."

He left with a dispirited look about him.

She'd ruined his good mood as surely as their mother had. Excellent.

Leda dressed, splashed her face with water and pulled her hair into a plait before making her way down to the sitting room. The sun had barely risen and she was already not having a good day. She moved towards the door.

Azaria appeared from nowhere in a magenta nightgown with a ludicrously high collar.

"Leda, I need—"

"No, Azaria. I'm busy," Leda said firmly.

Azaria regarded her through slightly narrowed eyes, seemingly weighing up what a response was worth to her. "Alright." She went back into her room.

Leda took a large bite of the apple she'd taken from the dining table and stepped into the corridor, noting that the guard at the end had swivelled to watch her as she emerged. Turning her back on him, she marched resolutely in the opposite direction.

It was early for the inhabitants of the palace. Leda could see servants cleaning and stoking fires but no sign of nobles or members of the royal family. They'd been up celebrating late last night, she supposed. She wondered how Princess Elina was feeling today.

Leda decided to check the classrooms first, taking advantage of the early hour, to see what selection of reading material they might offer. Then, she'd attempt the library. The royal librarian, Levi, had threatened to knock her down the stairs the last time he'd caught her trying to sneak in, so she needed a plan.

It was easy enough to make her way down to the third

floor without attracting any attention. She wore her plain wool dress, with a simple plait and bare face, drawing the eye little more than a servant would. Watching the guard who stood before the grand doors to the King's personal study clutching his spear, she waited until he craned his head to look to his left. With barely a whisper of sound, she slipped through the archway to her right and into the corridor that led to the classroom.

She'd only been in this wing once before, a few years ago, when Azaria had instructed her to bring her more paper from her rooms. It was empty here, too, the royal children didn't start their instruction until later in the day.

Leda peered inside the main classroom, her eyes taking a while to focus in the gloom. It was empty of people. The tables rose in rows from the front of the room like a theatre, and she could see Pyrrhus's desk and blackboard at the bottom. There was only one other door near the entrance, which led into a small cupboard filled with stacks of blank paper and quills, leading back into the corridor through another door. No books whatsoever.

Defeated, Leda shut the door with a snap and a sigh. How could the classroom not have a single educational book in it? Did Pyrrhus lock them away in paranoia at the end of each day? She wouldn't put it past her father to order him to do so.

Leda stepped out back into the corridor and froze, the hair at the back of her neck rising in warning.

A flash of red at the end of the corridor as the door opened; Thorodin. She could hear his low voice as he spoke to someone at the other end, and she knew she had precious little time before he approached the classroom.

He *couldn't* find her here. If he was loyal to her father he'd turn her in instantly for being in rooms that were forbidden to her. Why was he up so early?

Leda threw herself along the corridor away from his voice, turning the corner and stopping short before a dead end. It was a single, locked door.

With a low curse she sank down to her knees and pulled a couple of pins out of her hair, inserting one into the lock and pressing it downward while leveraging the other until she heard the click of it disengaging—a handy trick she'd picked up as a young girl after Dalev had started locking her in her room as part of his rages. After a while she always became too hungry to wait for Fayne to find out what he'd done and release her. It had taken her months of frustrating trial and error to learn, but had remained a useful skill ever since.

Hearing Thorodin's voice grow closer, Leda opened the door as quickly as possible with a creak that set her teeth on edge and slid inside, closing it with a soft click behind her.

She stood at the top of a polished, straight wooden staircase. Grabbing the bannister, she looked over the edge and inhaled sharply as she saw what looked like a personal study laid out before her. Shelves stretched all the way to the ceiling across two stories, lining an entire wall, breaking only to accommodate a fireplace where a small fire crackled. She'd never seen so many books in her life.

A polished mahogany writing desk sat to the right in front of the only window, papers arranged on it in neat piles. A few books were stacked on one side, each with a bookmark sticking out. A pot of expensive-looking quills sat on the other side, pinning down a large map. Leda's eyes widened as she squinted down at it. The map depicted the conquered kingdoms, a sight she'd never been allowed to see before. She could barely comprehend how far her father's lands spread, the scale of it absolutely flabbergasting.

He must have more favour than the gods had given any

other. Leda had heard the stories, the whisperings of the time before her father had come to power, when vengeful gods had torn towns apart with curses and plagues to show their displeasure to a dismissive population. Something in the bargain her father had made with them had brought that to a halt, and Leda burned to know what he had done to make it happen.

He was as likely to tell her as Azaria was to start hugging everyone she met.

In the middle of the room sat two red armchairs, and between them a chess table with the pieces resting in ruler-straight lines.

The room was thankfully deserted. Without a second thought about how dangerous this was and how she absolutely should not be here, Leda tiptoed down the staircase. The steps creaked, but she was too entranced by the hundreds and hundreds of books of every imaginable colour and size lining the walls to care.

When she reached the shelves nearest the fireplace, unable to help herself, she trailed her fingers over the spines. This room was obviously well cared for, she couldn't see a speck of dust anywhere.

The pointed sound of a throat clearing a few moments later almost sent her staggering into the fireplace. Trying to calm her furiously beating heart, Leda turned to regard the figure standing at the bottom of the staircase where she'd been only a minute before. Recognition flared through her, along with something else she didn't want to put a name to.

Pyrrhus, with his dark hair, dark eyes and dark coat—imposing as ever and so far above her in status, despite her birth, that having him focus all of his attention on her was something of a thrill.

"Oh!"

Her eyes moved down his stiff form. In one hand

Pyrrhus held a gently steaming tankard. The smell of rich, dark chocolate wafted across the room towards her.

Tearing his eyes from her, Pyrrhus strode over to his desk, put the tankard down and briskly rolled up the map that had been stretched over it. She watched as he carefully tucked it into a drawer.

That done, he leaned against his desk and arched an eyebrow at her, his drink seemingly forgotten.

"I ... I'm so sorry." Leda flushed to the roots of her hair and just barely resisted the urge to cover her face. How embarrassing that he would find her here snooping around what was clearly his office.

What reassured her most was that he looked relatively relaxed, not like a man about to sprint back up the stairs and report her to her father.

"I ... I'm Leda." She skirted around his chess table, hand outstretched in the way she'd always seen nobles greet each other. To her surprise, he took it without hesitation. She felt a flash of awareness somewhere in her chest at the smooth warmth of his skin against hers. She couldn't remember the last time she'd initiated touching another person.

He let her go almost instantly.

"Ledazaria," he said, nodding. "I know who you are."

His voice saying that name was just wrong.

"Oh, no, please—just Leda."

He made no reply to that. For someone so educated he wasn't an effusive conversationalist. Then again, that made him a perfect ambassador for Rivernesse; they were generally a reserved people, viewing the exaggerated emotions of inhabitants of Viridiana as self-indulgent and strange.

There was a strain in Pyrrhus's face as he looked at her, probably his discomfort at having her in his private rooms, and Leda clenched her hands as she realised she had no idea what to do with them.

With a small, nervous laugh, she started walking towards the staircase to leave him in peace. Maybe if she got out quickly enough he'd forget that she'd been trespassing.

"I'm sorry, I should go. If you could ... could consider not mentioning finding me here to anyone I'd be immensely grateful." Leda hated how weak her voice was as she clasped the bannister. Was this really what she sounded like? How mortifying.

"I have no interest in telling anyone."

She gave him a stilted nod as relief flooded her, turning once more to leave. "Thank you."

"Wait."

Leda looked back at him in surprise. "Yes?"

Pyrrhus opened his mouth and paused, seeming to change his mind on what to say seconds before he spoke. "Last summer I saw you teaching Counterparts to swim in the river, Markuselov and Amifessler. It was kind of you to pay them attention."

His words were stilted but his voice was so rich, how could the royal children concentrate when he was lecturing them?

Dear gods, Leda, please get a grip.

"Oh, yes, thank you," Leda said, one foot on the staircase that would take her away from this odd conversation and the danger of being found here.

The silence that followed made her want to squirm.

"I'm so sorry, I never would have come in here if I'd known these were your rooms."

What a lie, she'd have broken in two years ago had she known. She was fascinated by the pieces of him that this room revealed, this remote man who was so sparing with his words.

Pyrrhus had turned away, casting an assessing eye over

his desk. "Would you mind passing me that book on Viridian gemstones?"

Leda looked down at the two books on the side table at the foot of the staircase that she'd been a second from knocking over.

They both had beautiful green covers, embossed titles shining in the firelight. One book on gems, the other on nomadic Doviet travel practices. She picked up the book closest to her and brought it over to him. He took it with a nod of thanks, adding it to the stack on his desk.

"I'll leave you alone now, I know you're not allowed to speak to Counterparts. We can't have you accidentally giving me an education."

Leda returned to the staircase. She couldn't keep the dryness out of her voice at that last part, and something in what she said seemed to spark life in him as he stared down at the book she'd passed him.

Pyrrhus tilted his head to one side. "And do you always abide by every rule?"

His eyes glittered with the first hint of emotion she'd ever seen in them, and she was so surprised by that and by his words that she took her foot off the step.

"No," Leda said simply, scanning his face with an intensity she would be surprised if he didn't find alarming. "I'm becoming rebellious in my old age. It's a side effect of having one year left to live."

That had his brows pulling down into a frown. "You don't know that."

"Don't I?"

Leda touched a fingertip to the pointed head of one of the pieces on his chess table. She would love to learn to play. Fayne had never been taught so couldn't pass the skill on to her. Azaria had been sent a tutor from the village a few years ago during the winter, but Leda hadn't found an opportunity to eavesdrop.

It was probably for the best, anyway. If she managed to escape she'd be living in isolation for the rest of her life, away from the nightmare that was her family, and would have no one to play chess with even if she did know how.

Leda looked longingly at the hundreds of books lining the shelves around her, full of knowledge she'd never be able to access.

A whooshing noise sounded and she instinctively put her hands out, catching the small book that Pyrrhus had just tossed her from one of the stacks that lay upon his desk. A bookmark, which he'd clearly just removed from it, dangled from his hand.

"When you come down here I would recommend you begin by reading that. It's a brief history of the Five Kingdoms. It doesn't include much about Doviet given their culture; they practice oral history and don't like to see it written down, but the book gives an excellent account of the other kingdoms. You might find it … interesting to learn more about the lands your father rules."

Leda observed the desk where the map she had glimpsed was now hidden. She held the book like it was made of glass and she was afraid it would shatter if she gripped it too tight. He couldn't possibly know the gift he was giving her.

"When … when I come down here?" she asked, smoothing a hand along the embossed spine of the book.

Pyrrhus sat behind his desk, flipping the tails of his coat behind him as he did so. He didn't make eye contact with her, which was probably for the best given hers were comically and, to his view, surely ostentatiously, wide. With his usual precise movements, he picked up his quill and dipped it in ink.

"I hold lectures and discussion groups most days in the early afternoons, during which time this room will be unoccupied. No one is permitted access but me." His lips twitched ever so slightly at the corners. "And now you. Make sure no one sees you entering, I trust I do not need to elaborate on what the consequences might be for both of us."

Leda took a breath, refilling lungs that felt painfully empty. "Why would you allow this?"

It was such an unexpectedly kind gesture, something she wasn't used to from anyone aside from Fayne, and on occasion her Counterpart brothers and sisters. Leda wracked her brain and couldn't think of a single reason he might have for defying his King, even in this small way, for her.

The scratching of Pyrrhus's quill paused as he lifted it from the paper, though he didn't look up at her. He seemed keen to avoid engaging with her too much now he'd moved past the shock of seeing her there.

"It is no trouble to me," he said quietly.

Ah, so it was pity. His moral compass. He wanted to make the final months of a doomed young woman's life more palatable. Kind, thoughtful, sweet—it made her want to scream.

As Leda made to leave, a bolt of panic shot through her. She couldn't believe she'd almost overlooked it.

"How do you know I can read?"

It was a terrible secret, one that could get her in incomprehensible trouble and would mean certain death for Fayne for teaching her. A Counterpart could not be literate.

Pyrrhus lifted an eyebrow and pointed his quill to the book on gemstones she had passed to him, indistinguishable from the other green book on the table but for its title.

She hadn't been thinking, too overwhelmed by the situation she'd got herself into. She could kick herself.

Pyrrhus leaned back in his chair, eyeing her speculatively. It was the first time she'd seen him without his back ramrod straight. "I had my suspicions earlier. I have a rather extensive network of librarians throughout the Five Kingdoms."

Leda kept her face expressionless, deeply afraid that someone else might have deduced her secret as well as Pyrrhus. Her siblings had been whipped for less egregious rebellion.

"Books have been going missing for years from your village, despite the low literacy rate. Not remarkable on its own, books are stolen from libraries every day. However, those taken from that particular location always have a habit of turning up less than a week later, in pristine condition, on the correct space on their shelves as if they hadn't been away for a second. I simply put two and two together, and you just confirmed it for me."

"Please—"

"You have nothing to fear from me. I value learning above all else; I will keep your secret."

Leda sighed in relief, clutching the book he'd given her to her chest. She had started stealing the Leatherfell library books when she was young and stupid, not thinking about what might happen if anyone put the pieces together.

"And here I thought I was good at being invisible."

Pyrrhus had turned back to his writing. "You do yourself discredit, Ledazaria. You are more noticeable than you might think." His eyes narrowed slightly after he said that, and she felt a thrill shoot through her at the inadvertent compliment. "All of the Counterparts are. Good day."

She placed the book reverently on the side table beside the staircase.

"Good day, Pyrrhus."

CHAPTER 6

*T*he next day began, as it so often did, with the interminable boredom of the thrice-weekly gods' gratification ceremony in the palace temple.

Leda sat on the floor, legs crossed like a child, in the crowd of silent courtiers, and stared down at her prayer garland. She'd gone to the gardens earlier to choose the flowers to wind around it for this session, selecting the small blue-violet flowers of the amethyst shrub for its connection to clarity and wisdom—anything that might entice the gods to actually communicate with her.

She'd always found the temple to be simultaneously unbearably stuffy and chilling in its silence as the congregation spoke to their own personal gods in their heads.

Leda had never named her god, though most people took great pride in doing so when they reached adulthood.

She'd name hers if it ever bothered to speak to her.

The temple, which sat in the very heart of the palace, made the rest of the building look like a simple country tavern with its decadence.

It was enormous and circular. The floor and walls were covered in gold, so dazzling they were painful to look at. The ceiling was painted in an elaborate fresco of the spirits who did the bidding of the gods. Around the skirting boards were painted dark, curling flames and the leering, horned heads of the demons of the netherworld. These creatures were invisible to everyone, but apparently that hadn't stood in the way of whoever had painted them.

In the centre of the room stood six enormous marble statues that stretched twenty feet into the air. They were turned inwards towards each other, as though conversing about secret matters, and wore long robes that covered everything except their faces. Not that their faces were worth looking at, in Leda's opinion, given they were smooth circles without features.

No one had ever been able to agree on whether to depict them as human-esque or something more fantastical, and so the choice throughout the lands was to settle on neither.

On one side of the room stood a huge plinth upon which the Counterpart axe rested. Leda refused to look at it as a matter of course.

Opposite was a group of chairs for the priestesses to sit on when they weren't speaking with worshippers. From there they had a nice view of the final cluster of statues in the room.

This arrangement was smaller than those of the gods, of course, only standing six foot high. It was much like the painting in the entrance hall, the royal family standing tall and proud in an outward-facing circle. The King, largest of them all, and his queens and royal children rendered in marble. His mistresses in granite, and finally his Counterpart children. Their likenesses were composed of crumpled white parchment paper. They looked like something from the netherworld that might haunt one's nightmares.

Whenever a Counterpart was killed in the ceremony, their statue was ritually burned by the priestesses at the exact moment their body was cast into the Blainchill River. Piles of dusty ash were scattered at odd intervals within the structure.

Of course, paper was a difficult sculpting material to work with, and so one of the priestesses had needed to point out to Leda which creepy, shapeless mass depicted her. It drew her eye as soon as she'd entered the room, it always did, and she imagined what it would look like going up in flame, the light of it flickering off the marble of Azaria's likeness.

It would be reality, soon enough.

The statues were, like much of the palace, a sumptu-ously rendered lie. Princess Gabriell had been born shortly after the installation had been completed, the twelfth royal child. The King had a horror of odd numbers, and so was soothed enormously by her birth. Mistress Aina was now pregnant with what would be Princess Gabriell's Counter-part, completing the set.

Queen Verene, the King's first and most adored wife who stood beside him here, had been dead for years. When her children, the two eldest royals, had killed their Counterparts and left the palace to conquer new lands, they had fallen into a dispute over territory. Prince Fynn had conquered Saint-Trevale, and two years later his desperate sister, who had not managed to secure anything for herself, had tried to take it from him. The ensuing bloody battle resulted in both their deaths.

When she received the news of her children's deaths at the hands of one other, Queen Verene had died of heart-break, or so they said.

Leda turned away from the depressing sight and stretched out her arms as much as she dared; she didn't want to be told off by a priestess for disturbing the peace. Trying not to move her head too much, she looked around the gathered crowd, hoping to see something that might alleviate her boredom.

Something unexpected sparked in her chest when her eyes fell on Pyrrhus, who appeared to be frowning with concentration in the corner. Just behind him was Eber, who was staring up at the ceiling with his mouth slightly open. Prince Caspari lounged beside him and appeared to be counting his own fingers, so who knew what was going on there.

The King knelt upon a special cushion in the very centre of the six statues of the gods, a place only he was allowed to occupy. He was not to be disturbed there while praying, on pain of death or dismemberment. He clutched his own prayer garland, which today was an explosion of crimson red roses symbolising mourning.

As if he'd ever felt anything for Sofie at all.

Opposite Leda, Elina looked like she was having a full and animated conversation inside her own head, her features tense.

Leda frowned and screwed her own eyes shut tight, willing herself to concentrate harder. If she could reach that mythic level of focus the books and priestess' periodicals were always yammering on about perhaps she would actually hear a response for once in her life.

But she was just a Counterpart, her god had no interest in speaking with her. Elina would go forth and conquer kingdoms and rule over millions and would need the guiding hand of the divine to do so, and Leda would simply die. Not someone worth investing in, for a busy god doing ... well, whatever it was they got up to in the heavens.

She understood their disinterest in her, in a way. But it still hurt. And it was so exhausting to cover up, to ensure that no one was aware of this glaring flaw. To be abandoned by the gods was to be immoral, worthy of shunning by all who worshipped them.

Blowing out a breath, Leda looked once again to her father. His head was bowed at such an angle she would be very surprised if his neck wasn't in significant pain.

He was more fervent than any of the others in this room, but she supposed it made sense. These gods were the ones who had placed him on the throne, after all, and he was the one who had introduced formal worship of them to the masses. Before he had taken the throne all those decades ago the people had worshipped the gods as and when they pleased. They didn't need priestesses and prayer garlands and all the other pomp and pageantry forced on them.

Now, they had to attend the temples under the watchful eye of the priestesses three times a week. If they declined to go, they were flogged in public.

Whatever deal her father had struck, it was beneficial for most people who weren't his illegitimate children. The skies over the Five Kingdoms were serene and blue throughout the year, raining as and when the crops desired it. The temperatures were warm as needed in summer, and not so cold as to be too uncomfortable in winter. The harvests prospered and even the poorest of the people of the Five Kingdoms were reasonably well fed.

Well, when her father didn't take their resources for himself, that was. Fayne had always said that was his most effective strategy to stem any rebellion. He ensured that aggression was confined to fighting over resources within communities. He didn't want envious eyes turning on him.

If the people only knew how stuffed with gold his precious palace was.

Oh gods, how much longer until she could leave? Judging by the position of the sun out the window they must be nearly done with their mandated hour of worship.

Leda looked around to see Azaria staring, but not at her. Instead, those flinty blue eyes were fixed on Leda's sad paper likeness in the display of royal statues.

Sometimes Leda was certain that Azaria was fiendishly excited to kill her—other times not.

It wasn't as if Azaria had a choice. If she refused to go through with the ceremony, both she and Leda would be killed, so it would all be for nothing.

Their father held them all there like puppets on his strings, using his manipulative ultimatums to keep them all in line. Refuse to kill your Counterpart? You die too. Your Counterpart escapes or dies before the ceremony? Another unknown child of the King will be brought in from a secret location and sacrificed in their place.

Or so they were told; none of that had ever happened before. Leda wasn't sure they were more than just empty threats, but couldn't prove it either way.

That was the thought that curdled her blood when she considered escaping, that another nameless, faceless but utterly innocent sibling of hers might pay the price for her freedom.

Her father would get his blood sacrifice, one way or another. If enough time passed without blood spilt the gods would rebel and he would lose his kingdom. Though he loved his royal children, or seemed to, his kingdom was entwined with his very bones. He would kill every one of them, his queens, his mistresses, his beloved dogs, to keep it.

To the people of Viridiana, power was everything. And an unfortunate number of the royal children had inherited that predilection as well. Leda could see it in Azaria's determined gaze whenever she looked at the throne, in the way Elina threw herself into battle training, in the calculated stare Caspari directed at his siblings at dinner. She had seen it most clearly in the brutal faces of her older brothers

Prince Agon and Prince Elias as they had hacked their own Counterparts into pieces during their ceremonies.

Leda shifted restlessly, her leg was falling asleep. Azaria looked up at her only to mouth 'keep still' with a deeply unamused expression.

Leda felt her head turning, without her conscious approval, towards a certain dark-haired man she had no business looking at. She forced her eyes shut again.

Talk to me, you stupid, good-for-nothing, ignorant gods!

Nothing back, as always. Perhaps she should get more aggressive in her addresses to them and see if she could provoke them into coming back to her with something, even if only a harsh rebuke? She'd settle for that.

It was no different from how she felt in real life, always screaming into the void, no one really listening.

CHAPTER 7

*F*or the next few weeks Leda visited Pyrrhus's
study almost every day, always in the afternoon
when Azaria was distracted with archery or weaving or her
studies with her royal siblings. Occasionally Azaria went to
the King's throne room and they discussed politics and
philosophy and languages for hours with his courtiers.
Sometimes they feasted until dawn or threw elaborate
masques. It made it easy for Leda to complete her chores in
a rush in the mornings, slip into the study in the early afternoons, and spend the nights carving away at her chimney.

Pyrrhus was never there when she arrived, but she
noticed that every few days a new book appeared on the
table by the armchair she used. They focused on a range of
subjects, from botany to languages to politics, and she had
devoured each in turn alongside those she'd chosen from
his collection to aid her in her life outside the palace.

Every book she'd managed to steal from a library previously had needed to be read with frantic speed so she could
return them quickly.

Now, it was like being in a different world. Leda had time

to peruse, to go back to different tomes and cross-check concepts she hadn't understood. Her view of the world outside was growing richer, and the bitterness that she might never get to experience any of it was growing too.

When she'd read a book about her father's ascension to the throne of Viridiana all those years ago she'd had a particularly miserly expression on her face as she turned the pages. She read of the peaceful but poverty-stricken reigns of her grandfather and great-grandfather and those before them. Her father had apparently decided he'd had quite enough of that. Intelligent and brave and supported by the gods, the rumour was that he'd killed his elder brother with poison to ensure his succession to the throne. He'd tried to conquer foreign lands, to get more and more and more. He was always a glutton, it seemed; that wasn't a feature that had developed in him over time.

But he'd failed at first, been pushed back. He'd conquered Glisse, then lost it, and had forfeited vast swathes of Viridiana, his home country, to North Doviet. Only a desperate deal, struck with the gods at the cost of the blood of his own children, had given him the power needed to conquer and hold the Five Kingdoms.

What a depressing book; she'd throw it in the fire if it weren't utter sacrilege to do so.

Pyrrhus had found her a few times, she suspected. She'd feel the disturbance in the air from the door opening at the top of the staircase, and stared into the fire whenever she felt his presence behind her. Sometimes she could smell the scent of hot chocolate, seemingly his only vice despite the stiflingly hot palace. He would stand there for a few moments, before closing the door softly. She always left within minutes, taking that as the signal that he needed his room back.

On a surprisingly cool evening at the height of summer, Leda was sitting cross-legged on the rug in his study, flicking bemusedly through a tome on mathematics that barely managed to cling to her attention.

She'd just picked up Azaria's new archery equipment, a gift from their father, from the armoury. She'd tossed it carelessly on the floor next to her, perilously close to the fire.

The door above opened with a creak and Leda looked up to see Pyrrhus framed by the light of the corridor. A look out the window told her that she'd completely missed the sun beginning to set.

"Oh, pardon me, I didn't realise the time!" Leda leapt to her feet and overturned the book in her lap in her haste. Pyrrhus hadn't moved from his spot at the top of the stairs.

He held up a hand to stay her.

"Should I fear for my life?" he asked, looking at the bow and arrows scattered around her feet.

"Er ... oh!" Leda looked down with an embarrassed huff. "Azaria had a set of arrows made for her. They just arrived. The tips are silver. More lethal, you know?" She was rambling, she never knew what to say to him.

Leda shrugged to indicate she really had no idea whether silver arrows were functional or merely decorative. It wasn't like Azaria needed any adjustments to make her a more proficient killer, she could take down a fully grown human with two or three sharp twigs if she was minded to.

"And you're bringing the arrows to her?"

Leda crossed her arms, wondering whether she should tell him the truth. He looked so forbidding up there above her, but he'd proven relatively trustworthy so far. "I haven't decided." In all honesty she'd been considering turning them into kindling for his fire before he'd arrived.

The corners of Pyrrhus's mouth twitched as he leaned

over the bannister to get a better look at her. She'd surprised him. It was slightly unnerving watching him attempt to read her when she failed so miserably at reciprocating.

"Never mind," she muttered, leaning down to scoop up the quiver into one arm. Taking her shawl from the back of her armchair with the other, she hurried to the staircase.

Leda put her right leg on the lowest step and her muscles chose that moment to fail her, collapsing under her weight like paper. With a short, sharp cry of pain, she crumpled to the ground. The clatter of wood falling from her arms and on to the stone floor rang out.

"Ledazaria—" Pyrrhus was one step above her in an instant. He reached out as if to help her up and then withdrew his hand so quickly she questioned whether she'd imagined it. Her head was spinning so it was entirely possible. With a whimper, she clutched her thigh with one hand, letting her forehead rest on the cool wood of the step above the one she was sprawled across.

"Are you alright?" Pyrrhus's voice was steady, but he did seem concerned despite the respectable distance he was keeping from her.

Leda felt as if all the energy had been sucked out of her body, though her heart was beating frantically in her chest, like it wanted to burst out. Of all the times to have a hibcus episode, why did it have to be here, in front of *him*?

With a poorly stifled whimper, Leda pulled on what little reserve she had left and dragged herself to her feet, gripping the bannister with white-knuckled hands.

There was a spark of suspicion in Pyrrhus's eyes that she did not want to see there at all.

"Are you dizzy?" He made as if to reach for her once more, but again stopped himself. It looked like an intense battle was playing out in his mind. "How is your pulse?"

He had just alluded to two of the principal side effects of extended hibcus use and Leda scoffed to hide her panic that he might know.

She leaned back against the wall in what she hoped was a nonchalant fashion. In reality, she was using it to keep her upright.

"I'm not dizzy," she lied to his spinning, whirling face. Her pulse was thudding so fast he could probably see it in her throat. Thankfully he seemed to be scanning her eyes instead. Was he checking to see if she was trying to deceive him?

"Are you su—"

"It's an old injury," she said quickly, making sure to interrupt him. She slapped her right thigh for good measure, and instantly regretted the idiotic move as more pain shot through it.

"What kind of injury?" Pyrrhus stepped closer despite himself, eyes now on the skirts that concealed the jagged scar on her leg.

"None of your business," Leda said. She felt cornered, but wasn't as bothered about it as she would have been were anyone else caging her in against the wall. It was interesting to have the full focus of Pyrrhus's curiosity on her. This was the most attention anyone had paid her in a long time.

"I apologise, I did not mean to pry."

She felt the odd compulsion to tell him her secrets. To her surprise as much as his, what she gave him next was a truth he hadn't even asked for.

"When we were ten I stole Azaria's favourite doll, and accidentally pulled its arm off. When she found out, she went to the kitchen and got a knife. She made me apologise to her and then she stabbed me in the leg."

Leda left out the gruesome details of how Azaria had not stopped there, instead dragging the knife down the length of her thigh with a curious expression, ignoring her screams. Azaria had said she was sorry afterwards when Fayne had arrived to find them both drenched in blood, Leda half-conscious, and shattered the silence with a piercing screech.

"The, er ... the village physician treated me well; you can barely see the scar now."

Why was she lying to him? It wasn't as though knowing the extent of her scar would make any difference—he'd never see it, nor would anyone else if she could help it. But she didn't want his pity. "I just lose support in my leg sometimes; I don't think it'll ever heal completely."

She didn't tell him that ever since that day Azaria had kept a knife strapped to her boot. That way she wouldn't have to rely on going all the way to the kitchen for a weapon when she next needed one.

Leda slid a couple of inches down the wall, and whatever battle was playing out in Pyrrhus's mind seemed to reach its conclusion. He stepped forward and caught her sagging shoulders in his hands, keeping her upright. She hissed out a breath as he took the bulk of her weight off her leg.

"You need to see the royal physician."

Ambrose was his friend, or so she assumed given how often she saw them together at meals. Though for friends, they often appeared angry with one another. Then again, perhaps that was normal. Leda had no idea what friendship should look like, she'd never been allowed to keep any real friends of her own.

She looked down at Pyrrhus's arms, the strength in them evident under his coat as he steadied her. It was strange, she wouldn't have expected an academic to be so strongly built, but he held her up as easily as if she were made of feathers.

She shook her head. "No, no, I'm fine."

"I insist—"

Her fingertips sank into the soft fabric covering his arms as she, in a rather unladylike fashion, used him to claw her way back up into a standing position.

The feeling of another person so close overwhelmed her.

"Let me go."

He did so instantly.

"Allow me to take you to the infirmary," Pyrrhus said. "Please. For my own peace of mind, if nothing else."

She softened instantly. "I'm not allowed to see him; you know that." The rule about benefitting from the royal tutor matched the one about the royal physician. The King would ensure that his Counterparts didn't die so that they could continue to take part in his ceremonies, but if they were ill and likely to recover he had no interest in diverting his personal medical resources towards them.

"Ambrose will see you if I bring you to him." Pyrrhus drew one of her arms around his shoulders and put his arm firmly around her waist. He dwarfed her so much in height that she was nearly lifted off her feet. "He's only one floor away. Lean on me as we go up the stairs."

Mortified by her weakness, Leda stayed silent as they made their way slowly up the steps. The warmth of his body was shocking in such close proximity to hers, and she kept her eyes squarely a step ahead of her to make sure she didn't trip. Her leg throbbed in protest at each movement. If only she had access to her hibcus right now she could at least take the pain away, but she could never risk Pyrrhus seeing her with it.

Going to see Ambrose felt like a terrible idea, she had no idea how he'd talked her into it, but off they went.

The corridors were dark, candles flickering weakly in

their brackets. Pyrrhus took her to the nearest tightly spiralled staircase and helped her up it, bringing them to the fourth floor.

When Pyrrhus opened the door to the infirmary he was pressed so close to her that she actually felt his sigh of relief at what was inside. Edging over the threshold, Leda eyed the line of beds pushed against the left wall warily. Each had a heavily brocaded privacy screen next to it, but thankfully they all looked empty. A range of intimidating contraptions stood along the opposite wall, behind a desk piled high with a mess of books and papers.

This room recalled difficult memories. Azaria had injured a number of her siblings over the years and so she had often made the pilgrimage to the infirmary to offer her apologies, dragging Leda along with her as a witness. Leda remembered the time she had sat on one of the sofas in the far corner, watching her sister bending over the prince whose arm she'd severed during an argument, and barely repressed a shudder.

Ambrose was alone, sitting at his desk and polishing a set of round spectacles she'd never seen him wear. He sported his customary pristine silver coat. With his light hair, eyes and brows he was entirely without colour. He and Pyrrhus were stark opposites in every way. While Pyrrhus's face was aristocratic and austere, Ambrose had laugh lines and crinkles at the corners of his eyes.

That seemed incongruous, given Leda had never actually seen the man smile.

He was certainly not smiling at that moment, instead looking accusingly at Pyrrhus as he got to his feet.

"Ledazaria?" he said, though he was still looking at Pyrrhus.

Leda felt a flash of surprise mixed with pleasure, it was

still so rare that people knew who she was when she wasn't standing next to Azaria.

If Pyrrhus had noticed Ambrose's bad mood he didn't mention it, steering Leda over to the bed closest to the desk. She felt slightly bereft when he let her go and turned to his friend. "Her right leg is injured."

"Is that so?" Ambrose's eyes flicked to her and then back to Pyrrhus. "I am forbidden to treat her; you know that."

"I don't see anyone here who would stop you."

Ambrose's eyes narrowed, although he had taken a step towards Leda, seemingly unconsciously. His aura was cold, frosty as a deep winter's night. While Pyrrhus was cool in the way of someone who existed so much in his own mind he barely noticed those in the room with him, Ambrose looked as though he undertook a thorough review of all who approached him and found each and every one of them wanting.

"Why take the risk?" Ambrose asked.

"You know why."

Leda had no idea what either of them was talking about.

"Pyrrhus, I told you not to—"

A flash of anger appeared on Pyrrhus's face. "We are not discussing this now."

"Oh, for the sake of the gods." Ambrose threw his hands in the air and Leda saw that he wore three thick silver rings on one hand. "Lock the doors, then."

As Pyrrhus did so, Ambrose turned to Leda with a slightly less aggressive expression.

Ambrose looked into Leda's eyes and cocked his head as he registered her dilated pupils. She dropped her gaze in an attempt to disguise the common sign of hibcus use. He could attempt to treat her leg, but he would not learn of how Dalev had chosen to medicate her if she could help it.

Ambrose pulled a wooden tube out of his pocket and

crouched down to place it against her chest, making her flinch. He held his ear against it, presumably listening to the amplified beating of her heart, and she jerked away. He gave her a knowing look, but put the instrument down.

"May I see your leg?" he asked politely.

He looked deathly tired, which she supposed would be normal for someone with the stresses of his job. She'd watched him try to save Prince Elias's arm last year and saw, along with everyone else in the palace, how he'd taken the brunt of the King's fury when he'd been unsuccessful. Azaria, of course, had been passed over as favoured child that year, giving Leda a stay of execution.

Leda hesitated, glancing up at Pyrrhus, who was hovering nearby.

"Yes, of course," she said. "Pyrrhus, would you mind turning around?"

He went further than that, turning on his heel and walking to the far end of the room. He stopped in front of a depiction of a human skeleton which stood in front of a large window, his hands clasped behind his back as he inspected it.

Reassured that he had no intention of turning around, Leda gathered the plain wool of her skirts, carefully rolling them up so that Ambrose might see the jagged scar that ran the length of her thigh. To his credit, he didn't exclaim or show the slightest degree of shock, though his mouth tightened into a grimace. He had treated enough of her siblings to recognise Azaria's style. She'd always liked to play with blades.

"A knife wound, if I am not mistaken?" He peered down at the scar with a frown.

"Yes." She looked away from her leg, watching Pyrrhus, who had moved on to look at the model of a heart rendered in silver on the windowsill. "A kitchen knife. About a decade ago."

"And how was it treated?"

That was her chance to tell him about the hibcus.

She couldn't. They would take the hibcus away from her, and she'd be in constant, mind-numbing pain for the rest of her life. She'd never escape if she didn't have her wits about her.

"It wasn't properly treated," Leda said crisply. "The healer bandaged it up and then waited for it to heal and for the fever to pass. No ointments, medicine or stitches."

"Or pain relief, no doubt," Ambrose said, voice heavy with scepticism. She thanked the gods that he didn't give her time to respond. "It must have taken months to heal."

"Superficially, yes ... though ... I'm not sure that it ever really healed," Leda said with a pitiful attempt at a smile. "I can walk on the leg well now, and exercise on it for short periods of time, but I occasionally have episodes where it refuses to work for me. I usually just go to bed and it's back to normal by the next day."

Ambrose's mouth moved but no sound came out. He was silent for an uncomfortably long time.

"Tincture of orange willow," he said finally, drawing himself up to his full height and going to rummage in a large glass-fronted cabinet behind his desk. "Take half a teaspoon each morning. It should help with any pain. You'll need to strengthen your leg muscles to prevent them failing quite so often. Do you often take exercise?"

"Not really." Unless desperately hoisting herself up to chisel pieces of stone out of an old chimney counted.

"No," Ambrose sighed, handing her the bottle of tincture. "I suppose you'd be too tired for that." It was unspoken between them that he was referring to her hibcus use, which drained her of as much energy as it did pain.

Leda desperately wanted to get out of that room. Grabbing the bottle of orange willow from him with a tight nod, she got to her feet. Her leg wobbled but held her.

"Thank you, I appreciate your help. I'll head off now."

Pyrrhus turned from the window. "I'll see you back to—"

"No! No, thank you. I'm fine." Without waiting for a reply, she scurried from the room.

CHAPTER 8

*A*mbrose's tincture worked wonders on Leda, clearing the fog in her brain each morning and making her leg feel stronger than it ever had before. Being able to walk around the palace secure in the knowledge that her leg wouldn't fail and send her face first on to the floor was invigorating. Unfortunately the hibcus still made her weak as a kitten at times, but at least that applied to her whole body, not just her leg. She could cope with that.

Pyrrhus and Ambrose knowing who she was without her needing to introduce herself had been exhilarating, but now Leda was becoming better known throughout the palace, the idea of being noticed lost its lustre. Suddenly the servants were looking at her with mixed sympathy and fear, scurrying away when she entered a room as if she'd infect them with her bad luck.

Rumours raced around the courtiers that the King was once again pleased with his daughter Azaria, and had forgiven her for her past transgressions. They said she was likely to be back in his good graces and would be this year's favoured child. That meant that Leda would be next to follow in Sofie's footsteps.

The court had liked Sofie; she was pretty and docile and sweet. She had no temper tantrums or moments of rebellion, and appeared to accept her fate with grace.

Leda, they liked less. They saw her as icy, cold, and reserved. Too much like Azaria. She was distant from them, and they believed that was because she thought herself above them.

In a way, she did. If she had a choice like they did she would be living a fulfilling life away from the gossip and blackmail and blood of the royal court. She'd give anything for it.

If the courtiers were displeased with her behaviour, Azaria was even more so. Leda had always been a somewhat helpful aide to her, performing her chores with speed if not enthusiasm. Now, she dragged her feet. Her sewing on Azaria's new dresses was haphazard, her storage system for Azaria's weapons had fallen into disarray, and how Azaria's favourite flute had appeared in the fire one night Leda claimed to have no idea.

These were minor acts of rebellion, but Leda's thoughts were turning darker, towards actions she'd never considered in the past. She barely recognised herself. If she could find a way to get her sister to disgrace herself in front of the King once more, she could buy herself another year. She dismissed that thought relatively quickly—it would need to be something as terrible, or worse, as cutting off a royal child's arm, and it would mean one of her Counterpart siblings suffering. She couldn't bear that on her conscience, even if it secured her more time. She'd need to find another way.

When Leda was awoken at four in the morning by Azaria demanding that she go to the armoury and fetch her throwing knives for a hunt she wasn't at all surprised. She dragged herself out of bed with only a glare for Azaria and made her way groggily to the armoury.

When she entered it was like stepping into cool shade beneath a tree on a hot day. The room was made of dull grey stone, weapons of every conceivable size and shape covering the walls around the enormous and thankfully dormant fireplace.

Milos sat in the middle of the room on his stool, his back to her as he inspected a vicious blade on his lap. He turned to see who had dared interrupt him so early in the morning.

"Tell her no," Milos said gruffly, returning his attention to the sword. "Azaria's been at the palace all of five bloody minutes and I've had orders from her every time I open my eyes. Give me some peace, for the love of the gods."

He and Azaria did not get on.

Leda stifled a smile. Milos had never been particularly kind to her, but he'd never been cruel. She even thought sometimes that he might prefer her to her demanding sister.

Plus, he was the key to her escape—albeit unknowingly. She would forever view him with affection for that.

"She needs her throwing knives, please," Leda said politely. "She's going hunting."

"In the pitch-black?"

"She likes the challenge."

Milos sighed. "Don't know how you put up with her," he grumbled. "You stay here; I'll get 'em. They went into storage last winter." He hooked the sword he'd been inspecting on to the wall behind Leda and disappeared from the room, leaving her alone.

Leda slid a hand over the cool bricks of the chimney surrounding the enormous fireplace. She didn't dare to stick her head in when Milos was around, but she knew if she did she would find the series of painstakingly carved grooves just big enough for hands and feet to slot into.

She just needed to carve four more holds, a few weeks' work and then, finally, she'd be free.

She would hide letters in Pyrrhus's study for her Counterpart brothers and sisters for him to find after she was gone, praying that her instinct that he was trustworthy wouldn't backfire on her. If he found the information outlining her escape plan within and shared it with them, they would be able to get out the same way she had.

The plan had come into her mind when she was ten years old and she'd spent years refining it. It was insane, and that was why it just might work. Guards never patrolled the roof, it was too steeply sloped and there were no doors to it. Leda knew from scouting outside the palace that they wouldn't be able to see her between the mass of intersecting structures that made up the roofs.

Leda stroked her hand down the brick, her plan running through her mind as it had a million times before. It comforted her.

She would wait until everyone in the palace was distracted by some spectacle, a feast or a ball or some such, and would climb out of the chimney and on to the roof with her supplies. There, she would stay for a week as they sent out the search parties and dogs to find her. Then, late one night, she would rappel down the side of the palace. She would make her way around the areas the guards patrolled, which she had spent years learning, and disappear into the forest.

They would be searching for her in entirely the wrong place.

Her ultimate destination? The country of Saint-Trevale and the cottage on the beach that had once belonged to Fayne before her marriage to Dalev. Leda had a map tucked away that Fayne had drawn for her, years ago, with instructions on how to find the key she'd hidden in a hollow tree trunk.

But Leda needed to hold steady, until she was able to execute her plan.

Reading in Pyrrhus's rooms was an excellent distraction for her, but she couldn't keep going back. She'd frightened herself one day, when she was alone, curled up in front of the fire. The glint of a golden coin reflecting the light had caught her eye, and she'd lowered her book to observe it, mouth suddenly dry.

It lay innocently on a side table next to a bushy green pot plant.

Pyrrhus must have discarded it there without thought. He was unlikely to notice it missing, Leda had never got the impression that he struggled for money. She could take it, just as she had every other loose coin she'd found since she was ten years old. It would be another step to funding her independence, as abhorrent as she found the practice of stealing in the first place.

Something stopped Leda from moving forward to snatch it, holding her as still as if her whole body were wrapped in chains.

She couldn't take it from him.

That was a problem. A huge one.

She was getting attached. The almost magnetic compulsion Leda felt to be near him was beyond inappropriate, and it both thrilled and frightened her.

The good news was that Pyrrhus was uniquely skilled at keeping Leda at a sensible distance. She wouldn't be surprised if he was aware of her reluctant interest in him and was reticent to put her in her place, out of sheer pity. How embarrassing.

And while it was edifying to read the books he suggested for her, as well as the ones she'd chosen from his shelves,

Leda wondered if she was soaking up much knowledge that way. Perhaps she was missing out on the benefits of listening to an expert speak.

That was the logic she used to argue herself into listening in on Pyrrhus's discussion groups with the older royal children: Azaria, Elina and Caspari. The cupboard full of supplies that led into the classroom had a second door out into the corridor, and Leda made use of her lock-picking skills to get inside. She slid herself in between a box of papers and the wall so that anyone who opened the door from the classroom side wouldn't easily spot her. Then, she sat, wrapped her arms around her knees, rested her head on top, and listened.

She didn't dare make notes as she had nowhere nearby to hide them, and so tried to commit what she heard to memory.

Pyrrhus drew her brothers and sisters into debate on a huge range of topics, his knowledge seemingly infinite, his goal to challenge their thought processes. He referenced his study under the mathematics masters in Slofray and the great works of literature catalogued at the university in Saint-Trevale. They then all switched to speaking the main language used in Doviet for an incomprehensible thirty minutes.

The royal children all had much more expertise on these topics than Leda, with her stolen pieces of knowledge, but she was still entertained by the parts of their discussions she could follow.

One afternoon in midsummer, having completed her chores for the day, Leda was curled up in her usual spot. She listened to Pyrrhus and Elina talk animatedly about the various flora and fauna that could be found in the mountains around them. She hadn't seen him face-to-face for a few weeks. She missed being in his study, but she needed to distance herself. No good could come of trying to get close to him. He could not be her friend. Or anything else.

Being around him made her feel safe, and that was dangerous.

From what Leda could glean of Pyrrhus, he was a good-hearted man, despite his stand-offishness. Knowing that made her want to run as far and as fast away from him as possible. She couldn't understand an intrinsically good person, couldn't predict their actions. She was used to Azaria and her father and mother and Dalev, who all worked exclusively for their own benefit. Even her Counterpart brothers and sisters were preoccupied with their own survival. Those were the kinds of people she knew how to be around. Feeling safe with Pyrrhus was a luxury she couldn't afford.

So why did she feel so guilty for failing to tell him why she'd stopped visiting?

Leda knocked her head against the stone wall at the back of the storeroom and winced as it made a louder thud than she had expected. She waited with bated breath for a couple of seconds, but there was no pause in the flow of Pyrrhus's speech. She couldn't detect any whispering from her brothers and sisters; he clearly had no trouble holding their attention.

His speech was smooth and erudite in a way that wasn't as evident when he spoke to Leda. He had always been stilted when she had tried to engage him in conversation.

Maybe her proximity made him stupid, she thought morosely. He was better off without her visiting his rooms; he'd probably barely noticed that she'd stopped. Maybe he was even relieved.

Her self-pitying thoughts were abruptly interrupted when she heard the thudding of multiple sets of footsteps along the corridor. The door to the classroom squeaked on its hinges and she heard the chairs of the students scrape back in unison. There could only be one person who would have them hurrying to their feet like that.

The King had come to visit his children.

Heart beating unreasonably fast, Leda pressed herself forward to hear better, praying no one would think of a reason they'd need to access the store cupboard while she was in there.

"Azaria, I have come to check on your progress," the King announced in his booming voice, ignoring Elina and Caspari. They weren't in his favour at that moment, he had eyes only for Azaria.

Leda wanted to scream every curse word she knew at the top of her lungs, but kept silent.

"I am delighted to see you here, father." Azaria had surely sunk into an elegant curtsey, though Leda could tell from her voice that she didn't enjoy this surprise. Azaria hated nothing more than being caught off guard. She refused presents on her birthdays because she didn't know what they'd be.

Rolling her eyes, Leda shifted the box that hid her hiding place and crept forward to look through the crack between the wall and door into the classroom.

Most royal children could barely tear their eyes away from the King whenever he blessed them with his full attention. They marvelled at their luck. Their expressions were worshipful; some were even brought to tears. Azaria's face was, at best, indifferent.

"She is progressing well?" the King asked Pyrrhus.

"Princess Azaria is accomplished in all areas," Pyrrhus said, and Leda wondered if it was just her poor view of him through the crack in the door, but she could have sworn that he was annoyed.

"Rare praise from Pyrrhus," the King said with satisfaction, pulling a handful of sweets from the pocket of his heavily embroidered doublet and popping two into his mouth. He eyed his daughter thoughtfully as he chewed, oblivious to her mute companions who watched him, wondering if he might turn his attention their way. "I would be remiss if I did not reward my child for doing so well."

He bestowed a smile on her that was more terrible than anything else, yellowing teeth bared in a grimace.

"I thank you, but that is unnecessary, father." Azaria kept her head bowed, her tone gracious and deferential. Leda would have snorted had she not worried it would give up her position.

"Nonsense," the King said indulgently, stretching out his hand towards her.

Before Leda had consciously realised that their father was going to touch Azaria, she was up and out of the cupboard, emerging into the corridor. Spinning around, she grabbed the door to the classroom and yanked it open, executing a hasty curtsey as soon as she was inside. Her leg burned with the pressure she put on it.

"My apologies for the interruption," Leda said, looking straight down at the floor, still half in her curtsey. She was careful to keep her gaze averted from the King. He didn't like the Counterparts attempting to make eye contact. "Princess Azaria, your mother has asked that you come to her after you are finished here. She has a matter she must discuss with you urgently."

It was nonsense, but it was enough to distract the King from touching her sister with his outstretched hand. He didn't bother to look at Leda, she was beneath his notice, but she felt the twin gazes of Azaria and Pyrrhus burning into her.

Azaria relaxed noticeably as their father withdrew his hand. Leda had reached them just in time. She knew that the minute he made contact with her sister she would have lost her head completely. And an attack on the King meant death, no matter who you were. Only the King, who knew his daughter so little, would have dismissed the rumours that had circled her for years; to touch Azaria in any way was to invite injury.

Pyrrhus, damnably observant as he always was, was frowning at Azaria.

"Yes, of course. She mentioned it this morning," Azaria said. "I am finished here for the day, so I should find her immediately. Please excuse me, father." She swept a deep curtsey to the King and moved towards the door.

Pyrrhus crossed his arms in the corner. Judging by his slightly sour expression he did not share Azaria's conclusion that their discussion was over.

"Leda? With me," Azaria said, keeping the door open for Leda as she exited. Sighing a breath of relief that her sister had thought to rescue her from the situation, Leda hurried after her.

Azaria waited only until the door closed before rounding on her. "How did you know to enter at that moment? Were you eavesdropping?"

Leda took a deep breath and willed herself to remain calm. She met Azaria's eye. "Yes."

For a second Azaria didn't seem to know what to do with that information. She settled on an irritated expression. "That's against the rules. You know this."

"Do you care?"

"The King does. Do you think he didn't notice you appearing out of nowhere?"

"I did it to protect you from what he would do to a daughter who punched him in the face when he touched her."

Azaria's expression froze at that. "It was a possibility,"

she finally conceded. "Very well, I will return once the King has left and make excuses to anyone in that room who shows suspicion, and ensure later that he has no concerns himself. And I will never catch you lingering around the classrooms again. This area is forbidden to you, Leda."

"You won't see me here again, I promise," Leda said sweetly.

She just wouldn't get caught next time.

CHAPTER 9

*A*s the height of summer commenced the palace began to swelter. The King's dogs could be seen panting in the corridors, rolling on the cooler marble floors to keep themselves from overheating. The fashionable ladies of the court shortened the sleeves of their dresses and carried elaborate fans wherever they went, and the gentlemen shed their tailcoats, walking around in only their shirtsleeves. Still, the fires burned, all except the one in the armoury, allowing Leda to continue her work.

Azaria didn't cope well with the heat, she was much better suited to snow and ice. As the temperature increased so too did her temper, until everyone from the servants to her own mother went out of their way to avoid her. Leda sadly didn't have that luxury, but she hated the heat almost as much as her sister, so her own temper towered nearly in comparison to Azaria's. When Azaria sniped that her skirt had been mended poorly or that Leda had misplaced her hairbrush Leda had no problem telling her in no uncertain terms exactly where she could shove her complaints.

One night had ended in a ridiculous argument over nothing, with an antique figurine flying past Leda's ear and Leda then slamming the door to her room with as much strength as she could muster. It didn't create as much of a bang as she'd have liked, and that only made her angrier. When Azaria closed her own door, it was with a magnificent slam that rattled the rickety staircase Leda was ascending. She glared towards Azaria's room as though her gaze could burn through multiple layers of stone.

Leda woke early the following morning, before the sun rose, still in a foul mood. Her leg ached and her sister was unbearable, though that was nothing new. Sadly Azaria wasn't being awful enough to put the King off choosing her as his favoured child for another year. Leda would never be that lucky.

She yawned widely as she got up and pulled her riotous hair into a loose plait. Opening a drawer at the bottom of her wardrobe, she cursed. Her hibcus supply was empty. She could have shouted if she weren't afraid Azaria would wake up and yell back. Of all the days she needed it most, of course it was empty.

Having unearthed a basket from beneath her bed, Leda made her way out of her room and through the quiet corridors of the palace, out into the rose garden. Once there, bathed in weak orange light as the sun began to peek over the horizon, she picked a respectable amount of blooms from the rose bushes to cover the hibcus blossoms for when she returned.

That done, she hurried down into the small wood that encircled the right side of the palace. A nearby guard was watching her stonily, so she made sure not to stray too far into the tree line. Pretending to pick from the carpet of daisies around her, she stripped some nearby fat, ruffled hibcus flowers from their stems, burying them beneath the roses in her basket.

She'd picked too many, leaving a patch of plants conspicuously bare, but she found it hard to care.

They would only need drying for twenty hours before she could crush them into a fine powder with her mortar and pestle, with no one any the wiser.

She cursed when she heard the telltale growl.

Without looking behind her, Leda took off straight into the trees, darting between the trunks as she yelled over her shoulder.

"No, Creoste! Get away!"

The little beast was so close behind her that she could feel him snapping at her heels.

"Bad dog!"

There was an understatement if ever there was one.

Said bad dog's teeth grazed Leda's ankle and she let out a screech, making a rather impressive leap into the air by her standards. She seized the low-lying branches of a tree and used them to pull herself upward. Sweat appeared on her skin almost instantly and her hands scraped painfully against the bark as she ascended.

While she'd been good at climbing trees as a child and had built up her abilities with her activity in the chimney, she didn't have the energy to be doing this any more, though the adrenaline helped to compensate.

There had been a time growing up when escaping up into the trees had been the best way to avoid Azaria when she was in one of her moods. Azaria had never followed her up there, her fear of heights keeping her firmly on the ground.

Creoste sat on his haunches on the dry, cracked ground beneath the tree, looking up at her with those beady little eyes. She saw that he'd driven her in a circle back towards the palace, they were only a metre from the tree line.

"Making sure I wasn't escaping?" Leda said mockingly,

swinging her leg with difficulty over a horizontal branch a few meters above the ground.

"Ledazaria?"

Just the voice she wanted to hear when she was muddy, scratched, and halfway up a tree carrying a basket of illicit medicinal flowers.

Neither Leda nor Creoste had noticed Pyrrhus coming to stand directly behind the dog, far too immaculately dressed for the woods. How he could be comfortable in this heat with his tailcoat and cravat she had no idea.

Her eyes travelled over his coat. His tailor was clearly skilled; she was almost tempted to ask who it was and whether they gave lessons.

Leda shook herself. "Pyrrhus." She nodded, trying to smooth her skirts so as not to appear indecent. The slight amusement on his face told her she had failed, and she gave up with a faint huff. "Are you just going to stand there and laugh at me?"

It was the closest she'd ever seen to him laughing; she'd assumed he wasn't really capable of the act. The people of Rivernesse had always been a dour sort.

But Pyrrhus seemed perilously close to smiling, and it dazzled her for a moment.

"How did you manage to get up there?" He was clearly referring to her injured leg, which was beginning to pound with pain as the adrenaline wore off. Leda rolled her eyes, gesturing to Creoste, and Pyrrhus seemed to snap back to himself. He called the dog away briskly, and Creoste shot out of the wood and back towards the palace.

"Do you know how those dogs are trained?" Pyrrhus said, stretching out his hand to show her a short piece of thick silver chain curled in his palm.

Leda looked down at it, dumbfounded. "No."

"With chain. They'd rattle one when they administered

punishment for negative behaviours, forging an association in the dog's mind. When he hears it, he'll become docile. He'll retreat."

"I ... the sound of metal? That's been the key all along?" Leda said, gaping down at him.

"It would seem so."

"Right." Leda didn't know what to say to that. She'd have to negotiate some chain out of Milos as soon as possible, she supposed. Muscles protesting viciously at the movement, Leda lowered herself down through the branches as carefully as possible.

Pyrrhus eyed her curiously as she paused a metre from the ground, frowning at the flimsy branches beneath her.

"How did I get up here?" she muttered to herself.

With a barely audible sigh Pyrrhus stepped forward, offering his hand. Leda couldn't help but think that this would be the second time he had initiated touching her, though on this occasion she wouldn't be delirious with pain. Choosing not to analyse why her mouth went so dry at the thought, she lowered herself slowly to sit on the branch and clasped his hand. Surprisingly cool, the feel of his skin against hers sent a small shock through her, but it was over as soon as it began as, with his help, her feet made contact with the blessedly firm ground.

He stepped back immediately—tall and unaffected as ever.

Lingering with him was the worst possible thing Leda could do, he was too clever not to pick up on her hibcus use eventually. Her symptoms were painfully obvious.

"Thanks," Leda said, arranging the roses in her basket to make sure they blanketed everything else.

"That's quite alright, Ledazaria."

She fought the ugly urge to yank him back towards her by his sleeve as he turned away. She hated her full name at the best of times, but positively loathed it when it came out of his mouth.

"I'd prefer if you called me Leda." She didn't mean for her voice to be so sharp, but there it was.

He turned back. "I don't think that would be appropriate."

Well, that was that, then.

"Fine," she said stiffly. "I'm nothing more than Azaria's property anyway; why bother calling me by my real name when you can use the one that contains hers?"

Pyrrhus's expression didn't move an inch, but he took a step towards her. Just as she had once before sensed his loneliness, she now had the impression he was angry, but looking at him she could find no evidence to back it up.

"Why should I expect you to care?" she hissed, her anger ready to be unleashed as her circumstances coupled with the unbearable heat of the summer sun riled her up. "You're the King's puppet just like the rest of them." She gestured towards the palace.

Still, he said nothing. She couldn't believe that she'd started to become attached to someone like him after a couple of acts of basic kindness. He would reject and push her away just like everyone else did. So he'd given her use of his study, so what? Clearly that meant nothing to him. She was embarrassing herself. He was probably just standing there silently praying to the gods that she would leave him alone.

Well, that wouldn't be a problem.

She rolled her eyes. "Goodbye, Pyrrhus."

"Wait—"

Though the fact that he had called her back made satisfaction pound through her veins, Leda still turned away from him and trudged back up towards the palace, basket clenched so tightly in one hand it was cutting off the blood supply to her fingers.

As she ascended the steps to the rose garden, she hastily stifled a curse and drew back into the shadow of a statue of a large deer.

The King walked slowly down the main pathway, hands crossed over his broad chest as he surveyed the sun rising over the land around him. Each of his steps landed precisely in the centre of a paving stone. A palpable air of smugness radiated from him, as it always did. He was accompanied by two slender figures, heads down demurely, flanking him on either side. The sunlight glinted from Azaria's jet-black hair.

This time, Leda's curse was not so muffled, and she staggered backwards down the steps and out of their immediate view. A quick glance back revealed that Pyrrhus had disappeared from the edge of the wood. He must not have come back into the palace or she would have seen him pass her. He was probably trying to give her as wide a berth as possible and was walking aimlessly around the woods, hoping not to encounter her again when he emerged.

Leda turned her attention back to the King, who was now in muttered conversation with Queen Celandine as she drew level with him. Despite the heat she was dressed as though it were the depths of winter. Her sumptuous periwinkle gown fell in thick folds of fabric, diamonds glittering ostentatiously at her throat and wrists. A muffler made of abundant white fur wrapped around her head.

Celandine stretched out her hand to her daughter and Leda watched Azaria flinch, taking a smooth step sideways under the guise of appreciating a particularly luscious rose.

Azaria's back was stiff and straight, hands curled into fists in the folds of one of the dresses that Leda had made for her. They'd had a fight about how many ruffles needed to go on it. In Leda's opinion the dress made her look like a bad-tempered doily.

A pang of feeling hit Leda as the King smiled at Azaria, genuinely joyful. The smug look on Celandine's beautiful features was even more jarring.

Leda pondered the hibcus in her basket and cursed how long it would take her to prepare it. She could already feel the withdrawal headache coming on.

If there had been any possibility that the King was going to pass over Azaria once more in favour of one of his other children, this cosy gathering proved it was not to be.

Leda glanced up to see the guard by the palace door watching her, as though he hadn't taken his eyes off her once since she had left the building.

Something moved at the corner of her eye, in the shadowed doorway behind the guard, and she blinked. A dark figure watched her silently over the oblivious guard's shoulder. She couldn't make out his face, but it did not feel friendly. She shivered, catching a flash of crimson as the figure disappeared.

"You've changed over the past year, daughter," the King said in his booming voice, which carried easily over to where Leda was crouched. He could not seem to avoid speaking to an audience, even when conducting a small conversation. "I see maturity where there previously was none. I am proud of your development."

If Azaria bristled at the implicit criticism she didn't show it. Leda couldn't see her, but wouldn't be surprised if she were baring her teeth in one of her false smiles.

"I thank you, father."

"And you have expressed regret for the injury you did your brother," the King said sternly.

Azaria's voice was all sweetness and light. "It was an aberration, I assure you, father. I was sickened with remorse for what I had done. I took to my bed for weeks; I was not myself until Elias responded to my letters and gave me his forgiveness."

Leda snorted. Azaria had not been upset at all, and she had made Fayne write those letters for her. For all of her education, intelligence and cunning, she'd had no idea what to write to express her regret—mainly because she didn't feel any.

And Leda had seen their brother's reply. Though he spoke of forgiveness in a way that satisfied Azaria, Leda wouldn't be surprised if the next time they met he'd be looking to even the score. Elias was a petty and vengeful boy who had grown into something worse as a man. Leda was relieved not to see him visiting the palace this year, he must be off trying to conquer the next set of lands for the King.

"I may have overlooked you last year, but I will not do so again," the King said, and Leda could hear the smile in his voice. "I look forward to seeing more of you over coming months, daughter. I do miss you when you're away."

And there it was, as good as confirmed. Azaria would be his next favoured child; she and Leda would stay at the palace until the next summer. When the rest of the royal children and Counterparts would come back, and Azaria would slaughter Leda with the ceremonial axe.

Leda slid to the ground, her back against the stone wall of the rose garden. She could barely hear the sounds of the King, Azaria and Celandine returning to the palace over the roaring in her ears.

Her feet took her to the only place that had hope, without any conscious input from her. She moved like a ghost through the empty halls and up to the armoury, only to stop dead in the doorway.

A fire roared in the grate behind Milos, who was polishing one of the King's helmets.

He grunted a greeting at her, taking a minute to notice that Leda was fixated only on the fire behind him. Her face was a mask of horror.

"Bloody hot," he said, wiping the sweat from his face. "Still, King's orders to keep 'em burning, isn't it? So I've been reminded. We've got to suffer through. Are you here for Princess Azaria's bow?"

Leda staggered out of the room.

CHAPTER 10

*B*y the evening the heavens had opened above Gemdark and released weeks' worth of rain with more power than Leda had ever seen in her life. It thundered down on to the grounds, sending everyone running for cover inside the palace. As she watched it fall in thick sheets over the city from a window on the second floor, Leda felt a compulsion to be out there in it. Then it struck her that there was no reason why she shouldn't.

One wall of the ballroom was comprised of doors made entirely of glass to afford guests the spectacular view of the rose garden. Leda grabbed the handles of two doors and rattled them, gratified to discover they were unlocked. They opened with a bang. The warm rain hit her like a geyser, and she gasped as it soaked her hair and dress in seconds, tilting her face up to the sky.

The doors closed behind her and she looked back to see three guards huddled where before only one had stood, watching her closely. They were there to make sure she wouldn't try to escape now that Azaria was certain to be the next favoured child, but to have three watching her seemed excessive. Leda supposed she should be flattered.

Still, she gave them an incredulous look. As if she'd have a hope of escaping into the hills, soaking wet with only the clothes on her back? She'd be dead of hypothermia in days.

To their credit, the guards didn't seek to interfere as she trudged through the garden, stopping to extract a rose from one of the bushes and study it. It had wilted slightly under the force of the rain, but each petal was still vibrantly black. Leda knew from one of the books she'd recently read that black roses signified rebirth and new beginnings, and the thought caused her to yank the head off the stem and crush the velvet petals in her fist.

There were no new beginnings for her, only endings. Her only way out of the palace was on fire and there was no prospect of her getting in there in the short periods it was unlit to finish what she needed in time to be able to climb it.

Leda had to talk to someone, to rant and scream and pour out her emotions. She could go to Eber, but that would be selfish. How could she confide her panic and her grief in he who would be following only a year later? She'd traumatise the poor boy. He needed to see her strong, resolute.

She could try to talk to Azaria, but that would do her about as much good as conversing with the deer statue at the end of the garden.

The idea of discussing anything with her mother was laughable.

Who else did that leave?

Leda had had a real friend, once, a servant girl named Ismene with a sunny disposition and a wicked sense of humour. In their teens they'd been caught giggling together by one of the King's mistresses and the next day Ismene had appeared in the corridors with a red scar bisecting her face and had refused to look at, let alone speak to, Leda ever since.

That left one person Leda sort of, *almost,* trusted.

The one she'd shouted at in her frustration only hours earlier. Would he even want to speak to her?

The journey to his study went by in a blur, the guards losing interest in Leda as soon as she stepped back into the prison that was the palace. Before she knew it she was dripping water on the landing of Pyrrhus's staircase, looking down at that dark head bent over his desk.

"He chose Azaria."

Pyrrhus started and dropped his quill, his mouth falling open as he looked up at her. She supposed she must be quite the sight, standing at the top of his staircase, one hand curled around the bannister. Water streamed from her hair and her dress, which clung to her like a second skin.

She must look utterly mad, like a demon that had emerged from the river to drag him down into the netherworld.

Pyrrhus seemed to realise the state of her dress at the same time as she, his gaze dragging once down her sodden form and then away. Look at that, he was being respectful. Somehow, that only made her angrier.

"I'm sorry to hear that." He pushed back his chair and stood, shaking his head as if he knew his words were inadequate.

His room was cosy as evening fell, the soothing sound of rain tapping at the window behind his desk, a small fire crackling in the hearth.

They were silent for a moment, and Leda loosened the fist at her side, letting the black rose petals she held fall to the floor. Pyrrhus watched them go with an unreadable expression.

"Why am I here?" She wasn't sure why she was whispering, but he seemed to hear her all the same. "You don't even like me." His eyes seemed to flash at that, but it may have been a trick of the light.

Yet again, Pyrrhus seemed to struggle to decide what to say to her.

"There's nothing I can offer you that will make you feel better about this, Leda. You should"—he cleared his throat—"you should go."

She stayed still, stunned. She wasn't sure if he realised that was the first time he'd used her name correctly.

With a wet squelch marking every step, Leda descended the staircase until she was face-to-face with him, his desk between them. Tossing her mass of wet hair over her shoulder with one hand, she squared herself up to him. He was leaning back slightly. She wondered whether, if his window were open behind him, he'd be tempted to jump out of it to save himself from this conversation.

"Teach me."

"Teach you what?"

"Anything," she said. "I have a year left. There's nothing I've ever wanted more than the education Azaria had, and I wasn't allowed it. If I can get even a taste of it, it will help me go to the end of my life in peace. I don't want to die knowing nothing about the world I'm leaving."

Pyrrhus's hands were white-knuckled fists at his side. "Your sister is going to kill you and you want to learn mathematics? Geography? Languages? That would make you feel better?" For all his scepticism, she knew that deep down he understood what she was asking of him.

He was a scholar, and having dedicated his life to the pursuit of learning, he knew there didn't always need to be a purpose to it. That was why he'd allowed her access to his books and the sanctuary of his rooms, even knowing as they all did that her execution day drew nearer.

"And chess." Leda indicated his pristine chess set lying dormant on the table in the middle of the room. "I'd like you to teach me that too."

Pyrrhus looked absolutely nonplussed. "And why would I do that?"

"Because it would be the kindest thing that anyone's ever done for me." Leda's voice cracked, and she wondered whether showing him this vulnerable side of her would be too much. But she had to, she had no one else in the world to confide in. She was utterly isolated.

"My life has been … quite miserable for the last twenty years. My foster mother was kind, but I've been beaten and kicked and stabbed by my sister since we were children. I've been ignored by my parents, and I've watched six of my brothers and sisters slaughter my other siblings. I'm next, and I want to fill my head with something that's not fear over the next year. I want to know more about what's out there in the world, because right now I haven't the slightest idea."

She couldn't tell him that, if her escape attempt didn't work, this might be the only thing that would keep her sane.

Tears had welled up in her eyes again and she felt a tightness in her chest as she looked at him imploringly. "I need a *friend*. Please."

There was a screech of his chair against the stone floor as the normally calm, collected Pyrrhus shoved it out of his way. She watched him with wide eyes as he made his way around the desk and stopped right in front of her.

He took her in as she swayed on her feet, drenched and shivering. She was in direct contrast to his rather excellent impression of a marble statue.

"This would really help you?"

She nodded.

There was so much conflict in those dark eyes.

He shook his head slightly, turning as though about to move away from her, as though he had no idea why he had approached. She was therefore stunned when he made a sound of frustration and abruptly pivoted back, reaching out to her.

Bewildered, she felt herself being pulled into a hug.

It wasn't a polite, courtly hug involving minimal contact and the lightest brushing of limbs. Leda was surrounded by him. Her head tucked underneath his chin, his arms wrapping securely around her as her hands tentatively spread over the fine fabric of the coat across his back. He didn't seem to care that she was still soaking wet.

The warmth of him dazed her. The hug overwhelmed her senses, she had so rarely been touched, but her arms had locked instinctively around him. She doubted she could let go of him even if she tried.

Leda let out a shuddering breath. She'd never felt safe or shielded from the world like she did in that moment. Probably because all she could hear were the combined sounds of his heartbeat pulsing against her ear, the pattering of the rain against the window, and the snapping of the fire in the hearth. She couldn't see anything, her face buried in his coat, and she revelled in the darkness.

"I'll be your friend. We can discuss anything you want to know." Pyrrhus's hand caressed the back of her neck, just for a second, pushing aside her wet hair, before tension suffused his body. He released her and stepped backwards.

He was slightly flushed, and looked as though he was just as surprised by his actions as she was. This was not a man who *hugged*.

Leda shot him a slightly watery smile.

"You changed your mind very abruptly there," she said shakily, but she was cautiously optimistic nevertheless. She'd never had a friend before who wasn't a sibling, or a servant now forbidden from talking to her.

"I serve him faithfully, but I do not support your father's superstitions," Pyrrhus said calmly, as though he hadn't committed treason merely by uttering the words. "I wouldn't be able to justify knowing you had come to me for help and I had turned you away."

Leda felt a rush of affection for him unlike anything she'd felt before, but quelled it. This was not a man she could develop feelings for. He was too reluctant to be near her, too knowledgeable about hibcus not to guess at her dependence, and above all would not be someone she could take with her when she ran away. He would only ever be a fleeting part of her life. Friendship was all she could demand of him.

"I should go," Leda said, taking advantage of the opportunity to study him. Those dark eyes, set in such a handsome face, and the way he looked at her made her want to re-initiate that hug for reasons that were not entirely platonic.

Dangerous. This buttoned-up and respectable man was so very dangerous to her.

"Yes, of course. The confirmation ceremony is tonight," Pyrrhus said, clearly oblivious to the sordid direction her mind was taking her in. "You'll need to ..."

He trailed off as he gestured at her ruined dress, the wool clinging tightly to her body. She looked down at herself and shivered despite the warmth of the room. The corridors were cooler, and she wasn't looking forward to trudging back to Azaria's rooms soaking wet.

Pyrrhus seemed to be thinking the same thing. "Here." He lifted a thick, black coat off the back of his chair and draped it around her shoulders. "It's draughty outside these rooms; you wouldn't want to catch a cold on the way back."

Slightly stunned, Leda drew the fabric around her. It smelled like the room; mahogany and old books. That must be what comfort smelled like.

"That's very kind of you. I'll ... I'll go now."

"Yes, of course." He stepped out of her way and gestured to the door.

It took Leda a long time to get ready that evening, but when she emerged from her room it looked like she'd only bothered with her appearance for a few minutes. She was wearing a plain green dress that she'd made herself, and her hair was pulled into a rough bun. She hadn't bothered with painting her face, and she knew her eyes were red.

Azaria had gone in a different direction. She was sitting bolt upright on the sofa when Leda joined her, wearing a stunning sapphire blue dress. Diamonds dripped from her fingers and wrists and neck and ears. She was idly turning the pages of a book Pyrrhus had suggested to her a few days ago.

Leda felt a stab of jealousy and was promptly ashamed of herself.

"Are you ready?" Azaria said without looking up.

Leda jumped slightly, she'd had no idea her sister had sensed her presence. "Of course."

"You didn't do your chores today," Azaria said, her voice sharp with reprimand. She waved her book at the heels lined up on the coffee table. "I told you yesterday that these need mending."

Leda sighed. "You have hundreds of pairs of shoes, Azaria. You can wait a few days for those."

Azaria narrowed her eyes. "You will take them to be mended tomorrow, Leda. And I need you to hem my new nightgown, the seamstress here never does it as well as you."

Leda was faintly flattered by the compliment, but her mood turned sour when Azaria tossed her book aside. It slid off the arm of the settee and on to the floor.

"Alright," Leda said, bending to retrieve it and place it carefully on the side table. "Let's just go."

"You look ghastly," Azaria said, regarding her at last. "Are you ill?"

Leda shot her a withering look and pointed at the door.

Leda noticed the stares they were getting on the way to the throne room, but refused to meet anyone's eye. She liked to think the glances of fear and disgust from the other royal children and Counterparts were more targeted at Azaria than at her, but as they were walking side by side it was difficult to tell.

Leda might have had confirmation beforehand that Azaria would be chosen as the favoured child, but it looked like no one else in the palace needed verification. They had watched the King and his children over the past months, had already guessed what her fate would be.

As they rounded a corner to descend one of the staircases, Leda jumped. A hand had plunged out from the crowd surrounding them to grab hers and squeeze it briefly in what she hoped was reassurance. As Leda looked up, it withdrew.

Completely nonplussed, she whipped around to see who had touched her, but the cluster of people around her all averted their eyes. She had no idea who it could have been.

Leda was oddly touched, and took a deep breath to stem the tears that suddenly wanted to escape. She'd done a relatively good job of keeping herself together so far, she would under no circumstances fall apart in front of the entire court.

Azaria, showing rare perceptiveness, turned around to look at Leda as they descended the stairs.

"Pull yourself together, everyone is watching," she said out of the corner of her mouth. Leda rolled her eyes, which seemed to satisfy her.

Azaria stepped abruptly to the right to avoid colliding

with a statue in the busy corridor, and Leda leapt sideways against the wall, heart in her throat, to avoid touching her.

Azaria did not notice.

As they approached the throne room Leda saw Azaria widen her eyes threateningly as Elina ventured a little too close to them while trying to squeeze through the archway.

Elina eyed her with a mixture of fear and defiance. Her face was drawn and she looked gaunt, like she'd lost a lot of weight very quickly. She somehow looked even worse than Leda. Leda had wondered how she was coping with Sofie's death, and here was the answer.

It was the first time they'd been in the throne room since Sofie's execution, which might explain why Elina looked like putting one foot in front of the other cost her greatly.

Sofie's blood had been scrubbed from the floor and there were servants moving around, offering refreshments on mirrored trays. High on his throne sat their father, his outfit decadently bejewelled as usual, a crown jammed on to his head. He didn't look at them as they walked in, as he was deep in conversation with Ambrose, who looked worried.

Not that Leda had ever seen Ambrose *not* look worried.

The other royal children and their Counterparts were lined up beneath the throne on the dais, as they had been for Sofie's execution. Light-headedness hit Leda so hard she almost staggered into Caspari, haughty as ever in a ridiculous high-collared white tailcoat. He glared at her and refused to move out of the way so she could take her place.

Patience running low, Leda put out a hand to steady herself and shoved past him. She kept her expression resolute as she lowered herself to her knees, her back to Azaria.

The King got up and began to make his yearly speech. It was the same as every year before it, an outpouring of his love and devotion to his realm, to the gods—the sacrifices that he and his children had to make to ensure that the kingdoms were prosperous.

This year he turned his praise towards Azaria, gushing about her wit, her intelligence, her skill in battle. He knew that she above all others was worthy of the honour of going out to conquer her own country for him. He had complete faith in her.

And so it was confirmed that, in a little under a year, Azaria would kill her Counterpart.

When the announcement came with the blaring of trumpets, Leda felt the weight of the stares of everybody in the room on her, and fixed her gaze on the floor. She wouldn't give them the satisfaction of seeing her crumble.

CHAPTER 11

*A*s summer turned inexorably into autumn, Leda watched the hustle and bustle of her brothers and sisters packing up to return to their villages with a detached kind of dread. One of the last to leave, Eber had taken her hand on the palace steps and not let her go for a full minute before Caspari's yelling that the carriage was waiting became too grating to ignore. Leda fought the urge to cling to her brother and instead let him go with grace.

"I'll be fine. I'll work something out," she said with a smile. "I'll see you next year."

Neither of them mentioned that when he returned, it would be to watch her die. Just as she had with Sofie. The next year, it would be their brother Markus's turn to watch Eber's ceremony. An endless, tormenting, heartbreaking cycle.

Leda's chimney was nowhere near ready. Milos had been lighting fires nearly every day. Even when she managed to get in there, the higher she got, the more difficult the task became, and the more evident her lack of strength was.

As Leda watched the last carriage bearing her brothers

roll down the road to the palace gate, she felt a pang that she wasn't leaving with Azaria, as she had every other year.

The thought that she'd never see Dalev again brought her so much joy she could have jumped up and down, but knowing that applied to Fayne too felt like an icy dagger in her heart.

As Leda turned back into the palace she could feel the absence of the children. Subdued and well mannered though they may be compared to normal children, they still brought life and bustle to the quiet corridors. Now it felt like walking around a flamboyantly decorated mausoleum. As she strolled past the banquet hall she glanced in through the wide doors that had been thrown open, and what she saw stopped her in her tracks.

The royal tables had been rearranged. The King's table had been elongated on its dais, and Azaria's golden chair sat at the right-hand side of his throne. A matching chair for Queen Celandine took up the position on the left side.

The rickety wooden chair of the Counterpart stood alone against a tiny table in the back corner of the hall, facing out towards the long trestle tables. The whole court would be able to view her as they ate and know that she was alone, friendless and powerless.

Well, that wouldn't be happening. Leda's hands balled up so tight she could feel the sting of her fingernails in her palms. With a barely audible scoff, she turned on her heel and left. She'd rather not eat at all than be put on display like that.

The King was away hunting that morning, taking his favoured wives and mistresses with him, as well as Azaria. Leda supposed her sister would now be showing off her abilities by shooting their targets while on a moving horse.

Still, that presented an opportunity. Hurrying back to her bedroom, Leda drew a length of rough brown fabric that she had stitched into a sack out from beneath her pillow. Into it she stuffed some dried fruit wrapped in paper that she'd taken from Azaria's table of snacks in the sitting room, as well as a variety of nuts and seeds.

She'd been reading one of Pyrrhus's books on surviving alone in wild, harsh environments and had been making a list over the past few weeks of things she would need to take with her if she was able to escape into the hills behind the palace.

Every time Pyrrhus had entered his study she'd whipped the list out of sight. She was starting to trust him more than anyone she knew, except perhaps Eber, but this was something she needed to keep to herself.

It was too dangerous not to. She wouldn't make him complicit.

Leda took a tightly furled roll of silk she'd stolen from Azaria's wardrobe and treated with oil to make it resistant to water. She should be able to use it to keep most of the winter rain off her as she travelled. She had learned from another book how to create fire from sticks, so she should be able to use that to boil water for her to drink. She put a plain tin cup into the sack, which she'd hidden in her pocket after lunch yesterday. A knife she'd taken from Azaria's extensive collection followed it.

Finally, she shoved a scarf and hat that she'd knitted into the sack, as well as a few of the coins that she'd sneaked from various sources over the years, and her sewing kit.

There was more that would be useful to her, but she needed to keep this sack small and light. All it needed to do was get her over the border into Saint-Trevale; then she could pay for a night in an inn and go from there.

Lifting her skirt, Leda tied the strings of the sack around her left thigh. It dangled awkwardly, hitting her shin with every step she took as she left Azaria's rooms and made her way excruciatingly slowly through the palace and out into the rose garden.

She knew she was being watched now, a hundred times more intently than before. Leda was not the first Counterpart to have thoughts of escape. That helped her to temper her behaviour, she had to be cautious.

Leda nodded brusquely at the guards patrolling the rose garden, strolling as casually as she could down the steps on to the lawn, and approaching the river.

The day was crisp and bright, the leaves on the trees at the other side of the river turning a riot of beautiful autumnal oranges and reds. Leda walked to the shallowest part of the river, which she knew from her youth could be crossed with the water only coming up to the tops of your knees, though the current was strong. There was a cluster of large rocks there, and she sat down on the grass with her back against one, tilting her face towards the weak sun.

To any guard, it would look like she was taking a moment to sprawl on the grass and enjoy the weather.

Leda sat still for a few minutes before glancing surreptitiously behind her. They were still able to see her but had grown bored of staring directly at her. Provided she made no sudden moves, she should be safe.

Casually, she pulled Azaria's knife out of her pocket and began to dig a small hole in front of the rock to her right with one hand, keeping her body as steady as possible. The rock would hopefully shield the hole from view of anyone looking out from the rose garden. It took many minutes and sweat was glistening on her forehead by the time she'd dug a hole big enough for her sack.

Inching her hand under her skirt, she untied the strings and used her feet to push it out. She slid it into the hole with little difficulty, making sure it was tightly cinched so nothing could get in or out, before replacing the dirt back over it with her hand. Once that was done, Leda scattered a few pebbles and leaves over the fresh earth so it didn't stick out, and viewed it with satisfaction.

It wouldn't last long in there, particularly if it started raining soon, but having it there just in case she managed to complete her chimney in the next couple of weeks soothed her. She'd take a pack up to the roof to sustain her for the first few days, and then come down and retrieve this and escape while the guards were searching for her much further away.

That decided, Leda pulled a pair of small satin gloves out of her pocket and slid them on over her incriminatingly dirty hands. Rising as elegantly as she could, she made her way back towards the palace.

She'd wash her hands and then go and see what Pyrrhus was doing.

She had been sneaking up to his rooms a few times a week when Azaria was engaged with their father or the other members of the court.

The afternoons were bright and varied; on one day Leda and Pyrrhus might debate a book of philosophy that he had suggested to her, on another they would play chess. Once he brought her a tray with vials of medicine from Ambrose's lab and they discussed the manufacture and properties of each in detail. When he'd pointed out the hibcus she'd worked very hard to appear nonchalant.

When she had freshened herself up, Leda made her way into Pyrrhus's study. He was rolling up the large map he sometimes perused, though never talked about, and his eyes brightened infinitesimally as she came in.

She smiled at him as she descended the steps. "Good afternoon."

Aware that Pyrrhus was watching her as he murmured his own greeting, she looked at the cover of the book he'd left by her chair for that day. It was a slim yellow tome that focused on the history of Rivernesse, the country that had been invaded ten years ago by her brother Prince Fynn before his death.

Fynn's initial takeover had been brutal. Rumour had it that he had executed every member of the royal family, even the children, and displayed their heads on pikes along the border with Saint-Trevale, showing them that they were next. Sure enough, Prince Agon had conquered it a couple of years later.

"Chess?"

Pyrrhus was suddenly opposite her, settling into his own chair and moving his first pawn forward, starting the game without waiting for a response. Unable to resist the challenge, Leda scoffed and sat down.

"I'll get you this time."

That was unlikely; they'd been playing for weeks and she still had yet to beat him, but she still greatly enjoyed each game. She liked that he never let her win out of pity. When she finally did win, she would have earned it.

Fifteen minutes into their battle, she was hunched forward with her elbows on her knees, engrossed in the pieces.

She lifted a pawn, Pyrrhus's head shook minutely, and she put it straight back down again. Grabbing her castle instead, she moved it forward by two squares, placing his queen in jeopardy. The white knight she had just captured from him was still clenched in her fist, which tightened around the wood as he smirked.

"Checkmate."

"What!" She dropped the knight and leaned forward, as though having her nose next to the pieces would help her figure out how he had beaten her so easily. *Again.*

She never failed to get drawn into his traps. With a rueful smile, she pushed over her king with a clink.

"Reset it," she insisted, sweeping her pieces back towards her. "I won't fall for that this time."

He was oh so perilously close to smiling at her.

A not-quite smile from Pyrrhus was so rare that she stored up every appearance in her memory. He was so serious that he made Leda seem positively light-hearted by comparison. She liked it; it was uplifting not to be the most subdued person in the room.

Though a feather-light rain sprayed the windows, it was a warm evening in Pyrrhus's study. The fire sparked and spat in the hearth, and she felt cosy and safe.

Curled in the armchair she'd come to think of as hers, it struck Leda that she felt so relaxed she could easily lean her head back and go right to sleep. She watched Pyrrhus as he contemplated his pieces and a thrill of affection went through her.

"Alright, let's go again." She sat forward and moved one of her pawns forward two spaces. The heat of the fire had sweat prickling on her forehead, and the thick fabric of her dress clung to her uncomfortably.

Still fixated on the game, Leda rolled both of her sleeves up to her elbows.

"Aha." She reached across to take his castle with hers, and let out a gasp as Pyrrhus shot forward in his seat, grabbing her wrist. He exerted very little pressure on her, but still she froze, her other hand braced on the table.

He wasn't looking at her face, his focus instead on the five fingernail marks embedded in her forearm. They had faded over the last few days from an angry red to pink, but were still visible. Flushing profusely, Leda yanked herself backwards. Pyrrhus let her go without issue, settling slowly back into his seat. He pinned her with a sharp look.

"Where did those come from?"

Leda thought about lying, then decided against it. They were friends now, right? And friends told each other the truth. Besides, he'd been at court for over two years, he knew about her sister. And he had taught Azaria for long enough to know that the rumours he'd heard about her were probably true.

"Azaria," Leda said dismissively, rolling her sleeves down so they covered her to her wrists once more. "I thought she was about to trip and grabbed her. Turns out she wasn't. I didn't think." She gave a rueful smile to the pieces on the chess board, unable to look him in the eye.

There was a forbidding silence from the seat opposite her.

"So she scratched you?"

Leda shrugged. "That's a subdued reaction from her, actually. She didn't even get her knife out." She kept her voice light and quirked her lips at him as though that were the end of it. Judging by his expression, he did not agree.

"Leda, you—"

"That's enough."

"But—"

"Do you know *why* Azaria is the way she is?" Leda said with a sigh, reaching forward to move her knight.

Pyrrhus seemed to have forgotten that they were playing, and looked down at the board as though surprised to find it there. "No, though I've been curious since I arrived here."

"You wouldn't be the first," Leda said, leaning back to study him when it became clear he wasn't about to move any of his pieces. He was tense in his seat, as though he wanted to get up and start pacing around. She'd quite like to see that, she'd so rarely seen him agitated.

"I've been asked over the years, why is she so cold? Why does she let no one touch her? Why is she so violent?"

"And what did you answer?"

"Nothing," Leda said simply. "They'd only use the information against her."

Now Pyrrhus was visibly bothered. He got up at last and circled his chair, bracing his hands on the back of it. "Why would you defend someone who behaves this way towards you? Ambrose told me last year that she *cut off* Prince Elias's arm."

Leda got to her feet so quickly she staggered slightly. "He was tormenting her!" she said hotly, not entirely sure why she was defending Azaria.

She could remember that day like it was yesterday—the hot sun beating down on their backs, Prince Elias's mocking laughter and then his screams as blood splashed on the rocks by the river.

"They'd had a rivalry since they were children; I always thought it was because they were each other's only full siblings. Azaria had beaten Elias at archery, he was teasing her, she shouted back. He punched her. Then he picked her up and tried to drop her in the river." She remembered Azaria's inhuman shrieks as she was manhandled towards the water. "I told you she always carries a knife in her boot. We heard a yell and him dropping her, and then before we could stop her his arm was dangling from his body by an inch of skin. She'd cut clean through the bone."

"And you condone that behaviour?" Pyrrhus said. She got the impression that her answer to that question was an important one. He was watching her intently, as though trying to detect elements of her sister's violence, her father's cruelty, her mother's indifference.

Leda was unreasonably desperate that he find no evidence of her family's influence in her at all.

"Never," she said passionately. "I'm not like her." He, of all people, needed to understand. "I've been through some terrible, damaging things in my life. But Azaria ... even I can't comprehend what she's experienced."

Pyrrhus looked sceptical at that. "A princess of the blood? What could possibly have happened to her that's worse than what she puts you through?"

Leda failed to hide her irritation. She wanted to tell him the shocking truth, wiping that know-it-all expression off his face with her words. Childish, perhaps, but that didn't stop her. There was something cathartic about telling him all of this. Precious few people knew what she was about to say.

With a sigh, she sat back down in her chair. After a second, he mirrored her.

"When we were five years old, Fayne took us to the market. She turned her back for a second, just a moment, and when she looked around I was the only one there." Leda took a deep breath. "A band of militants had kidnapped Azaria. They held her for a month before the King paid the ransom. Before that she was so ... bright, and happy. Always laughing and smiling, full of love." She twisted her hands in her lap. "Or so I was told, my memories are fuzzy. They spent a month torturing her." She swallowed heavily. "She has more scars than I do, actually, but she covers them well. When she came back to us, she was a different person. Cold, cruel, emotionless. After a few months she started lashing out physically. It got worse over the next few years until she learned to control her temper better."

Leda paused, swivelling in her seat and lifting up her hair to expose the back of her neck. There sat a thin, jagged scar that ran parallel to her hairline.

Pyrrhus seemed to be struggling to hide his contempt, his mouth a grim line. "She did that to you as well?"

Leda let her hair drop and turned back to face him. "It's not who she is," she said. "It's what they did to her. We hoped she'd grow out of it, but she hasn't."

"Did you ever talk to her about what happened?"

Leda laughed bitterly, caressing the back of her neck gingerly, though the wound had healed many years ago. "How do you think I got this? I've never dared to bring it up since."

Pyrrhus took a book from the table beside his chair and strode over to a bookshelf in the corner, sliding it into place between two other thick tomes. Or what he thought was its place, clearly, as he had grabbed a book on geography and put it back in the middle of the fiction section. Leda decided not to remark on it.

"I may be able to understand why she is the way that she is," Pyrrhus said quietly, his back towards her, "but I cannot condone her hurting you."

"Then you'll probably want to skip next year's ceremony," Leda said with a wry smile.

"Don't joke about that," Pyrrhus said stiffly. "She will not kill you, Leda."

"Oh, really?" she said with a snort. "Says who? You?"

He ignored the question, returning to their chess match and taking one of her pawns with aggression as he sat down. Leda moved her knight defensively to protect her queen, fighting the urge to smile at the idea that someone might feel protective over her.

"You never talk about your family," Leda said. "What are they like?"

"My family are dead," Pyrrhus said stiffly. "Plague." The word sounded like it was forced from his mouth. "I was away studying when the contagion swept through the cities that summer. They wrote to me and begged me not to come home in case I was caught up in it. I followed their advice, and I never saw them again." His tone was matter-of-fact, but his words were heartbreakingly sad.

"When you say 'they'?"

"My mother and father, and my brother and sister. I was the eldest, their great hope for the family. It's why they sent me away to study." He shook his head. "I had a talent for languages at a young age, they had hoped that I might become a diplomat."

"You would have made a good one," Leda said softly. He was intelligent and articulate enough, though his evident aversion to most people, especially courtiers, might have held him back. "I'm sure they'd be proud of you now."

"I hope that they would be. Nowadays, at least." Pyrrhus's face had relaxed as he looked at the chess board, and she felt a leap of triumph at having made him feel even a little better. Perhaps she had the makings of a good friend after all.

"And did they love you?"

Pyrrhus looked up at her as if that were a strange question to ask. "They did."

Leda nodded, glad for him. "You know, my father has never once looked at me."

"He hasn't?"

"Never in my memory." She shrugged. "He considers me beneath his notice. I'm chattel raised for slaughter, no better than the cows and pigs in his farms. You don't love the livestock."

She tipped over her king. He hadn't called checkmate, but she knew it was over for her in a few more moves. Why delay, when it was hopeless?

CHAPTER 12

*I*n every encounter with the King over the following days, Azaria positively sparkled. She was quick-witted and erudite, able to turn a piece of philosophy into a clever play on words that had sycophantic courtiers howling with laughter. She led the King's favourites on a series of gruelling hunts, always at the front, riding her horse to exhaustion. They roasted their catches for the evening banquets. And when Azaria rode out, they always came back with a kill.

Naturally, the increased attention on Azaria bled over to Leda. Courtiers felt comfortable loudly discussing whether Azaria would be glad to be rid of her, or whether she might miss her. Leda never reacted, merely leaving whatever room she was in as quickly and unobtrusively as possible when the gossip started up.

She spent most of her days in the sanctuary of Pyrrhus's study, reading. Aside from ensuring she wasn't trying to escape from the palace, the guards seemed content not to follow her around too closely, and so she went in and out undiscovered.

One afternoon Leda sat curled up in her armchair, a

heavy book balanced across her lap. It was one she'd been studying with increasing frustration for months, a dry and wordy book on the language of Saint-Trevale. She'd need to familiarise herself with it if she wanted to live there, and while the alphabet was easy to learn, the verb structure had been designed by someone with a particularly cruel streak.

The autumn rain drummed relentlessly against the window. She knew her sack of supplies buried outside was probably in a sad, sodden state, but still the noise calmed her. Pyrrhus was sitting opposite her, also engrossed in a book. The dancing orange light from the fire flickered over his features.

He'd seemed at a loss when he entered his study to find her there. Leda had recommended a book from his vast library that he hadn't read, and had beamed at him when he picked it up.

She trailed a finger down the margin of her book, pausing with a frown on a word she didn't recognise. Glancing up, she saw Pyrrhus watching her thoughtfully, his book dangling from one hand. He looked thoroughly distracted, as if he'd forgotten he'd been reading.

Leda flushed, wondering how long he'd been looking at her. And how hadn't she noticed? Did she have something on her face? Or was she making a ridiculous expression as she tried to understand the more complicated words?

"Adumbreile," she said.

Pyrrhus shook his head slightly, as though waking himself up. "I—excuse me?"

"Adumbreile." She gestured to her book and prayed her face wasn't red as a tomato, because that was how it felt at that moment. "In the language of Saint-Trevale. What does it mean?"

"Apathy ... or lack of concern." He reeled off the answer as though he didn't need to consult anything in his brain to find the meaning. He looked distracted, but Leda was floored as usual by how fast his mind worked.

"Interesting." That certainly made the sentence she was attempting to read easier to decipher. "Thank you."

Idly, Leda extended her arms in the air to stretch them. Pyrrhus watched her over the top of his book with a raised eyebrow.

"I need to take Azaria's shoes down to the servants so they can take them to the cobblers." Azaria could have ordered the servants to collect them from her rooms, but she had proclaimed that she liked Leda to feel useful, and so the task was hers. The idea of an exhausted Leda traipsing around the palace all day to bring her reading material, polish her weapons and have her clothes altered appeared to give Azaria great satisfaction.

"Why should that be your job?" Pyrrhus asked. When his eyes landed on the sparkly gold heels on the table beside her, his expression darkened further. "Those are uniquely hideous."

Leda chuckled; she couldn't agree more.

If she didn't know better she'd think he didn't want her to leave.

They said goodbye, and she sneaked out of his room into the corridor and down the stairs to the underground rooms where the servants lived and worked. The palace got darker and gloomier the further down she went.

"Oof!" She almost lost her balance and staggered down a step. A pair of arms shot out to steady her.

"My apologies!" She saw a flash of blonde and looked up in surprise to see Ambrose clutching her upper arms.

He wore his usual pristine silver outfit, too clean for a physician when she really thought about it. As usual, he had the air of someone in a hurry and nodded at her with a muttered 'Ledazaria' before releasing her and taking the steps two at a time until he had reached the bottom. He disappeared around the corner.

When she reached the place she'd last seen him, Leda looked along the dark, narrow corridor in both directions and saw a chef from the palace kitchens striding in the opposite direction, bearing a huge silver tray of petit fours.

She jumped when a click sounded behind her, whirling to find a single servant coming out of a nondescript door. She was a petite young woman with angular eyes and dark hair, and she nearly jumped out of her skin when Leda approached her.

A scar bisected her face. Oh gods.

"Ismene?" Leda croaked. They hadn't spoken in so long, and the way Ismene's face dropped when she recognised her sent a bolt of pain through her.

Ismene recovered remarkably well, however, and smiled at Leda as she stepped away from the doorway she'd emerged from.

"Leda," she said, her voice as sweet as ever. Leda had never met anyone as kind before, or anyone who had such a lightness about them. Ismene could enter any conversation and instantly soothe the participants, her disposition sunny and positive. She spoke to people with such focus they felt like they were the most interesting people in the room.

"How are you?" Leda asked, determinedly not looking at the scar that made her feel sick with guilt.

Ismene gave her a wan smile and reached out for the shoes Leda clutched. "I'm not bad, thank you. Are these Azaria's?"

Leda let them go and scrambled to collect her thoughts. "Oh, yes, they need to go to the cobblers."

Ismene bobbed a small curtsey that Leda did not deserve.

129

"Consider it done." She cast wary eyes around the corridor. "Bye, Leda."

With a dip of her capped head, she turned and fled in the opposite direction.

Leda watched her go with a frown. She should have apologised again, but she could understand why Ismene wouldn't want to be anywhere near her.

Leda glanced at the sliver of the room that was revealed by the door Ismene had just come out of, now ajar. Looking hastily up and down the corridor, Leda saw that she was alone, and pushed the door open so she could poke her head around it. It led to a dark, dank passageway with the candles bracketed to the walls producing faint light.

She would ordinarily have turned around and gone back the way she came, but Leda could swear that, even underground as she was, she could almost smell fresh air. A slight breeze ruffled the flames on the candles, and her decision was abruptly made for her.

Leda opened the door wider so she could slip inside, a bolt of excitement shooting through her. Was this a passageway that would lead out of the palace? Could Ismene have inadvertently led her to her escape?

"Ledazaria." Pyrrhus's assistant Thorodin appeared at the bottom of the staircase Leda had just arrived from, holding an orange in one hand. He didn't seem to be phased by her stricken expression as she closed the door behind her and tried to look casual.

Leda hastily rearranged her features into a smile. "Good afternoon, Thorodin."

"What brings you down to the servants' quarters?" he asked curiously.

"I ... Azaria had some shoes that needed repairing. She sent me down. What about you?"

He held up the orange. "Quick trip to the kitchens for a

snack. I worked up an appetite hunting this morning." He looked curiously at the door behind her. "I suppose we'd both better hurry along, dinner will be served soon and I'm sure Azaria needs her Counterpart to help her get ready."

The words were fastidiously polite, though incorrect.

Something felt amiss as Leda nodded and walked away with him at her back. Thorodin had been looking at her just a touch too intently, his smile fixed upon his face. She could only pray that he had no idea what that door led to, but why would he? It wasn't as if he would need to make use of such a passageway. He was only here to go to the kitchens and get some food, no more, she shouldn't be paranoid.

Reassuring herself that all was well, Leda went back to Azaria's rooms with a spring in her step. She needed to return later to fully explore that passageway, it could prove the answer to all of her problems.

CHAPTER 13

*L*eda spent the next morning in a state of pure excitement, she may have found another way to get out of the palace undetected that wouldn't risk breaking her neck trying to get up a chimney and down the side of the palace. She needed to gather her provisions, find an excuse, and slip away when everyone would least expect it.

It couldn't be today, when the rain fell in buckets and the entire court was cooped up on top of one another inside. The best day would be tomorrow, when the King held his jousting tournament in honour of his favoured child. No one would expect to see Leda there, so it would take hours for them to realise she was missing and send out their search parties. She could do this.

Leda's hope was so all-encompassing that she even found herself going willingly to the palace temple. Ignoring the priestess who looked up in surprise at her entrance, Leda strode to the centre of the enormous circular room.

She'd held the prayer garland she'd strung through with dried poppies for hope.

If you can hear me, and if you care, whichever of you gods is mine, I need you to listen to this. You don't pay attention to what goes on down here anyway, but I need you to turn a blind eye to this. You will not interfere, you will let me leave here. I have never asked you for anything before now. I don't want riches or fame or glory, I just want to live. I'll do anything if you'll just let me live.

Please.

~

The royal children and their Counterparts were making a brief return that week for the autumn festivities and a ball that the King had planned for Azaria, who had bemoaned the lack of dancing at court and the absence of her brothers and sisters. Why she had done so Leda had no idea, as Azaria famously didn't care for any of them. She had on more than one occasion declared them to be a menagerie of chattering twits with barely a brain cell to share between them.

It benefitted Leda, though, as she would have a much easier way of communicating the escape routes to the other Counterparts if they were here.

Leda sat at her little table at breakfast, alone as always, in a fairly good mood. Glancing across the room, her eyes immediately found Pyrrhus. He nodded tightly at her over his cup of hot chocolate and turned to speak to Thorodin, who laughed as though he had told a hilarious joke. Leda looked down at the small stack of waffles drizzled in sticky honey on her plate, her favourite breakfast, and promptly devoured the rest of them. She'd need all of her strength to execute her plan.

But there was one thing she needed to do today. Having finished her food, she went back up to Azaria's rooms to retrieve the small package. By the time Pyrrhus joined her in his study she was sat comfortably in her chair, her 'good-bye' gift for him folded neatly on his own seat.

His greeting faltered as he stared down at the package, and he lifted it carefully into his hands.

"What's this?"

"Oh." Leda coloured immediately and shrugged. "It's a scarf. I knitted it." Her knitting was not quite on the same level as her sewing, but she was improving with practice. The scarf she'd created for him was a deep green, almost black. She'd made it with a soft, decadent wool she'd taken from the palace seamstresses' room. They'd never miss it, and it had helped Leda make a soft and pliable scarf that she was really quite proud of.

This was the second version, the first having gone into the fire when she'd realised how many strange lumps she'd knitted into it.

"I know you're not necessarily a 'colours' person," Leda said quickly, trying to read the expression on his face and coming up empty. "I went for green because I thought you might ... I thought you'd like it." It had been difficult to figure out what colour he might be partial to, given he only ever wore a combination of black and white. His room had a green rug by the hearth and vibrant green plants were scattered around at intervals, so she had taken a guess based on that.

Pyrrhus ran a hand along the soft wool.

"It's getting colder outside, I thought ... Anyway, if you don't like it that's fine, I can take it back and give it to Eber, I just thought ..."

She reached out and, quick as a whip, Pyrrhus pulled the scarf away from her. He looked mildly affronted. "It's mine."

"Oh."

"I like it."

She froze. Coming from Pyrrhus, that was a huge compliment.

"Good."

"Thank you." He was studying the scarf with entirely too much intensity, in her opinion.

Leda sank back into her seat and gestured at the basket he'd put down when her gift had distracted him. "What's that?"

He laid it on the chess table, and it seemed to be his turn to be unsure about her reaction. "It's for you."

"Don't tell me you knitted something too?" she teased, but he didn't smile along with her. He looked serious as ever.

"You skip every meal you can get away with in the banquet hall. This morning was the first time I've seen you there in over a week. You're getting smaller by the day. I was by the kitchens on my way up here." He opened the basket. "There's bread and cheese in there with some smoked ham, and a little mead. I also got some apples as a gift the other day." He looked up, as if only just remembering. He crossed the room to a golden bowl on the chest of drawers, filled to the brim with fat, crisp green apples. He threw one to her and she caught it by the tips of her fingers.

Leda knew instantly that he was lying about happening to be by the kitchens. His last meeting with the royal librarian must have ended very recently, and instead of going straight next door to meet her he had detoured by four flights of stairs down to the basement kitchens and back so he could bring her something to eat. How he'd managed to convince the servants to let him take so much she had no idea; he must have been very popular with them. Or an outright thief.

"I ..." Leda was embarrassed to feel herself getting a little choked up. "You noticed that?"

Pyrrhus quirked a brow as though the idea that he wouldn't was patently ridiculous. "Of course I did."

He didn't say anything else, but the look he was giving her demanded that she elaborate.

Leda took a bite of the apple and sighed. She really should have gone to the kitchens herself to build up a food supply for when she skipped dinner. The servants were looking at her with so much pity nowadays she doubted there was anything she could ask for that they wouldn't give.

"People just ... didn't use to notice much about me. I blended into the shadows, you know? For most people that's still the case. If you asked Azaria how many times I'd been at dinner this week she would have said every day without the slightest hesitation. If the guards thought of me the same way, trust me, I'd be able to walk out the front door and they wouldn't even realise."

Pyrrhus looked as if he didn't believe a word she said, and she ploughed on.

"I mean it, if you'd asked any courtier here to point out Leda before this summer almost all of them wouldn't have been able to ..." She trailed off, affected by the intensity of his gaze and realising that she wasn't quite right. "That doesn't include you, though, I suppose. You recognised me."

Pyrrhus had resumed studying his new scarf, which he had absent-mindedly twisted around one hand. "I did."

She was suddenly desperate to know what it was that had made her noticeable to him. "You saw me by the river."

He looked up sharply at her. "Yes, from here." He gestured to the window behind his desk. "You were teaching Markus and Ami how to swim. I was never very proficient, myself, I was curious. I remember you standing in the river shouting about water safety. It was the first time I'd ever heard you speak. It ... made an impression." He smirked, and the sight of it made her cheeks heat.

"I didn't see you interacting with Ami and Markus this summer." He said that with such confidence that Leda knew he'd been actively paying attention.

Leda smiled sadly. "It was time to pull away," she said. "It's best not to let them get too attached, they're so young."

"As you were, when your older brothers and sisters were killed?"

Leda nodded. "I was ten when Sira and Elea were killed, they had just turned nineteen." She remembered her eldest Counterpart sisters as clearly as if she'd seen them yesterday. They were twins, Counterparts to the King's oldest and second-oldest royal children. They were born in the time just before the King's horrific ceremonies had been dreamed up.

"Were you close with them?"

"Yes," Leda said briskly. "Too close. I was very affected by their deaths." Their conversation was formal, but she liked it that way. It made her feel stable, and not like she was about to dissolve into tears like she so often wanted to when she thought about them. "Sira helped me learn to read; she'd learned in secret, too. You would have liked her."

"I'm sure I would have."

Leda opened her mouth, emboldened to ask more about his family now that she had shared a little more of hers, but stopped when she heard a loud bang from somewhere above them.

She and Pyrrhus shared an equally bewildered look, and she glanced out of the window. It was getting dark, and she needed to prepare for dinner. She also needed to pack her essentials so that she could make her escape.

There was no point bonding with Pyrrhus further, they were never going to see each other again, so why was she so reluctant to leave this room?

Throwing her apple core on to the fire, Leda rolled her

neck to relieve some of the tension and turned back to face Pyrrhus.

"I should go and ready myself for dinner."

She went to move for the stairs, then abruptly changed her mind and turned back. She crossed the room in a few strides and slid her arms over Pyrrhus's shoulders, drawing him into a hug.

For the first few seconds it was like hugging one of the rocks by the river, and Leda almost let go before she felt his muscles loosen infinitesimally beneath her hands. Delight surged in her as she felt his arms come around her waist.

"What's this for?"

She smiled into his coat. "No reason." It was odd, fighting the dual compulsions to laugh and cry at the same time. She was stunned to realise that, of all the people in this miserable palace, he was the one who she'd miss most. Her heart hurt at the thought of never seeing him again.

Pyrrhus broke away first and stepped back, though his hands trailed along her arms. "I will see you at dinner, Leda."

Leda had a harder time controlling her expression as she retreated and climbed the stairs, giving him a small wave at the top, which she instantly regretted.

Chastising herself for never being able to keep her cool, Leda slipped out of the door and into the empty corridor. As she closed it behind her, she jumped as a loud crunching sound and a scream echoed along the walls. She could see shadows moving around the corner at the end of the corridor.

Tentatively, she stepped towards it, until she heard a yell that was unmistakably Azaria. Before she knew it, she was running.

It took Leda seconds to understand the situation as she rounded the corner.

"Azaria!" Leda shouted, sprinting along the corridor. "No!" With an almighty yank she wasn't entirely sure she had the strength for, she pulled her sister away from Caspari, whom she had pinned up against the wall. His face was an ugly puce colour. A little further along the hall, eight-year-old Prince Fessler sat curled into a ball, bawling.

As soon as Azaria had been prised away from her brother, Leda hastily drew her hands back. Luckily for her, Azaria was in such a towering rage that she appeared not to have noticed Leda touching her.

Gasping for breath, his face screwed up with pain and humiliation, Caspari drew himself up to his full height.

"What is going on?" Leda cried, kneeling down to see if Fessler was alright. He cowered away from her and cried harder. "What did you do?" She looked at Azaria and Caspari with equal suspicion. Both had a cruel streak, though Caspari's was based more on enjoyment of others' suffering than Azaria's, which often seemed to accompany complete detachment from reality.

"Caspari hit me," Fessler sobbed into his legs, and Leda felt a strong urge to tell Azaria to continue what she'd started.

Caspari opened his mouth to defend himself and Azaria shot him a look that silenced him instantly.

"Caspari is sorry, Fessler," Azaria said sharply. "And now we are done with the matter. Brother, I trust you will keep your hands to yourself when it comes to the children of this palace." She gestured at Fessler, and he got to his feet and ran off in the opposite direction. "Come, Leda."

Her voice was imperious, and Leda was loath to disobey when she was actually quite impressed by her sister's show of morals. Then again, Azaria always had a soft spot—her only one—for the younger children.

"It was kind of you to defend Fessler," Leda said quietly as they made their way through the bustling corridors.

"Caspari is less than worthless," she spat, and Leda barely refrained from rolling her eyes. It was always one step forward and two steps back with Azaria. "If our father let us choose who we could kill at our ceremonies I know who would be my choice for next year."

Azaria punctuated that interesting statement by slamming the door to her bedroom, leaving Leda standing in shock. It was nice to know that perhaps her sister wasn't anticipating her murder with fervour. One never really could tell with Azaria.

Dinner that night started off as it did any other evening. Musicians played a lively jig from their spot behind the King's dais, and in the gaps between songs the lively chatter and clinking of cutlery against plates rang out.

Leda sat at her little table facing out into the hall, sliding her spoon listlessly through a pale blancmange. She had arranged to meet Eber immediately after dinner, where she would tell him everything he needed to know about the two escape routes, and then she would leave.

A strange whisper of excitement swept the room. The guards who normally stood sentinel outside the doors had come in, and were blocking the exits with their spears.

Frowning, Leda turned to scan the rest of the diners. Her mother sat with her back to her on the table with the other mistresses, hair glistening in the candlelight. Azaria was alone on the dais next to their father's empty throne. It took Leda a few seconds of searching to find the King, who was at the Queens' table. Celandine giggled, sitting on his lap as she fed him grapes.

Pyrrhus was deep in conversation with Ambrose at the very end of the trestle table in the corner, Thorodin sitting next to them with a pinched expression on his face.

Leda wondered what entertainment the King had planned for them this evening. When he was in a good mood he would display his royal children's talents at dancing, singing or poetry. Once, even Eber had been allowed to play the flute for them all. The King hadn't looked at him while he was playing, but he'd seemed to enjoy the music at least.

Sometimes they brought in wise men and women from around the kingdoms to talk about the stars or philosophy, or a priestess to speak of the gods. When the King was feeling malicious bear-baiting and dog fighting were the order of the day.

Leda normally managed to slip out of the room well in advance of the violence. She hoped the higher-than-usual number of guards circling the room didn't mean she'd be made to watch whatever entertainment the King had in mind. She wanted to leave early to prepare her supplies. It would be difficult to do that and meet Eber if they were kept there until midnight.

Leda jumped as she realised that Azaria was suddenly standing beside her, looking out across the room just as Leda had been. Instead of the courtiers, she was watching the guards with narrowed eyes.

"What's going on?" Azaria said, reaching for Leda's wine glass and draining it.

Leda sighed but didn't answer. Something *was* off.

With a grunt, the King pushed Celandine away and got to his feet. Returning to his dais, he beckoned the guards towards him. They approached as he bid them in perfect, practised formation, two symmetrical lines filing down the pathways between tables. Leda's feeling of unease grew as, instead of approaching the King, they turned to encircle the table that she was sitting at, gently ushering Azaria aside.

She wanted to cry out when a guard wrapped a firm

hand around her upper arm and tugged her up from her seat, but seemed to have lost her voice.

Leda went to her feet, dropping her napkin on to her chair. Another guard grabbed her other arm and together they pulled her into the middle of the room so that she was facing her father on his throne. The rest of the King's guards fanned out behind him, affording a better view to the spectators.

The guards who held her forced Leda down to her knees. She hissed as they collided painfully with the floor.

Her father did not look up as he sat on his throne, instead beckoning Azaria to ascend the steps and join him.

The musicians had stopped playing, holding their instruments aloft uncertainly, as though they weren't sure whether they should be.

Azaria's heels clicked against the stone as she approached their father. With an elegant sweep of her dress, she sat next to him. Her face, beautiful as ever, might as well have been carved from stone for all the humanity it showed.

"Father," she murmured.

He turned to her, a malicious gleam in his eyes that had Leda rearing back. "You need to keep a better eye on your Counterpart, my darling," he said, his voice carrying across the room as courtiers waited with bated breath. "She has a mind to escape. Betraying you and our family like that, and our people ... unforgivable."

It was then that Leda felt a guard's hands gathering in the fabric of her dress on either side of her spine.

"No!" she cried out, trying and failing to extricate herself. A deafening ripping sound marked the back of her dress giving way.

She felt cool metal against her back and then another, more muted tearing as a knife split the back of her corset.

Her skin prickled unpleasantly in the open air and she gasped.

"What are you doing?" she demanded, her eyes on Azaria. "For what am I being punished? Tell me!"

Azaria was reading a scroll that their father had handed her, brow furrowed.

"Abandoning your duty. Attempting to escape," Azaria said quietly, and if Leda didn't know better she might have read her sister's expression as conflicted. "What is her punishment, father?"

"She is to be whipped, it is the usual way," said the King. "Thorodin," he called.

Leda looked over her bare shoulder to see Thorodin walking towards her. His bearing was confident, a coiled whip held in his gloved hand. All the blood seemed to leave her head, but Leda redoubled her struggling against the guards. As she twisted she caught a glance of Pyrrhus, standing in a different place from where he had previously been sitting, his face a mask of white.

Ambrose stood behind him with a fistful of the back of his coat in one hand.

"No, no!" Leda shouted, letting out a muffled scream as her arms were forced out either side of her, holding her prone on her knees, back almost parallel to the floor. "Father, please! I didn't try to escape! I didn't!"

It was true, she had never tried. Only plotted and planned. And carelessly, it seemed. What an idiot she was to ever trust Thorodin. How could she be stupid enough not to realise that he was one of the King's spies, trying to gain her trust and ensure that she would never do anything to jeopardise Azaria's ceremony?

"How old are you?" the King asked Azaria.

She took her time to answer, her face calculating. The

King did not like to be kept waiting, and narrowed his eyes as she deliberated.

"Twenty," Azaria replied stiffly, her eyes on the whip in Thorodin's hands. Leda couldn't tell if her sister wanted to stop this at once or grab the whip and take out her frustration on Leda herself. Two decades they'd lived side by side, and still Leda couldn't read her.

She wondered if that was down to Azaria's complete lack of emotion or if she was just a terrible judge of other people.

It would make sense, she could never figure out what might be going on in Pyrrhus's head either.

Leda wondered if he was still looking at her, watching her humiliation with disgust. She wouldn't blame him, she'd never been brought so low before, and in front of so many people.

Azaria looked up at their father like she'd never seen him before.

"Twenty lashes, then," the King said.

A murmur rippled through the crowd. Tears slid silently down Leda's face but she was frozen in position, her arms already aching. She closed her eyes.

She just needed to get through this; she'd dealt with pain over the years. She'd been punished before. The hibcus already in her body would hopefully numb some of the worst of it.

She just needed to survive the next ten minutes.

Twenty lashes, she could do it. It would mean yet more scars, but she had developed quite the collection over the years, and no one would ever see them anyway.

The whip came down for the first lash. It was a streak of searing lightning down her back, a caustic pain that had her crying out in a ragged voice.

She raised her head. That one was fine, she could cope. Nineteen more to go.

The crowd's jeering didn't help her, but by the fourth lash the combination of unimaginable pain and blood rushing in her ears had drowned it out. By the time the fifth stroke landed on her back, her throat was hoarse from screaming. Looking up at the dais through swollen eyes, she saw both the King and Azaria missing. Neither had bothered to stay and watch her suffering. She wasn't even worth that to them.

Each one of her senses was on fire. Her vision was blurred with tears, pulse pounding in her ears. She tasted her own blood, she must have bitten her tongue. The stone beneath her bruised her knees. And she could smell burning.

Burning? Even as foggy as her mind was, that one didn't seem quite right.

A scream that was not her own pierced the air, and the arms that held her loosened. Taking advantage of the slack, Leda looked to her right to see thick, black smoke curling from the corridor that led to the ambassador's waiting rooms. There was a great scramble as courtiers, nobles and servants alike turned their tables over in their haste to get out.

The guards were scared, too. They dropped her like a stone and hurried towards the exit. Thorodin appeared to be long gone, he must have fled at the very first sign of danger. He was quite the coward when his whip became useless, it seemed.

Now lying prone on the floor, eyes watering as smoke filled the room, Leda dragged herself forward on her elbows with a groan. She would not die here, not like this.

She hadn't lived this long, put up with Azaria and her father and her mother and her brothers and sisters, tricked and lied her way into educating herself, only to die here on the floor.

She made it to the door, the last person in the room, slippery with her own blood, when she felt strong hands encircling her arms. Whoever her saviour was he was tall, with dark hair, and inordinately strong given the way he picked her up as though she was nothing and slung her over his shoulder. He avoided putting his hands anywhere near her back.

As he carried her away, she felt herself slip into the welcoming arms of unconsciousness.

CHAPTER 14

*L*eda awoke in an unfamiliar, dark room. The wind shrieked against the walls. Judging by the muted light, it was closing in on dawn. She could feel the cool air trying to push its way through the narrow window near her head.

Leda was on her front on a soft, narrow bed. The room, or what she could see of it, was plain, with a small desk and a chair under the window, a wardrobe by the door. A thin bookshelf stuffed to bursting with books stood in between them. That instantly told her whose bedroom this was.

A shadow moved out of the corner of her eye, and Leda whimpered as Pyrrhus moved into her line of sight. She let out a shuddering sigh of relief. She was safe.

He looked like he hadn't slept all night, his normally immaculate shirt creased, sleeves rolled up to his elbows, tailcoat crumpled in the corner as if he'd ripped it off and dropped it there sometime in the night.

He crouched beside her, his face inches from where hers rested on the pillow of what she was quickly realising was his bed. It smelled like him.

It took her a few tries to make her voice work. "Did …
did you set a fire?"

Pyrrhus smoothed away a matted curl of hair that had
come to rest over her face. "No, but I took advantage of it."
His expression was soft, though it didn't quite reach his eyes.
They looked so *very* angry. She prayed it wasn't at her. "You
have a habit of getting hurt, Leda."

Her back was flaring with pain, but it wasn't enough to
stop the irritation rising in her. "That's hardly *my* fault."

Pyrrhus stood and busied himself with something at his
desk, and she groaned when he pulled apart the frayed
edges of her ruined dress to expose her bare back. He let out
a low curse as he saw what was presumably the mess of
blood and welts marring her skin. He ran a hand lightly
over the uninjured skin at the base of her neck, and she
relaxed slightly.

"It will heal," he said softly. "You'll have minor scarring, I
cleaned the wound and mixed a solution of karascus oil and
ibur. I managed to apply it soon after your injuries were
sustained. You'll be back to functional in a couple of weeks."
Leda knew he found comfort and order in his detached
words, his mechanical language. She thought it must keep
him feeling in control.

She felt the sudden, ridiculous urge to roll over and get a
good look at his expression. Perhaps there would be some
rare emotion there.

He had performed miracles on her back, the pain was
fading faster than she could believe, but the mounting
feeling of hibcus withdrawal had started to spread through
her stomach. She couldn't remember when she'd last had a
dose. Her midsection burned, a different kind of pain
consuming her.

"I'll wait a while before applying the dressing." Pyrrhus's
voice sounded very far away.

She nodded into his pillow, which smelled of paper and something rich and dark, like chocolate. Tears began to prick at her eyes as her muscles clenched.

"Leda, what—"

Pyrrhus's question was abruptly cut off as she, with an almost inhuman spurt of strength, propelled herself off the bed.

Ducking around him, she fell to her bruised knees over his waste bin and vomited into it. The last thing she saw before losing consciousness once more was the look of mingled horror and realisation on his face as he moved towards her.

When she awoke, once again sprawled on her stomach on the bed, she wasn't surprised to find herself in his room this time. The pain in her body had faded into a dull ache, for which she was grateful. Reaching back with a shaking hand, she felt the smooth fabric of bandages criss-crossing her back.

Judging by the weak light filtering into the room through the rain, she'd been asleep for a few more hours.

"*Hibcus*?" The word was harsh, and she looked around to see that Pyrrhus was kneeling by the side of the bed once more. This time he didn't look caring, and she was quite sure that the fury in his eyes was now directed at her.

The room was dark and gloomy despite the daylight, but Leda could see Pyrrhus's glare as easily as if the sun had been streaming in through the window. Slowly, he brought a hand up to show her the empty hibcus pouch he must have found in her pocket.

"What gives you the right to rifle through my pockets?" Her voice was calm, but she could feel her temper rising once more to match his.

"I had a theory that prompted me to search," he said darkly, his face inches away from hers. "I have studied medicine and botany extensively over the years. You think I wouldn't recognise a hibcus dependent when I saw one?" He ran a hand distractedly through his hair. "I forced myself not to believe it before, but it all makes sense now. The weakness, the dilated pupils, the vomiting and fainting. And standing in the middle of a hibcus patch with a basket was the clue I absolutely should not have ignored."

She eyed him defiantly. "So what?"

"So what?" he hissed, dropping the pouch to the ground. "What have you *done* to yourself, Leda?"

That did it. "Excuse me?" she seethed. "How dare you!" Ignoring the muted pain in her back, she hauled herself into a sitting position with great effort. She declined to think about the fact that if she were able to move around this much, it meant he must have given her some hibcus. "You have no idea what I've been through, what led me to this! Sitting up in your ivory tower your whole life, cosseted and protected and given everything you could ever ask for. For all your books and your studies you know *nothing*," she spat.

Pyrrhus stayed admirably calm in the face of her rage, though his eyes had flashed as she insulted him. "You'll be dead by thirty if you keep taking it like this, you'll waste away."

Leda's laugh was close to hysterical. "Who cares! I'm dead by next year no matter what I put in my body, if this gets me through it then how is there a problem?"

"You're not going to die," Pyrrhus ground out, rolling down the cuffs of his white shirt so that they covered his forearms once more. She noticed the remnants of orange karascus oil on his hands and his shirt and guilt and fury welled up in her in equal measure. "I'm not going to let that happen."

"Oh, I'm sorry, are you going to ask the King for clemency on my behalf? Are you going to overwhelm his

150

compulsions with your academic arguments?" Leda scoffed, hands curled into fists around his bedding. "Like you have any power here at all," she said witheringly.

He ignored that. "Why did you start taking hibcus? And when?"

"So the royal tutor is curious, is he? I'm surprised you weren't able to tell immediately from the shape of my eyeballs or the length of my hair given your *extensive studies*." He didn't rise to her bait, and she couldn't help but be grudgingly impressed by his self-control. She hadn't been around many people who held that much power over their tempers. Azaria would have knocked her head against the wall by now.

"I'll tell you, but only because of this." She gestured at her back, the pain of it receding by the second. The karascas oil, ibur and hibcus seemed to have formed a potent painkilling combination.

It probably wasn't prudent to ask Pyrrhus for the recipe.

He stood up and leaned against his wardrobe, arms crossed as he waited for her explanation. With a sigh she bunched up her bloodstained skirt in her hands, rolling it up until her right thigh was visible. The thin, jagged white scar ran from her upper thigh all the way down to her knee.

"I told you that Azaria cut me when we were ten years old. Our foster 'father', Dalev, gave me hibcus when I returned from the physician in pain. He had a garden full of it. When he decided to start beating me for his own amusement, he gave me enough hibcus to heal me and take the pain away. He decided no one would care if he hit the Counterpart, but Fayne might, so she could never see the evidence. By the time I was twelve I was taking so much I didn't even feel him strike me."

Her cheeks were wet. She hadn't realised she'd started crying.

"Fayne noticed the weakness and the fainting, like you did. She followed Dalev to my room one day and saw him beat me with a poker. She screamed at him; I've never seen her so angry. I've never seen him afraid of her, come to think of it, except on that day." She stared down at her hands, covered in dried blood. "He never hit me again, but I was dependent on the hibcus. I can't come off it completely without being in considerable pain and barely able to use my leg—I'm on a lower dose now, I had to be to scrape together the brainpower to try to escape, but I've never been able to end it. So"—she sniffed—"are you going to tell me I'm pathetic now?"

The sound of the rain was deafening in the pause that followed.

"No, I'm not," Pyrrhus said, casting her an inscrutable look that sent a shiver down her ruined spine before turning and making his way to the door once more. It appeared he considered their conversation over.

"Don't tell anyone," Leda murmured, watching the hands that had balled into fists at his sides. "I can't bear anyone else judging me too."

He was silent for a second.

"I am not judging you. Get some rest," he said, closing the door with a snap as he left.

It took him over an hour to return, and she knew by something very much like instinct that he'd not gone far from her. He was avoiding her presence but seemed preoccupied with keeping her safe, so she assumed he had mostly stayed out in his study to brood. When he did come back he was calm, and she watched warily as he came to sit at the foot of the bed.

"I need to go," she said. "The palace must be crawling with guards looking for me, they'll think I've tried to escape again—"

He placed a hand on the first uninjured part of her he could reach, which happened to be the top of her head, and pushed her gently back down on to the bed.

"Eber helped me bring you up here. He's claiming to everyone who will listen that you're in his room, but he won't let anyone in but the physician. Ambrose verified it and the guards trust him, so they're currently standing outside the wrong door. He and Eber will distract the guards once you leave here, it'll be as if you were there all along."

"Oh, thank you." She was glad they had the savvy to come up with that plan, as her brain was half shut down by that point. "So what were you doing before you came back?"

"I was in the infirmary. Ambrose will help you," he said. "I've spoken to him and he can prescribe you the correct dosage of hibcus mixed with yaranthen berries to counteract the symptoms. It will reduce the side effects and you can take it safely for now. It will ... it will help. But eventually, you'll need to come off it completely."

Leda sat up gingerly. She knew the offer was generous. It was miraculous, even, and something that she hadn't known was possible. Then again, it wouldn't have been in Dalev's interest to offer her a healthy way to manage the pain, and the village healer back in Leatherfell knew next to nothing.

She wanted to be grateful, but found herself struggling with it. Pyrrhus was looking at her expectantly, as though she should fall about in thanks that he and Ambrose had deigned to help.

"Alright," Leda said tightly. "Though I'm not sure I'm happy about you sharing my circumstances without my knowledge or permission with a stranger."

He quirked an eyebrow at that, his lip curling maddeningly. "You're not sure?"

"Scratch that,' she hissed. 'I'm very sure I'm not happy about it!"

"Ambrose is not a stranger, he's your physician."

"He isn't really, and that's beside the point," she insisted.

"How?" Pyrrhus had edged closer to her on the bed, they were now no more than a foot apart. "He knew anyway, before I told him. He recognised the signs of excessive hibcus use, he's seen it many times before. Most of the court is on it in some form or another."

"It's still a terrible incursion on my privacy to—"

He threw his hands in the air and looked up as though appealing to the gods for the patience to deal with her. "I was only trying to protect—"

At that she stood up from the bed in a rage, towering over him. She was sure she must look quite a sight in her bloodied, torn, half-open dress, but couldn't bring herself to care.

"Stop. Trying. To. Save. Me," she gritted out. "I am not a child; I am not a damsel in distress for you to sweep in and rescue. I may have very little life stretching ahead of me, but *I* decide what happens to me." She thumped a hand against her chest. "Not you!"

She could practically hear Pyrrhus's teeth grinding together as he fought himself back from saying whatever he really wanted to say.

"Do you understand me?" She reached down and cupped her hand around his jaw, lifting it until he looked up at her. His skin was burning hot.

He froze as soon as she touched him. She waited for him to throw her off or chastise her, but he was quiet.

"I understand." His tone showed her quite clearly that he wasn't happy about it.

Silence stretched between them and she withdrew, clasping her hands in front of her. She couldn't touch this man, she couldn't get close to him. She wasn't going to escape, she was going to die, and she had no business pursuing anything with him.

"I'm so envious of you," she admitted. "You grew up in a happy family, you were educated and loved and had the freedom to do whatever you liked. You had the ideal upbringing."

"Don't make assumptions, Leda," Pyrrhus said flatly. "It's time for you to get some more sleep. You're not going back to Azaria's rooms until I'm happy with the state of your back."

Leda thought it wise not to fight him on that, particularly as weariness was already pulling at her eyelids once more.

"Fine." She stifled a yawn, crawling on to the soft sheets. As she closed her eyes, she could feel him adjusting the duvet so that it was properly tucked in under her waist.

Leda slept for a few more hours, until the sun was high in the sky and the rain had cleared. Pyrrhus was gone when she awoke, and she could hear the sounds of the jousting tournament from the gardens outside. This was the day that she was supposed to be escaping. The thought brought an ache to her chest that had nothing to do with her injuries.

Gingerly, Leda got to her feet and stretched the parts of her body that would allow it. Despite the sleep she'd had she felt absolutely wretched, an unpleasant stinging across her back and a dearth of energy in her veins.

She pulled the back of her dress together as best she could and stepped out into Pyrrhus's study. It was empty, the fireplace unlit, sunlight streaming in through the window behind his desk.

As she made her way through the palace, Leda was incredibly thankful that it was close to deserted. There were servants milling about to clean and stoke fires, but they kept their faces turned away from Leda as she trudged through the corridors, well aware of how awful she looked.

One of the two guards outside Azaria's rooms took one look at her and then turned and walked away, presumably to report on her whereabouts to whoever might like to know. She watched them go with a glare.

Unfortunately, she found the one person she'd not wanted to see stood in the middle of their rooms, a dour expression on her face.

Azaria was pulling on a pair of gloves, dressed in her favourite riding dress. A ridiculous feather bloomed ostentatiously from her hat—a gift from her mother, no doubt.

Azaria had always had a distaste for garish accessories that weren't jewels.

"What are you doing here?" Leda said, too tired to employ any kind of politeness in her tone.

"Changing my dress," Azaria said. "My last one caught on a hedge and tore."

Leda had the strong suspicion Azaria wasn't telling the truth, but couldn't find it in herself to care.

Next to Leda, Azaria looked angelic, hair perfectly coiffed, face smooth and well rested, her dress immaculate. Leda looked like she'd been dragged backwards through a thorny bush. She scanned the princess bitterly, pulling at the fabric of her dress as she did so. It was tied so loosely at the back to avoid contact with her skin that it had started to fall off her shoulders.

"You had a good night's sleep," Leda observed, crossing her arms and then rapidly uncrossing them as the stretching sensation screamed across her back. Every now and then another sharp spark of pain fired up her spine, but she was able to bear it with only a grimace.

Azaria looked confused, flexing her hands in their new gloves. "My sleep was as it has always been. You were with Eber last night? He healed you?"

"None of your business," Leda snapped. "You would have let me burn to death on the floor, what do you care?"

"You would not have burned to death," Azaria scoffed. "Smoke inhalation would have killed you first. But I checked the room as the fire burned and it was empty. I knew you had escaped." She took a step closer and sniffed the air, clearly detecting the thick, potent smell of karascus oil. "Who healed you? Eber can't tell grass from a pine cone so it couldn't have been him. Ambrose?"

Leda thought it best to let her believe that. "Yes. And I'm fine, completely healed. Do they know who set the fire?"

"They're interrogating everyone they can get their hands on; father and his advisors are furious. They haven't caught the perpetrator yet. Do you think he meant for you to die there?" Azaria didn't need to specify which 'he' she was talking about as she abruptly changed the subject. Their father loomed large in both of their minds.

"Of course not. Why deprive *you* of the pleasure?" Leda snapped, aware she was taking a tone she rarely dared use with her sister. Azaria seemed to realise this too, and her expression turned cold.

"You will excuse me, I must rejoin the festivities," Azaria said, pulling her cloak tighter over her shoulders. "We shall resume this conversation when you're in a more amenable frame of mind. There's extra hibcus on your bed for when you need it." Revealing the momentous fact that she knew about Leda's habit in her usual dismissive manner, Azaria walked away. "See to it that my clothes are laundered."

Leda groaned and began to drag herself up the stairs to her room. She almost jumped out of her skin when she saw Eber sitting on her bed, his face white.

"Leda!" He leapt up and crossed the room to her, pulling himself back at the last second in horror. "Sorry!"

"It's okay," Leda said tiredly. "I'll be alright."

"Yesterday ... Caspari and I weren't at dinner so we didn't see ... I came in just as the fire started. I'm so sorry, I would have stopped them if I'd known."

Leda placed a comforting hand on his shoulder, noting the dark circles under his eyes that indicated he'd slept even less than she had. "I would have been really upset if you'd tried. We both would have been punished and you know it. And thank you so much for covering for me while I recovered."

Eber's face was sullen, and he looked younger than his years. "I hate him."

Leda tightened her hand painfully on his arm. "I know, but what you say is treason. Don't repeat it to anyone else."

He nodded glumly and shook his arm out of her grip. "I understand that Pyrrhus knows his stuff but *how* are you walking around right now?"

"I'm fine." She stuck with the completely incorrect platitude she'd given Azaria. Eber seemed to believe her about as much as her sister had.

"Right." He rolled his eyes the same way she did when Azaria was being especially unreasonable. Leda did not enjoy seeing that.

"I need you to listen to me, Eber. There's a secret passageway down in the servants' quarters, third door on the left at the bottom of the Asqueth staircase. It's probably locked but I checked and it's not a complicated one to pick. It leads outside. I was planning on using it."

"And someone saw you," Eber said flatly.

She nodded. "Thorodin." What she would give to throw that man right into the Blainchill River. Or better yet, to set Azaria on him. He'd seemed so nice and normal whenever she'd spoken to him. That was the lesson she apparently still needed to learn; there wasn't a person in these kingdoms who wouldn't come running when the King snapped his fingers.

Leda gestured to the ratty armchair and Eber sank on to it as she settled herself on the bed.

"They'll be watching me more than ever, but there's nothing to stop you using it to escape. Just take Markus and Ami with you. Mira's only three, I'm not sure how you can get her out as she's constantly watched in the nursery, but you can find—"

Eber was already shaking his head.

"There will be guards permanently posted at either end of it this morning and you know it. If Thorodin knew it was an unguarded exit then he would have given its location to the King when he reported you," Eber said with a grimace. "That's not an option anymore."

Leda felt the bottom drop out of her stomach. He was right. And her fireplace was lit up every day despite Milos's objections, blocking that avenue of escape.

"So ... that's it?" she said quietly, her voice thready. "We're just accepting it? I'll be dead in nine months' time and you most likely the year after?"

"We always knew it would come to this," said Eber, once again displaying wisdom beyond his years. "It's what we were born for. Hope was the only thing that kept us moving forward, but it's done now. We need to accept it and make the best of what's left of our lives."

Leda rubbed her eyes and her hands came away wet. "Nine months is not enough time to finish everything I want to."

The image of Pyrrhus appeared, unbidden, in her mind. He was not for her. And yet, as she cried she didn't want Eber to be the one who comforted her, she wanted him. The thought made more tears spring to her eyes. What an idiot she was.

Stupid, stupid moron.

"You need to find a way to fit it all in," Eber said, reaching forward to squeeze her shoulder gently as he stood. "I'll help."

She gave him a watery smile. "I appreciate that."

"Get some rest. I'll tell Azaria to leave you alone for a few hours."

Leda snorted at that. "Well, you can try at least."

CHAPTER 15

a few days later found Leda sitting in the cupboard beside Pyrrhus's classroom, listening to the sound of him arguing with Caspari about the merits of the strategy Prince Fynn had used to conquer Rivernesse. The land had been Pyrrhus's home, so she was surprised at how dispassionately he spoke about the battles, massacres, and indignities perpetrated on the population.

Then again, he was an academic; he seemed to have that ability to divorce his feelings from facts. Leda smirked at the not-at-all-bitter thought. She wondered if he would tell her about his own personal experience of the invasion if she asked.

Leda wasn't sure she'd be welcome in Pyrrhus's rooms after the awkward way they'd left things the previous day, so now she was in this cupboard once again. She couldn't rest her back against the wall as she usually did, so she sat awkwardly upright with no support. In her hand was a small quill and piece of paper, which she balanced on her knee. It was difficult to see in the dark, but she was managing reasonably well.

She was making a list. Eber had put the idea in her mind

during their discussion the previous day. If Milos kept her chimney inaccessible and Azaria was going to end Leda's life in less than a year, then she needed to write out every experience she'd ever wanted to feel, every skill she'd ever wanted to learn, and find a way to get it done before the end.

Leda had become so absorbed in writing that she completely missed the sounds of Azaria, Elina and Caspari leaving the classroom. Elina and Caspari were sniping at each other, Azaria ominously silent, but Leda barely paid attention. She was sucking idly on the tip of her quill when the door opened and light streamed in.

"Good gods!" Pyrrhus jumped three inches into the air when he found Leda sitting there, his arm outstretched to grab a sheaf of papers sitting on a shelf. "What are you doing here?"

Leda gave him the wide-eyed look of someone who had been caught. "Oh, hello," she squeaked, before clearing her throat, furious with herself. "I ... er ... wasn't sure if I was welcome in your rooms. After yesterday."

Pyrrhus dropped the papers, utterly forgotten, back on to their shelf and leaned down to offer her a hand.

"Don't be ridiculous," he said stonily. "You're always welcome there, no matter whether we argue."

Leda took his hand gratefully and he pulled her to her feet.

Silently, they went down into his study. He didn't waste a second in seating himself behind his desk, snapping shut the book that lay there and flipping open the one beneath it. He seemed to be in a bad mood, but spending two hours with the dysfunctional nightmare that was Azaria, Elina and Caspari being snide towards each other would do that to anyone.

Leda saw a tankard of her favourite mead on the small

table by her customary armchair. Her heart clenched at the sight.

Pyrrhus took a minute or so to notice that she hadn't crossed the room to her chair and was instead standing in front of him. Her thighs touched the edge of his desk as she stepped closer, her shadow falling over the pages he was trying to read.

"May I help you?"

"No."

"Then why are you hovering?"

Leda toyed with the paper in her pocket. "I made a list," she said, her voice more confident than she was feeling.

Pyrrhus looked immediately interested, his curiosity piqued by anything in written form.

How dare he be so adorable.

Wordlessly, Leda handed the folded piece of paper she'd drawn from her pocket over to him. He spread it carefully on his desk.

She felt a flush creep up her cheeks as he looked down at her words. He probably found her handwriting childish and unrefined. She'd never learned to do the elegant script that he and Azaria could. Fayne hadn't been able to teach her that, and she'd had fewer opportunities to practice writing than she had reading while she was growing up. It produced too much evidence.

Still, her list was legible and that was what mattered.

"Learn to ride a horse, swim in the river in springtime, wear a proper ballgown, shoot a bow and arrow, find out what gold leaf tastes like ... what is this?"

"A list," Leda said simply. "Of everything I want to do before I die. Eber inspired me to make it. I have nine months to check off everything on there."

A furrow appeared between Pyrrhus's brows but he said nothing, smoothing a hand over the paper even though it already lay completely flat. Leda fidgeted as he continued to read. She knew she was looming over him, not giving him a moment of privacy, but found it difficult to care.

She watched his dark eyes continue to move down the list and detected the moment they stuttered and froze.

"You ..." She saw that his colour now matched hers, his normally pale face flushed. "You wish to kiss someone?"

Leda refused to be embarrassed.

"Yes," she said, quite impressed with herself that she was still able to look him in the eye. She'd come far over the past few months. "I've never done it before, and I don't want to die without knowing what it's like. I hardly think that's unreasonable."

Leda was very glad that she had decided not to write down who she wanted as her partner in that particular experiment. Something told her that if Pyrrhus had read his name on that piece of paper he would probably have thrown her out of his rooms and she would have expired from sheer mortification.

Unfortunately, Pyrrhus seemed to guess at the direction of her thoughts. He finally lifted his gaze from her list and leaned back in his chair, eyeing her speculatively.

"You have somebody in mind for that task?"

Leda couldn't stop herself, sudden boldness overtaking her. "Is that an offer?"

His calm demeanour disappeared in an instant and she had the distinct impression that if he hadn't been sitting down he would have been physically bowled over by her words.

"I ... Leda ... it's not, no."

"Right." If Leda had thought she was blushing before, that was nothing compared to now. Was it possible for a person to die from embarrassment? She'd certainly find out.

"I'm sorry, I ...," she trailed off. She had no plan for what she was going to say next, hoping he would cut her off, but Pyrrhus seemed just as struck dumb as she. Intending on leaving the room as quickly as her legs would carry her, Leda went to take her list back from him.

"I didn't mean—" Pyrrhus sighed in frustration, whipping the paper out from under her hand when she moved to grab it. "You'll have far more than nine months to do all of these things, you'll have a lifetime. There's no need to rush any of this."

Leda rolled her eyes. "Not this again."

"I'm telling you, you won't need this list," Pyrrhus said abruptly, folding the paper back along its original lines and shoving it unceremoniously into his desk drawer. As though to underline his point, he produced a key from somewhere, turned it in the drawer's lock, withdrew it, and put it in his pocket.

Leda could only gape at him. "Gods, you're more in denial than I am!" she exclaimed. "I have limited time to get all that done and I'm going to do it, you hiding the paper from me won't change that. I wrote it, you can be assured that I'll remember it."

Pyrrhus's face wasn't quite so handsome when he looked like he was chewing on a wasp.

"We'll see," was the only cryptic thing he said.

With a huff, Leda stormed across the room to take her usual seat. It no longer occurred to her that she'd like to leave, she was quite happy for him to see how irritated he had made her. Picking up a book for all of two seconds, she lowered it and twisted, getting on her knees to look over the high back of her chair at Pyrrhus.

"Has my father ever spared a single one of his Counterpart children?"

He'd been the palace historian for the past year, and had

seen some of the ceremonies first hand. He knew better than anyone.

Pyrrhus didn't look up from the book he was reading. "No."

"Then stop saying I'll have the rest of my long life to do these things. You know what's happening to me and that there's no way to stop it," Leda said. When she twisted back around, her spine touched the back of her armchair and she whimpered, pulling away.

The movement sent a sharp shock of pain across her back, and she poorly disguised the sound she made with a cough. Pyrrhus, as always, was too observant and therefore thoroughly unconvinced. Sometimes she missed the times they were so out of sync and awkward with one another that they could barely carry a conversation.

"Have you been using the oil on your back?"

She flushed hotly. "Of course I have."

"Then why are you still in pain?"

Leda glared at him for a moment before relenting. "I can't reach properly, alright? I'm not very flexible. It's not as if Azaria will help me with it."

"Surely one of the servants—"

"Who work for my father?" Leda cut him off with a snort. "I wouldn't trust them as far as I could throw them." Well, most of them at least.

"Ambrose?"

"Same problem."

Pyrrhus seemed to disagree with that, but he responded only with an infuriatingly neutral "I see." She heard a drawer opening and closing and thought that was the end of it.

Perhaps he was getting his map out and would spend the evening perusing it as he had done so many times before. When she felt a hand on her shoulder she started violently.

"Sit sideways in the armchair."

Leda obeyed without protest, moving to curl her legs underneath her. The warmth of the fire caressed her face and she closed her eyes. She stiffened as she felt Pyrrhus's fingers undoing the laces at the back of her gown with quick, efficient movements. The cool air hit her skin.

Nothing happened.

Leda looked around to see Pyrrhus staring at her back, entirely silent. She'd forgone a corset, it had been too painful. She probably should have warned him about that.

"It … looks much better." Seemingly forgetting himself, Pyrrhus trailed a finger down the line of her spine, charting the skin that was still pink from the whip, but well-healed thanks to his earlier efforts.

It was a shocking kind of intimacy that had Leda's eyes slamming shut as she forced herself to suppress a shiver.

She reached trembling hands back to make sure her mass of hair was neatly swept over her shoulder, and jumped a little when she felt the cold ointment touch her skin. It warmed almost instantly under Pyrrhus's hands as he pulled them across her shoulders in long, soothing strokes. Her sore muscles luxuriated in the sensation, and she could feel her head drooping forward of its own accord. Her skin was still a little painful, but she didn't care. She needed him to keep touching her, his focus entirely on her and nothing else.

As Pyrrhus's hand settled on the curve of her spine at her lower back, he paused. She heard him swallow.

Oh gods. It wasn't just her.

She felt bereft when he moved away, and after he retied her dress Leda turned in her seat to watch him cleaning the oil from his hands with his handkerchief.

"I keep ruining your shirts."

He seemed surprised at the orange oil that covered his cuffs. She doubted he would have even noticed if she hadn't pointed it out. "It doesn't matter."

"I'll sew you some new ones. My stitching isn't always straight, but at least they won't be orange."

She didn't think anyone had ever looked at her the way he did. She wished she could know what he was thinking.

"You spend a lot of time sewing?"

"Most of my spare time, actually, I've loved making things since I was a child. Azaria kept ripping all her dresses so it became a very useful skill."

"What do you like about it?"

That gave her pause. She'd never really thought about it before. "How methodical it is, I suppose. I find the repetitiveness soothing. That makes me sound extraordinarily dull, doesn't it?" Leda laughed, but he didn't, and she quickly sobered. "I've always loved to create beautiful things. They're a legacy, in a way, aren't they? Something positive to leave behind when I'm gone. Proof that I was here," she trailed off. "Why are you looking at me like that?"

Pyrrhus was sporting the oddest expression, but made no response. It seemed that words had failed him.

"Help me up?"

He stood in front of her, pulling her to her feet. When he made to step back to a respectable distance, she tightened her grip on his hands.

Their faces were inches apart, and she was seized by the thought that that was too far.

"I would ask you," she said quietly, painfully aware of the lack of distance between them, the fact that his breath was stirring the hair at her temple. He didn't move away.

"I beg your pardon?"

"The entry on my list, about kissing someone? I would ask you." Leda paused. "I trust you."

Now Leda knew what *this* expression meant. She'd read the word *tormented* in books before, but hadn't seen it realised on a person's face until that very moment.

She'd never known someone to be so confident and articulate but at the same time so thoroughly repressed. Everything from Pyrrhus's clothes to his manners to his accent was tightly and perfectly controlled. His whole body was tense, as though he was holding himself back from movement through sheer force of will. But she didn't know if he was restraining himself from moving towards her or running away. If the former, she wanted nothing more than for that ironclad will to fail.

"I think you know that I would want to," Pyrrhus finally admitted, eyes fixed on hers.

It was an enormous confession, almost incomprehensible.

He said it simply, as though his feelings about her hadn't been a source of mystery to Leda for months. Her heart felt like it had jumped up into her throat, and her fingers tightened around his.

"But that is immaterial," he finished.

"Immaterial ...," Leda murmured, watching the tension play out in the muscles of his neck. "What do you mean by that?"

"I'm here for a single purpose, it is not my place to fraternise with any of the royal family. Especially ...," he trailed off.

"A Counterpart who will soon be dead," Leda finished for him, stepping aside, suddenly business-like. He looked frustrated as she crossed her arms, and swayed on his feet as though he were seriously contemplating pulling her back towards him. "I'm not worth the investment."

"No!" he snapped. "Don't say that. You are worth everything. You are better than everyone inside this palace, including me, and deserve a life free of any of us."

There was a pointed silence as Leda's mind whirred. She had the distinct impression he had said more than he had meant to.

"Including you? You think I'm better than you? At what?"

"I've already—" Pyrrhus cut himself off in frustration, all markers of the sophisticated and urbane royal tutor gone. He ran a hand through his hair, ruffling the perfect style until it was unrecognisable. "We shouldn't be having this conversation, Leda."

"Stop that!" she snapped. "Why do you keep bringing things up and then shutting me out?"

"Why?"

"Yes! Why?"

He laughed at that, a bitter sound. It angered her even more, she so rarely got to hear him laugh that she couldn't stand when it wasn't genuine.

The tenuous control on his temper snapped, and the words came out in a flurry.

"Because I want to *save* you, Leda!" he said, and he looked disgusted with himself. "As if I'm a knight from a fairy tale and you're a damsel in distress. I want to get you away from here, and cure your illness and keep you safe, away from Azaria and your father. But that is not how life works!" He let out a shuddering breath. "Aside from treating you like a child who cannot fix her own problems, the only troubles I would be solving would be yours. I'd take you away but I'd leave behind a mad king still slaughtering his own children, wielding his favoured ones as a weapon against the others. He'd still strip all of the wealth and prosperity from the kingdoms he invades, leaving their populations destitute and starving. He'd still stamp out any hint of rebellion with soldiers and swords and blood."

Leda stared at him, dumbfounded. "And just what exactly are you planning on doing about all of that? You're not in a position to save the kingdoms from my father."

"What kind of person would I be if I failed to try?"

It was the loudest and most aggressive she'd ever seen him, but still he kept a distance from her, careful not to pose the slightest physical threat.

There was a horrible silence, and Leda felt all the blood drain from her face. She had wanted to get into further discussion on his apparent compulsion to be her rescuer, but his last exclamation had wiped that entirely from her mind.

"You're ... you're *trying* something? You're moving against my father?" she croaked.

Pyrrhus's face told her clearly that, once again, he had said too much.

"Don't be ridiculous, of course I'm not," he said curtly. "I forgot myself, my apologies. I shouldn't have shouted at you."

"Pyrrhus—"

He was already moving towards the door, tailcoat whipping around his legs as he hurried up the stairs.

"I must go, I am meeting with your father this evening."

Panic flooded her. "What—"

The door thudded shut, and she was alone.

CHAPTER 16

*E*verywhere Leda was, Pyrrhus suddenly found an excuse not to be. She was becoming frustratingly accustomed to seeing the back of his head as she entered whatever room he was in. She sat alone in his study when she went to read, he kept his distance at meals in the banquet hall, and when she was walking by the river one morning she could have sworn she saw him stride into the woods to avoid her.

Every night she threw caution to the wind and sneaked into the armoury, daring to douse Milos's fire long after he'd gone to bed and frantically digging away at the final holds in her chimney, trying not to choke on the residual smoke. It was tantalisingly close to being complete, and it wouldn't be a moment too soon judging by the unnerved ambience that had settled over the palace.

When she wasn't frantically carving at her chimney, she was steaming with rage and anxiety. Just who did Pyrrhus think he was? She needed to find out what reckless scheme he had developed against her father. He was an intelligent man, surely he knew how well protected the King was?

Rebellion meant death, everyone knew that.

So many questions, and Pyrrhus wouldn't let her anywhere near him to get answers. It was infuriating. Worse, it was lonely.

Leda was also coming to the unwelcome realisation that she was not the only one who appeared to be unravelling. Her father had abruptly changed from relaxed and always available to his court, hunting and feasting and dancing, to something of a shut-in.

Whispers swirled throughout the corridors of the palace, courtiers speculating about what might have put him in such a reclusive mood. The guard detail around him doubled; he spent hours of each day ensconced in his offices with his advisors. He even skipped meals, completely unheard of, to spend more time communing with the gods in the temple.

The more jumpy and suspicious her father got, the more Leda became so too.

Late autumn had brought a chill across the palace, and Azaria had taken to wandering around in increasingly elaborate furs.

She had stained one of her sleek mink cloaks and tossed it at Leda one morning. Leda had been sitting at the dining table eating an apple, staring out the window, and huffed when the heavy fabric hit her on the side of the head.

"What are you doing?" she snapped.

She had slept poorly, counting down the months she had left until the ceremony. She'd considered the list of experiences she'd wanted to have and felt rising panic at how she'd barely ticked any of it off. The further the days rolled on, the faster time slipped through her fingers.

Azaria smoothed back her hair, eyeing herself critically in the mirror.

"I spilt wine on that last night."

Leda let out another sigh as she dragged the cloak off

herself and laid it on the table to inspect it. There was a patch of red that looked distastefully like blood marring the inside, not visible if it was worn.

"Well, that's never coming out," Leda said, sifting her fingers through the soft fur.

"Fine. You can have it if you like. Or throw it away, it's nothing to me," Azaria said. "Perhaps you can wear it to dinner. It will be cold this evening."

She was not wrong, the weather outside was turning icy. But Leda doubted they'd be too cold at dinner, given the height to which the palace fires were being stoked—as if they would do anything to burn away the evil spirits.

Leda shifted in her chair with a groan. Azaria had made her accompany her while she was hunting that morning. Her back was aching from the awkward position she'd had to maintain to keep the quiver of arrows upright as she walked. The most exhausting part was the argument they'd had when Leda had refused point-blank to hold the squirrels Azaria had shot.

"Have you noticed any changes in the King recently?" Leda asked.

The quickness of Azaria's glance to her confirmed that she had. "What do you mean?"

"He's looking ... twitchier than usual."

Azaria felt no need for such subtlety. "He's losing what little remains of his mind," she said with absolute dismissal. She did not fear a treason charge, as if anyone would dare attempt to arrest her. The thought was laughable. "There is talk of rebellion in the conquered kingdoms. Something the gods should be preventing for him but aren't. He's paranoid and looking over his shoulder at every moment. He is a bear to be around."

"Why would the gods forsake him, he's given them the Counterpart blood?"

"I'm not a god, Leda," Azaria said. "How would I know?"

"You're very entitled, for someone who claims not to be one," Leda hissed back.

"Funny," Azaria said with a face that had never displayed the slightest hint of laughter. "He can't walk through a corridor without accusing everyone he comes across of betraying him. He even ordered Pyrrhus out of his antechamber yesterday."

It was interesting how one word, one name, could take over Leda's entire consciousness with such all-consuming ease.

"He suspects Pyrrhus of betraying him?" she said with the worst attempt at unconcern she'd ever managed.

"He suspects his dogs of betraying him nowadays," Azaria said indifferently. "Last week it was his chief advisor, Ecgred, then it was Thorodin, yesterday it was Pyrrhus. Tomorrow it will be the head of the guards, no doubt." She waved a hand to indicate it would go on and on.

"Pyrrhus hasn't done anything, then? He has no evidence?"

Azaria stood up. "The man you don't know and have never spoken to will be fine. You're boring me now. I'll see you at dinner."

Dinner that night was one of the worst that Leda had ever experienced, and she had quite the backlog of awful memories to compare against to give it the distinction.

There was the time Prince Agon had smashed his tankard over the head of his Counterpart when he'd dared to talk back to him, and the time her father had brought in dogs to fight while they ate. And of course no one could forget the time the chefs had undercooked the lampreys and one half of the court had explosively vomited over the other half.

This dinner was worse than all of those three, combined.

Leda had already been out of sorts when she sat down at her table in the banquet hall. She'd been scanning every face as they entered the room, balanced on the edge of her seat. When Pyrrhus walked in, her relief was so acute she actually wobbled her chair. He hadn't been thrown in the dungeons, that was a promising sign.

His eyes met hers and he gave the tiniest of nods to acknowledge her.

She looked away.

Despite the brightly burning fires in the grand fireplace, Leda's table was very near the window, and the cloak Azaria had given her did guard nicely from the icy breeze that filtered in through the gaps.

When the King arrived and sat at his table upon the dais, Leda found herself fixated on him.

He was calm.

His hands did not tremble around his cutlery as they had done for the past week. He called forward only one taster instead of the six he had recently been employing, his paranoia so advanced he'd inadvertently ensured his portions of food were tiny by the time he got to them.

This evening he sat with his elbow propped on the table, chin resting on one hand, and smiled benevolently at his court.

It was chilling.

No one else seemed to notice. The courtiers weren't used to fearing their King, that was for others, people who had displeased him by being poor or self-governed or not gods-fearing.

"I care so deeply for you all, I would not see you injured."

He spoke at a normal volume, as one might over a table to the person sitting opposite. He sat alone on his dais, no one remotely close, but every head in the banquet hall swivelled to him as one. It was as though he'd spoken the words directly into their ears.

Leda slowly set down her cutlery, her appetite disappearing so fast she could barely remember how hungry she was when she'd stepped into the room. Her plate might as well have been filled with sawdust.

The King had continued to speak, his tone low and measured. 'I keep you all in opulent lifestyles, do I not? I allow you rooms in the most beautiful palace in the Five Kingdoms, I fill your coffers, I entertain and feed you day after day. I provide the wine in which you soak yourselves, night after night. And I sacrifice my children, year after year, to keep you safe.'

His words cracked on that last sentence, as though he cared—as though it cost him anything to order the Counterparts killed. Leda took in a sharp breath as hundreds of eyes focused on her.

"I confess myself ... surprised, that any of you would choose to betray me."

Leda forced herself to exhale as fear, bright and sharp, speared through her.

He knew that a rebellion had reached the palace, that traitors sat amongst his biggest supporters.

"I have done nothing but provide for the Five Kingdoms." Emotion stirred the King's voice, and Leda gaped at him as she realised that he actually believed every word he said. He had cast himself the hero in his own story, and in the stories of any of them unfortunate enough to be trapped in this room with him. "I have served you all, faithfully, for decades." When he shook his head his crown glinted menacingly in the candlelight. "And this is how you repay me for my tireless work on your behalf?"

No one was brave enough to respond. If someone had dropped so much as a hairpin on to the ground it would have rung discordantly through the silence. The court barely breathed.

"Do not think that anything any of you do will ever slip past me. I have complete control over this country, this palace, and its inhabitants. You live because I and the gods allow it. Some of you have forgotten that. Perhaps you would like to return to the widespread calamity and poverty and starvation that marked the days before my reign. Some of you require a reminder of the power against which you attempt to stand, small and pathetic and morally bankrupt as you are."

If a shudder could ripple contagiously through a crowd, Leda would wager that was what she saw then. It was a jarringly refreshing change not to be the most vulnerable person in this godsforsaken place, if only for a moment.

But if the individual who was now most in danger was Pyrrhus …

The thought seized her by the throat and did not let go. What could she do? She didn't know what scheme he was involved in, for how long, what power he held in the structure, or what their numbers were. She was utterly useless.

She refused to look across the room at him. She couldn't do it.

"Bring him in."

Bring? The traitor wasn't already in the hall?

Leda's relief, mixed with a splash of guilt, utterly curdled when she saw who was now marching into the banquet hall.

The man led by chains wrapped around his wrists she did know, she believed he was one of the higher-ranking palace chefs. He'd given her bread and cold meats once when she'd snuck down to the kitchens after missing dinner. He'd been kind.

The ruddy skin of his face was marred by a blooming black eye and a split lip.

But he wasn't the one who struck that cold, ugly fear into her heart. No, it was the two men who flanked him. They weren't palace guards, as she had expected, but something infinitely worse.

She'd not seen them for years. It had been such a blessing.

"My sons Prince Agon and Prince Elias are here to bring me a rebel spy from within my own palace."

Agon was tall and thin, like a reed, his face and arms horribly scarred from battle. He'd never seemed to mind that though; in fact, he was proud of it. He was draped in so many weapons it was a wonder he could summon the strength to lift one foot in front of the other. But Leda had seen him fight with an arrogant swiftness and fury that made even Azaria's skill fade by comparison.

Elias was shorter, squatter, and missing an arm. That was courtesy of Azaria, who did not show a flicker of emotion as he entered the hall. He showed emotion when he looked at her, though. It was a kind of bubbling, roiling hatred that threatened to ignite if they encountered each other without the watchful eye of their father keeping them in line.

Agon was supposed to be ruling over Saint-Trevale, and Elias over Rivernesse. What in the gods names were they doing here?

Whatever the reason was, it brought their father comfort, and so Leda knew it could not be good.

Agon gave a swift tug on the chains he held and the chef was thrown to the ground by the force of it, crying out as his knees cracked against the floor.

Leda had seen that look on Agon's face before, that sadistic pleasure at watching another living creature suffer. She'd seen it years ago, when they had found his Counterpart Erdil's pet ferret hanging from the doorway to the banquet hall at breakfast one morning. Agon had absorbed their tears and their screams like they were his lifeblood.

Elias was two years Agon's junior, and a brute. While he was threatening to his core, only Agon was the one who struck fear in those who had never met him. His legend preceded him, these days, even larger and more awe-inspiring than Azaria's.

"Bring out the whip."

Thorodin had been promoted from his lowly position teaching younger Counterparts and noble children, it seemed, for he was the one who emerged from a shadowy corner of the room. A whip lay curled around his elbow. He was dressed more richly than he used to, in foppish maroon satins, and Leda fisted her hands in the tablecloth at the sight of him.

When he brought the whip cracking down on the chef's bare back the sound reverberated through her like a physical blow, snapping open the memory of when she'd been in his place. It took all she had to keep the bile from rushing up her throat.

The sound, more than anything else, provoked the trembling of her arms that she couldn't control. The memory, the ghost of the pain. It was excruciating.

This poor man, she couldn't watch this.

Her wild eyes found Pyrrhus in the crowd without her conscious direction. He looked perfectly composed, and when they made eye contact, he shook his head minutely from side to side.

He was telling her to calm down, to control herself, that it would all be over soon. Or at least that was what she assumed. She released the death grip she had on the table-cloth and blinked back the tears that had gathered at the second crack of the whip.

The King waved a hand lazily. "Enough for the moment, Thorodin. Lucas, perhaps you're more amendable to speaking now? In front of the people whose lives you would have forfeited in order to depose me? My closest friends and family, whom you would have ordered slaughtered by the soldiers you have been sneaking in disguised as palace staff."

Murmurs rippled through the crowd at that, and the air of sympathy abruptly evaporated.

Lucas was strong, stronger than her father had antici-pated. Spitting blood on to the ground, he cocked his head challengingly at his monarch, as though asking if that was all he had to give.

The King saw value in warriors and battles, not in the lower classes who cooked his meals and cleaned his palace. His eyebrows quirked a little in surprise.

"Tell us who your accomplices are, and all of the pain will stop. You've been sneaking blades into the palace in our food. Who are you supplying them to?"

Lucas merely grinned, and Thorodin struck once more.

Uncaring of what anyone who might see her would think, Leda put her face in her hands to block out the sight. But she could still hear the screams as the whip fell again and again.

Lucas was barely conscious by the time it stopped, slumped face down on the floor. Not one word had passed his lips.

Leda chanced a single glance at Pyrrhus, seeing his fists clenched on the table where he sat. Something was clutched in one of those fists. A scarf.

Her scarf.

He'd been wearing the scarf she'd made for him.

Leda looked at Lucas once more and the tears made their way down her face at last. He'd been put through unspeakable torture and he'd not revealed any of his collaborators. That was a kind of loyalty the King would lay claim to in public but never be able to truly feel.

And Lucas would die for it.

The King was that terrible mixture of enraged and bored now that it was clear his interrogation was not having the desired effect.

"Let's see what you have to say when Ambrose has fed you his remedies, hmm? I hear he can mix herbs into a concoction that will make you feel like your lungs are tearing themselves from your body. Much worse than the whip, I promise. Shall we see what you have to say then? These turncoats are not worth your life, Lucas."

They all watched as guards approached and dragged Lucas's limp body out of the room. His head bowed, Ambrose rose from his seat and swept out behind them. Leda watched him go with narrowed eyes.

He was a healer, surely he wouldn't be dabbling in torture for her father? She didn't particularly like him, but she'd thought him above that, at least.

No one in the court, no matter how nauseated they might feel, was brave enough to rise from their seats and leave with her father still watching. They might as well have declared themselves one of the rebels if they dared to do so.

Instead they all played their roles, as they knew they must, slowly returning to indulging in the food and drink and telling great jests. Roars of laughter were rippling up and down the trestle tables within minutes.

All the while the King sat there, staring suspiciously at the food on his plate without taking a bite.

Leda was among the first of the diners to decide she'd

had enough of the meal. Fifteen minutes after her father's scapegoat had been dragged away, she set down her napkin and got to her feet. Slowly, with no sudden movements that might attract attention, she made her way towards the door.

As she crossed the halfway point she slowed her pace even further.

Something felt horribly wrong, like an icy hand had seized the back of her neck, but a careful graze of her fingers over the skin showed that nothing was there. Trying and failing to repress a shudder, Leda's gaze followed where her instincts told her to. She twisted to look behind her and the air froze in her lungs.

The King had bright, penetrating blue eyes, full of intelligence and a peculiar form of madness that stared straight into your soul. Or at least that's what Leda had heard from others, given she'd had no experience. Even when she was being punished for her sins against him and the gods, he'd stared down at the ground with half annoyance, half boredom.

That was not the case now.

For the first time in her life, her father was looking at her.

When Leda visited the temple the next morning, groggy with stress and lack of sleep, it was one of the first times she had done so of her own volition. She even got there early enough to find Elina with a hand resting reverently on one of the statues as she spoke with two of the priestesses.

Elina cast her a deeply suspicious look when she noticed her presence, eyes moving to the prayer garland clutched so tightly in one of Leda's fists that the dried flowers were crumbling off the frame. Thankfully Elina said nothing, merely jerking her head as though allowing her in.

Leda certainly didn't need her permission to enter, but refrained from saying so.

She sat down in a dramatic puff of skirts on the floor by the statues of the gods and addressed the nearest one, letting loose a torrent of panicked thoughts, curse words and entreaties for help.

No matter that they weren't listening to her. She'd shout into the nothingness for as long as it took to make her feel better.

After twenty minutes Leda had exhausted every bitter, terrified thought in her brain, and unsurprisingly felt no catharsis. If anything, she was even more tired than she'd been when she'd woken up. She should have just slept in. A headache was already beginning to pound at her temples.

There was something, an innocuous feature of the room, that demanded attention. It took a few seconds for her to notice. It was odd, considering it was the lack of something that drew her attention, rather than a new and interesting object.

The ceremonial axe, the one stained with the blood of her Counterpart brothers and sisters, usually stood on a plinth at the end of the room.

It was gone.

Leda scrambled to her feet so fast she nearly tripped over them, dropping her prayer garland to the floor. She barely noticed that she kicked it halfway across the room in her haste to flag down a priestess who was walking nearby bearing a tray stacked high with fruit.

"Where's the axe?" There was no time for preamble.

This priestess was young and beautiful. A condition of employment in the palace temple, it seemed. Something like sympathy creased her features as she took Leda in.

"It has been removed to the priestesses' chamber, for the preparation and the blessings."

Leda's blood might as well have been ice in her veins. It was the first time she could empathise with the priestesses who thought this temple was too cold. "But you only do the rituals six days before the ceremony." She had every step of it memorised, had done since she was a little girl.

The priestess hesitated. "Indeed."

Leda didn't know her name, and yet this young woman, this stranger, was the one who was telling her that her execution date had been moved forward, and that in a week's time she would be dead. She'd suddenly become one of the most impactful people in Leda's life, and she had no idea who in the world she was.

"It is the gods' plan."

On second thought, this woman was an idiot and Leda wished she'd never met her.

Luckily she was prevented from the consequences of speaking her caustic reply by Elina stepping into view, face as expressionless as Azaria's usually was.

"Leave us, please," she said with all of the gravitas of someone who had not had many people say no to her in her life. The priestess seemed relieved by the reprieve and bobbed a short curtsey before disappearing through the double doors into the priestesses' wing.

"Six days?" Leda croaked.

Elina's face was as solemn as she'd ever seen it, not mocking as it usually was. That in itself was more alarming than anything else she'd witnessed since entering this temple.

"And there's no way out," Leda said on a shuddering breath. Her chimney was not ready, there was no other route. Fate had come early for her, and it was making a mockery of her attempts to avoid it.

Elina frowned at that. "You've considered running away?"

"Of course I have," Leda hissed. "Why wouldn't I?"

"Then they'll just kill someone else instead of you. The gods won't be happy but it'll tide them over until the next ceremony. You're content to allow another to die on your behalf?"

"Forgive me if I don't believe everything our father tells us to keep us in line," Leda said acidly. "It's never happened before, who's to say that's how it would work? Have you ever heard of other secret progeny, locked away somewhere waiting to be used as alternatives?"

"Well, no, but—"

"Then don't judge me for not deciding to stake my life on that."

"But what if it *is* true?"

Leda didn't need to stop to think. "Then I'm hardly the one killing them, am I? And you're a hypocrite if you say you wouldn't think the same in my position."

That seemed to offend Elina more than anything else given how she planted her hands on her hips. "I believe in sacrificing for others."

"That's easy to say when you never actually have to do it."

It took a moment for that statement to fully sink in, and Leda was suddenly aware of how much taller Elina was than her. "You think I haven't *sacrificed* anything?"

Elina looked incensed enough to grab her, to take her by the shoulders and shake her, and Leda took a hasty step backwards. She didn't know whether it was to her benefit or not that someone chose that moment to slam the doors to the temple open.

Elina froze and Leda watched blankly as a stream of guards poured in. All ten of them swerved towards her, their armour clanking with sounds that would echo in her nightmares.

Elina was suddenly refusing to meet her eye, focusing on her shoes as though they were the most interesting pieces of apparel she'd ever come across.

"Ledazaria." The oldest of the guards, with grizzled grey hair and faintly lined bronze skin, came to a halt in front of her. "My team and I are bid to accompany you wherever you go over the next week."

She looked warily over the impassive faces of his 'team'. "Why?"

"Your ceremony has been brought forward."

"Why?"

But she knew why, this stranger did not need to tell her. She knew that the very reason for her doom surrounded her as she stood in this temple of gold and decadence, a shrine to violence and blood. Her paper effigy stood in the corner, just waiting to be burned, to erase any hint of her existence.

The King's gods had stopped protecting him from the rebellion, and so he needed to appease them with more blood. The schedule must therefore be moved up.

She wondered if the gods ever felt guilty, if the reason her god never spoke to her was because they were too ashamed.

Likely not.

It was very possible she was going to be sick all over this guard's metal breastplate.

"Am I under arrest?"

The guard shook his head, something that might be sympathy crossing his face. "You're under our protection, madam, until the time comes for your ceremony. It will take place six days hence."

Leda could barely hear him over the roaring in her ears.

This was it. She'd tried and she'd tried, for so many

years. So many desperate plans and schemes, and even as each had failed, falling in an endless line of dominoes, there had always been some part of her that was so naively sure that she would succeed. That she would triumph, somehow, through her wit or her brains or even through dumb luck.

But she would not, she was finished.

All was lost.

CHAPTER 17

The old guard who shadowed Leda's every move was named Xander. He barely spoke, so Leda knew only three things about him after that first day trapped in his presence: he liked to crack walnuts in his palms between meals, he relentlessly tapped his feet when forced to stay in one place for too long, and he thought it was appropriate to follow her into the bathing room in case she tried to climb out the window.

Leda's response to that last decision had ensured that the two of them would never be friends. She'd nearly taken his head off in her rage. The rest of his team had drawn their swords in panic at the raised voices, but Xander had eventually managed to talk her down.

Leda was almost surprised by how rapidly she turned into a shell of her former self. All personal care and hygiene had gone out the window; she'd lost any concept of herself as a corporeal being when the life that stretched before her had been compressed from months to days. Her hair was ratty and unkempt and she felt grease on her skin, but was unable to locate the desire to care.

The news of the early ceremony had spread through the

palace, as had the whispers. They spoke of rebellions in the conquered kingdoms, armies massing in every location that was of strategic disadvantage to Viridiana. The court worried that the King was losing his influence with the gods, and that he only had so many royal children and Counterparts left to offer. If he dispensed with them all to smooth over this blip in his reign, what would come next?

Leda wasn't interested in speculating about that. She'd spent most of her day contemplating attempting to slip out of sight of her guards and find Pyrrhus. She needed to talk to him so badly it was an ache that sat continuously in her chest, no matter what she was doing.

Unfortunately, whenever an outlandish idea like that entered her head Xander would meet her eye and crack those stupid walnuts in his fists. His gaze said that he knew exactly what she was thinking and that it was damnable nonsense.

Her guard detail did, however, allow her to talk to Azaria.

That was not helpful.

Their first day together had seen Azaria spread dramatically over the settee in her rooms, one arm cradled in the other. "I don't want to do the ceremony next week."

Leda had eaten close to nothing the previous day and so had nearly overbalanced and fallen down the stairs that morning. She was therefore forcing herself through a bunch of grapes at the nearby table. She briefly contemplated spitting the seeds at her sister.

"Why's that?"

"I injured my arm hunting yesterday." Azaria pointed at it. "I can't lift the axe." She snapped her fingers at Xander, and Leda realised her sister's words were not for her benefit. "You, tell my father he needs to move the ceremony back. I'm not able to perform."

Xander pursed his lips like this was not the first nonsense he'd heard from her.

"Nothing will delay the ceremony, Princess Azaria. You'll simply have to do your best. Are you ready for the feast this evening?"

Azaria eyed him shrewdly for a moment as she got to her feet, smooth and sinuous as a cat.

"Yes, but I want my Counterpart with me."

Leda nearly choked on a grape. She couldn't think of anything worse than attending a feast hastily pulled together in celebration of the return of her two least favourite brothers. Spending the night being gawped at by a court that was trembling in morbid excitement about her death? No, thank you.

Xander looked reluctant. "It's much easier to guard Ledazaria when she's confined to these rooms."

"Then how lucky it is that you are a competent guard. Or so I presume, given the level of seniority my father has entrusted you with?" Azaria's voice was pure ice, and her words landed with exactly their desired effect as Xander puffed himself up.

"I most certainly—"

"Excellent," Azaria said, as though he had not spoken. "Leda, run a comb through that rats' nest you call hair, put on a dress less than a hundred years old and be back here in five minutes. Do not follow her," she said to Xander, who had started to move across the room. "She's not a toddler; she is capable of changing her own dress without assistance."

"But the window—"

"Is five floors above ground and she is not a humming-bird. She's going nowhere. I tire of this conversation." With that said she swept imperiously back into her own bedroom.

It was very rare but, sometimes, Azaria could be magnificent.

~

The smell of the feast turned Leda's stomach, and she wasn't even in the banquet hall. She resisted the urge to kick the statue of the gods that took up a chunk of the corridor outside it and made to go in.

Eber caught her arm before she could. Blinking in surprise, she allowed him to pull her aside. He was dressed in the same formal style as everyone else, though his clothes were shabbier, and he looked like he'd barely bothered to run a brush through his hair.

His eyes were bloodshot.

"Hey!" Xander said, stepping forward.

"WILL YOU GET OUT OF MY WAY!" Azaria bellowed so loudly her voice reverberated off the walls. "I haven't been able to move an inch without falling over any of you the whole way down here. Now you're getting in the way of our guests." She pointed at the opposite wall as the pack of guards quailed. "Gather over there and do not embarrass the royal family in front of dignitaries and diplomats, is that so difficult to understand?"

Xander indicated how much he did understand with the speed at which he chivvied his men over to the other side of the corridor. He settled there and watched Leda and Eber with baleful eyes as Azaria stormed into the banquet hall.

"Eber, are you alright?" It was a redundant question for Leda to ask another Counterpart, perhaps, but she couldn't help herself.

"I heard this morning about your ceremony. I'm so sorry." He looked it too, like the news had destroyed him. It was the very thing she didn't want to see, the reason she'd avoided close bonds with her siblings for her whole life.

She could not cry. She *would not*. It was not how she would spend her final days.

"I'm sorry, too."

Eber grabbed two glasses of champagne from the tray borne by a passing servant and pressed one into her hands, his own shaking slightly. "Smile, like I'm telling a funny story."

She made an attempt to do so, watching in alarm as he downed his drink in three swallows. He wiped a hand across his mouth and leaned in to avoid them being overheard.

"If the opportunity presents itself tonight, I want you to run."

"Run—what are you talking about?" she hissed, her smile disappearing. This close she could see the sweat beading on her brother's forehead. Oh gods, he was planning on doing something stupid. "Eber, talk to me, what's going on?"

"Nothing," he said, eyes following the sumptuously dressed courtiers as they milled past them into the banquet hall. "But if there's a ... distraction this evening, if something occupies your guards' attention, I need you to take the opportunity. Go out through the rose garden, cross the river and get into the woods."

He had guessed at her previous plan with an accuracy that made her mouth dry. "Don't be silly, Eber, the guards will be watching me all night. I'm surprised they're not attached to me with chains at this point."

"In one hour they won't be watching you," Eber muttered. He made to grab another champagne flute from a nearby servant and Leda slapped his hand away.

"That's quite enough alcohol for you," she said, putting her own untouched glass on the servant's tray. "I need you to tell me exactly what you're talking about. You'd better not be putting yourself in danger to help me escape. That will not work."

He flashed her a guilty look and dread clutched at her.

"An hour," he said. "Be ready."

"No! Eber—"

He disappeared into the crowd before she could catch him. She wrapped her arms around herself, suddenly cold.

Leda was so unaware of her surroundings that she collided with a woman just outside the banquet hall. She was tall and inordinately beautiful, with flaming red hair and draped from head to toe in heavy furs. She murmured an apology and drifted off into the party before Leda could reply with her own. With a huff of annoyance Queen Celandine appeared on her heels and hurried in after the woman.

Leda was once more knocked aside, only this time with no apology.

Without any real plan on what to do next, Leda drifted into the banquet hall. A full orchestra was playing a beautiful, soaring song, and the floor was filled with a crush of chattering courtiers, their finery gleaming in the light of the chandeliers. One long table passed through the centre of the room, groaning under the weight of more food than she'd ever seen in one place.

The King was out to show off his wealth tonight.

Azaria stood by the doors overlooking the rose garden, a glass of untouched champagne in one hand, engaged in conversation with their fourteen-year-old brother Prince Elov, who looked a little upset. Though she could never be accused of being comforting, it looked at least like Azaria wasn't actively making him feel worse.

To the right, their father sat on his throne, surrounded

by a throng of wives, mistresses and advisors, all fighting for his attention.

Leda stopped and looked at him. He didn't look back. So they were back to that, then. That age-old instinct that told him he was being watched never seemed to work when it was Leda who was doing the watching.

Prince Elias stood in prime position by the buffet, clutching a plate stacked high with food. He watched Azaria over the top of it with mean little eyes.

Their other guest of honour, Agon, was comfortably channelling their father given the cluster of women he had managed to gather around him. He made a joke and his audience's laughter spilt out over the music.

As her eyes travelled over the crowd, Leda noticed that no one was making eye contact with her. Whereas previously it had been because she was beneath their notice, now she had the feeling it was because they knew exactly who she was and did not want to be seen associating with her. They had all watched avidly, thoroughly entertained, as she had been whipped before them. Now, they couldn't muster the courage to acknowledge her.

Leda started when she saw Pyrrhus had entered the hall and was speaking to Ambrose, who looked like he last slept about a decade ago. They were both the very definition of tense, as though expecting someone to attack them at any moment. As Ambrose scanned the crowd with an angry expression, Pyrrhus turned and looked directly at Leda, as if he'd been aware of her position in the room throughout his conversation.

Leda feigned interest in the musicians instead. She'd show her face enough for everyone to know that she had attended, which would hopefully take no more than half an hour, and then she'd go back to her room and ... well, stare at the ceiling of her bedroom, she supposed. She had so little time left, she didn't want to waste any of it on sleep.

"Leda."

She started in surprise, Olora was suddenly at her side.

"Mother," she said blankly.

"Are you well?"

No. "Yes."

"Your ..." Olora faltered slightly. They both stared out at the gathered crowd as though they weren't having a conversation. "Your back ... it's ... you're alright?"

That was perhaps the first glimmer of concern her mother had ever shown for her, and expressing it clearly caused her great discomfort.

Leda fought the wave of gratefulness that cascaded over her. It was tempting to grasp her mother's interest and tug with all of her might, but all it would ever bring her would be disappointment. She had to remind herself that her mother had been among the hundreds who watched her being whipped and had done nothing. And she had also done nothing to convince the King to push back her ceremony.

Olora was a proud, selfish woman who cared little for her own children; that was what the King had made her. He had no patience for wives and mistresses who loved anything more than they loved him. He was as greedy with love as he was with fine meats and rare wine.

"I'm well. Not that it matters," Leda said, careful to keep her voice as free of bitterness as possible. Still, she wasn't going to sugar-coat this. "Azaria needs me alive to cut my head off next week. It won't matter what state I'm in when the time comes."

She felt Olora gasp beside her, a tiny intake of breath. "I will be devastated to lose you."

Leda didn't believe her for a second. This was one of the

longest conversations they'd had in her life, and she'd been in the palace with her mother every summer since her birth. What could Olora have to lose, if she didn't know her?

"I'm sure you'll be able to endure it," Leda said drily. "If you'll excuse me." She didn't wait for Olora's response, striding away towards the doors that led to the rose garden.

The crowd had thickened, and she looked around in surprise to see that there were many people there who weren't part of the regular court. In fact, a good half of the men clustered around her she was quite sure she'd never seen before. Perhaps she was just unobservant, or, as was more likely, they were Agon and Elias's entourages as well as visitors from the King's more distant lands.

As she passed one sumptuously dressed man, she caught a glance of what she could have sworn was a dagger attached to his belt. But surely she was mistaken, these great men never bothered to arm themselves when guards wandered so close to them. The court was complacent and glutted on food, alcohol and excitement.

A distinctive clanking told Leda that Xander was by her side. In an act of chivalry she wasn't expecting, he opened the door to the rose garden and allowed her through before him. He and his guards followed.

They weren't the only ones to do so. The cold air hit her like a slap at the same time as she saw Pyrrhus slip out of the door behind them.

To Leda's everlasting shock, Xander's face transformed into a smile. "Pyrrhus, my boy! I owe you your book back, I've not forgotten."

Pyrrhus was all charm in response, reaching out to shake the older man's hand with a rare smile. "Keep it, I insist, I'm sure your son will enjoy it as much as you did."

"He will at that," Xander said, grin widening.

"Apologies for interrupting, but I need to speak with

Ledazaria. There are some aspects of next week's ritual she needs to be made aware of in advance. Duty of the royal historian, you know." He phrased it as if it were all so deadly boring, just another courtly ritual that he'd like to skip.

Xander had been nodding before Pyrrhus had even started speaking. "Of course, we'll stand over here to give you some privacy." He and the other guards moved just out of earshot.

Leda ensured she was standing a respectable distance from Pyrrhus and clasped her hands behind her back.

He stood still as a statue before her, features remote.

"Did you make that up?" she asked.

If any emotion was gripping him, the only way it showed was in the flex of his jaw. "There is a script for you to follow, as you know, but it's not my responsibility to teach it."

So many eyes watched them, it was an itch all over her skin. She was so worried her feelings for this man were written all over her stupid face. The want and the resentment and the worry and the hunger. But she couldn't put him in danger from his association with her, particularly if he was involved in any doomed schemes against her father.

She forced her gaze to the ground.

"What did you want to say to me?"

He was looking at her so strangely. "I, yes, I wanted to say ... I ... it's ..."

This man, with the most extensive vocabulary she'd ever heard, was struggling to form a sentence as he looked at her.

It eased something in her chest to see him that way, proof that he was just as affected as she was, no matter how proficient he usually was at hiding it. If he had any grief he wanted to express at the prospect of her imminent death, he didn't seem to be able to translate it properly into words.

So she did it for him.

"I suppose this is goodbye," she said with what she hoped was a smile and not a grimace. "Thank you for—"

His eyes flashed.

A scream rent the air.

Pyrrhus was right in front of her so fast he nearly knocked her backwards into a rose bush, but then his hands were around her waist to steady her and the world tilted back on to its proper axis as he pulled her into his chest.

He was an assault to her senses, the solid warmth of him in front of her, the drugging scent of him instantly surrounding her. His hands dragged across her hips as he removed them from her.

She couldn't allow herself to focus on that.

Instead she stepped sideways to get a clear view through the doors and back into the banquet hall. She let out a muffled cry as she took in the scene unfolding in front of her.

Azaria stood in the centre of the room, brilliantly lit in her black dress by the chandeliers, skin white as a sheet. Eber stood next to her, a diamond necklace he had clearly just ripped off her neck in one hand. Jewels rained from his fist on to the ground in a sparkling shower. In the other hand, he held Azaria's upper arm in a tight grip.

All was silent for a moment, and then Azaria struck. With a shriek that was barely human, she leapt on their brother, scratching and kicking and punching and biting like a wild animal.

Leda started forward. "Oh gods!"

"Stay here!" Pyrrhus was past her like a shot, sprinting into the ballroom as the crowd swallowed up the fighting duo. He grabbed Xander's arm and yanked him in with him. All atwitter, the guards from his team followed him into the palace, swords drawn, as though that would help with anything. She heard the added shrieks as other royal children and Counterparts joined the fray. The King was nowhere to be seen.

So this was Eber's distraction. He was risking his life attacking Azaria, who just last year had severed the arm of another sibling, to help Leda escape. She could have cried. She wanted to scream at him.

Leda stood stock still, as though her feet were glued to the floor.

The guards stationed in the gardens behind her were emerging, the ones who Xander and his team must have been relying on to keep an eye on her while they entered the fight. But instead they were drawn by the noise, the incessant screams, and as they saw the commotion worsen they began to run towards the banquet hall doors.

Leda frowned as she looked back into the fray; something else must be happening to make them leave their posts. The screams and shouts had increased and were no longer coming from Azaria and Eber. It looked like there was a disturbance in the crowd itself.

There now seemed to be twice the amount of people who had previously been in the room, and the newcomers were easy to pick out from the courtiers. They wore rough homespun clothes with metal breastplates and were brandishing swords. Guards had begun to engage them in vicious battle, drawing them further inside the palace.

Leda staggered back and looked around, cautious hope spreading through her. She was alone in the gardens, the guards had all joined the fight in the palace and the guests had scattered. She had the sack of her belongings buried by the river and a route over the hills and into Saint-Trevale in her mind. Once there, she could disappear. This was her opportunity.

But oh, what it would cost. She would live with the guilt of knowing someone might have to be sacrificed in her place. She would have to leave Pyrrhus, and Eber, in danger. She wanted to storm back into that ballroom and pull both of them out to make them come with her, but she couldn't see either of them. The minute she stepped back over the threshold she would be part of that battle, and though she had no idea what it was about, she wasn't keen to find out.

Leda's heart jumped into her throat as she looked out into the darkness and back towards the melee. This was it. She would never get this chance again. She would never forgive herself if she didn't take this opportunity.

With a sharp intake of breath, Leda lifted her skirts and sprinted down the steps. Her heels clattered loudly on the stone and then were quiet on the damp grass.

She dropped to her knees by the edge of the river, uncaring of the mud streaking her dress, and scrabbled to pull up the dirt that covered her sack of supplies. Throwing a panicked look over her shoulder, she saw no one had exited the palace, though screams and cries were still echoing across the grounds from the open doors.

She let out a small cry of triumph as her desperate fingers found the sack, and she yanked it from the dirt, pulling the string hastily over her shoulder so that it came to rest on her hip.

Not allowing herself a further thought, she rose up and threw herself into the gushing river. The freezing water swallowed her up to her knees. She knew this was the shallowest point and she'd be able to cross it, but hadn't considered the weight of her voluminous skirts dragging her sideways, or the temperature of the water feeling like a thousand knives stinging her legs.

"NO!"

CHAPTER 18

*L*eda didn't get a chance to turn before she heard a splash behind her and felt a hand twisting in her hair. She let out a strangled shriek as she was yanked backwards, and she and her assailant fell to the shallow waters by the riverbed she'd just left.

Leda gasped for breath as the freezing water surged around her chest, splashing around to find herself face-to-face with Azaria.

Her sister's skin was a bloodless white, her eyes crazed. Hair fell in wet black ropes around that perfect face, her gown just as soaked as Leda's. Her elaborate diamond earrings glinted menacingly in the moonlight.

Leda could have screamed with frustration. "No! Let me go!"

She tried to get to her feet, but the weight of her dress was more formidable than the muscles in her legs. With a growl she grabbed the rocks of the riverbed beneath her and tried to use them to drag herself to the other side.

Azaria lunged forward, seizing her by the arm and pulling her back with an almighty splash. They struggled for a minute, each finding it difficult to gain the upper hand as the water swirled around them. Leda felt her strength draining by the second, shivering violently at the dual effects of the water and the frigid night air.

Her sister was stronger, better trained and apparently unencumbered by a conscience. Where Leda pulled back blows at the last second that might hurt her, Azaria did not feel that same compulsion.

However, their being in a river reset the odds somewhat. Knowing the most important thing to do was strip Azaria of her weapons, Leda grabbed her sister's flailing ankle and ripped the knife she always carried there out of its holster. With a small cry of triumph, she hurled it aside, the swirling current picking it up and carrying it on its way.

Leda shivered as Azaria wrestled her foot free of her grasp. Azaria's indignation seemed to be keeping her warm, and with a screech of fury she resorted to the basest tactic she knew to get her way. Dragging one of Leda's hairpins from her head, ignoring her scream of pain as she took a chunk of hair with it, she wrenched Leda's right leg towards the surface of the water and jammed the sharp end into the top of her thigh. Just as she had done when they were children.

Leda's scream of agony pierced the night, ringing across the grounds and momentarily obscuring the ruckus from inside the banquet hall. Blood bloomed beneath the water in a cloud of red, and she watched her sister stare down at it, as if she couldn't quite fathom where it had come from.

"Do. Not. Leave. Me," Azaria said, her voice guttural. She was as panicked as an animal, and Leda felt a spike of pure loathing shoot through her. Azaria was incapable of thinking about anyone but herself, unable to see past her own fear of abandonment to understand that Leda would be gone the following week anyway.

Leda suppressed a groan and spoke through gritted teeth. "*I hate you.*"

Azaria said nothing to that, instead grabbing her around the neck and dragging her back over to the riverbank on the side of the palace. Leda went rather than struggle, the pain in her leg excruciating. All the fight was leaving her as though it were stored in the blood seeping out into the water.

They struggled through the reeds and on to the bank and Leda fell to her back with a squelch of fabric as her ruined dress settled around her. It was the same colour as her blood, which was now spreading to stain the grass around her legs.

Now that Azaria had incapacitated her she seemed less inclined to cause further injury. She was on her knees, panting as she pulled the curtain of soaking hair out of her eyes. Her own dress was also beyond help, ripped from their struggle and slicked with mud and grime.

Leda's hand closed around one of the rocks that littered the river's edge, reassuringly smooth and cold against her palm.

"Get up. The palace is being attacked, we need to get out of the open," Azaria said, staggering to her feet and offering Leda a hand, as she never normally would.

Only momentarily stunned, Leda took the opportunity to grasp Azaria's cold hand, using it as leverage to yank her downwards. At the same time, she swung her other arm up with all of her strength. She hit her sister in the temple with the rock, producing a thud that felt much quieter than it should have been. Azaria reeled back and then froze, staring down at her with blood dripping down her face. She looked faintly dazed, but unfortunately not incapacitated.

Worst of all, she did in fact seem angrier than before.

Azaria dropped to her knees with a squelch, all reason

having left her eyes, and both of her hands curled around Leda's throat.

"Azaria—," she choked, trying to yank on her sister's vicelike grip and failing miserably. Her eyes watered, she tried to kick Azaria away but her legs didn't seem to be working. Her vision was blurring at the edges, the only thing she could see clearly was her sister's intent expression as she drained the life out of her.

"Go to sleep, it will be alright," Azaria said coldly.

"ENOUGH!" The word could have been shouted right next to them or all the way back in the banquet hall for all Leda knew. The blackness was spreading across her vision, and she could feel Azaria's hands leave her abruptly as every one of her senses began to fade.

Leda couldn't have been unconscious for more than a few seconds. She came to with a gasp and a hacking cough, hands flying up to her tender throat.

Azaria was kicking and screaming a few feet away, lifted clean off the ground by Ambrose, who was incandescent with fury. With a yell he threw her like a rag doll, and she hit the ground with a thud.

"Don't!" Leda said, words muffled by the grass as her head rested on the ground like it weighed twice as much as it did. With a groan and great effort she lifted herself upright on shaking arms.

Ambrose thoroughly ignored her, calling over a few guards who hovered nearby and ordering them to take Azaria away. Leda watched her limp form be picked up.

Before she could say anything more, Ambrose had approached and was kneeling beside her, a knife in hand. She watched, perplexed, as he used it to cut the heavy, sopping lengths of skirt that covered her leg so he could reach her injury. He cursed roughly when he saw the damage.

He wore a white tailcoat that had been pristine at the start of the night and was not so anymore. Using his knife once more, he sheared off a clean part of his coat and used it as a makeshift bandage, tying it tightly around her thigh to stem the bleeding. With his hand, he applied pressure on the wound. Leda let out a hoarse cry.

"It's shallow, it'll be alright," he said.

She looked up at the guards circling them, fear stirring her into a frenzy. "Don't let them whip me again."

"They won't," he gritted out, making pointed eye contact with one of them. "You're too injured, they won't hurt you."

Of course, they couldn't risk her dying before she could be sacrificed. There was no point risking her health now.

"Where are they taking Azaria?" she whimpered. Ambrose looked at her as though she'd lost her mind.

"Never mind that, she was trying to rip you apart," he hissed. He shook his head, as though he'd never been able to understand a single thought she'd ever had.

Leda clutched his wrist, tense from exerting pressure on her. "Promise me they won't hurt her, Ambrose."

His mouth was a grim line and he wouldn't meet her eye. "They'll take her somewhere to cool down, until the battle's over; they won't hurt her unless she becomes a threat."

That did not comfort her whatsoever.

"She's always a threat," Leda gritted out as Ambrose stood up and pulled her to her feet. He studied her neck but didn't appear to be too worried by the damage there.

Neglecting to respond to her, he directed her arm around his shoulders and took the weight she would have placed on her injured leg. Together, they began to hobble back to the palace at an agonisingly slow pace.

"Where's Eber? What happened to him?"

"They took him to the dungeons just before the attack began. Azaria gave him a concussion, but he'll be alright."

"Who attacked the palace? Are they winning?"

He shook his head grimly, and did not seem inclined to answer further questions as she heard the sound of armoured guards surrounding them. If they were free to encircle her, whatever invading force had made their attempt that night must have failed.

Brutal, unrelenting disappointment gripped her as tightly as Ambrose was.

The carnage of a quick, one-sided battle lay around them, unnaturally quiet. Bodies and blood and weapons were scattered through the grass. More rebel bodies than guards, judging by their clothes.

Leda kept her gaze upright, barely suppressing a grunt of pain as they staggered up the stone steps and into the rose garden. Most of the neatly trimmed bushes and plants had been destroyed, ripped out of their beds or cut viciously by sword swipes that had gone awry. Elina would be furious when she saw it.

Their feet crunched loudly on the gravel. They appeared to be the only ones outside, from what she could see in the pitch-black night. Light spilt from the banquet hall, and Ambrose shoved their way through a broken glass door.

The fighting continued here, though dead and injured rebel soldiers and guards littered the floor. Leda looked desperately around to see if she could find anyone she knew, but could see no signs of any member of her family, or Pyrrhus.

"Where are we going?" She screwed her eyes shut as she put too much weight on her injured leg.

"The infirmary," Ambrose said brusquely. "I'll be able to treat you there."

As they passed the throne room, Leda brought them to a halt with a hand clenching the fabric of Ambrose's coat.

Agon and Elias both held an arm of their father, dragging him across the ground towards the exit. He looked dazed and confused, as though he'd suffered a blow to the head, but he was otherwise unharmed.

"AMBROSE!" Agon roared when he saw him. "Get over here now!"

Neither Leda nor Ambrose was stupid enough to ignore his command.

"Go, I'm alright," she muttered.

Ambrose didn't need telling twice, and between the combined strength of him and her brothers, the King was quickly removed from the room and to safety. He would be alive and prosperous as he always had been.

More's the pity.

Leda scanned the ragtag groups of remaining fighters and her heart stuttered when she saw Pyrrhus in the corner. He was alive. He was covered in about as much blood as she, and she watched him dive between the cowering figure of her mother in the corner and two rebels who had approached her, his expression furious.

Pyrrhus held his own remarkably well as he fought them away from Olora. One went down with a grunt as Pyrrhus grazed his sword over the fleshy gap between two of his armoured plates and kicked him away.

Leda stumbled into the room, clinging to the wall with bone-white fingers. Pyrrhus hadn't seen her, he was shouting something incomprehensible at the other rebel that made him stop in his tracks. Still, she felt safer just being in the same room as dizziness overtook her. She knew she had mere minutes before she would collapse;

she wouldn't be able to ascend the stairs in her current state.

As she watched Pyrrhus it occurred to her that she had no idea where he'd learned to fight like that. There was confidence in his movements, his footwork precise, and he held his sword the way aristocrats were trained to. He didn't seem highly skilled, though, as though he'd had significant training while younger and had got somewhat out of practice.

"You!"

The only warning Leda had was a hand twisting in the back of her hair for the second time that night, brutally pulling her back a few steps. She went with a cry, trying to balance on her good leg while turning to see who had hold of her. She caught a glimpse of red. Thorodin.

His arm settled bruisingly tight across her chest, holding her in place while he brought a knife up to her throat with his other hand. Though he panted behind her, he said nothing, and she knew he didn't mean to give her a drawn-out death. He would slit her throat before letting her say a word.

"You had something to do with this, I know it, you scheming tramp. You know what? Your father can make do with a replacement."

She stamped on his foot and threw her elbow back into his stomach, but he did nothing aside from growl in pain.

Leda struggled in vain, eyes locked desperately on Pyrrhus, praying that he would turn around and realise what was going on. If she shouted he wouldn't be able to hear her through the cacophony of fighting, so all she could do was think, *Please. Please turn around.*

At that moment Pyrrhus's opponent ran from him, and he immediately swung around to get his bearings.

Thorodin started to draw the blade, excruciatingly slowly, across her throat, and she felt the wetness of her blood running down her chest. Though he stood metres away, she thought she could see all of the colour drain from Pyrrhus's face as his eyes finally met hers. He started towards her.

There was a whoosh and a thunk and Leda gasped as Thorodin's head snapped forward beside her, a bejewelled knife sticking out of the base of his skull.

Thorodin's grip on her slackened as he fell, but Leda went down with him. While he was dead before he hit the floor, the mysterious knife embedded deep in his throat, she was stunned and battered, but alive.

She tried to ease herself out of the tangle of Thorodin's limbs and traced her suddenly smarting shoulder with a hand that came away red. The knife had nicked her as it made its way to Thorodin, but it felt like a tolerably shallow wound. It bled less than her throat, anyway, which she was staunching with her other hand.

Pyrrhus was on his knees at her side in an instant, foolishly ignoring the fight at his back as more guards poured into the room to flush out the last dregs of the rebels.

"What happened?" Leda twisted around to see Elina panting in the doorway behind her, face a mask of blood, arm still out in the motion she'd used to throw the knife. She gave Leda a grim look and turned away, joining the flow of people in the corridor.

Had her sister just saved her life out of the goodness of her heart? Or to preserve her for the ceremony? She wasn't sure she'd believe Elina whether she told her either way.

Pyrrhus, in contrast, paid no attention to Elina whatsoever. "Where are you injured?" he gritted out, hands spanning her ribcage as he pulled her away from Thorodin's body. His fingers and thumbs almost closed around her middle, and she noted with bewilderment that she was still wearing a restrictive corset, which probably wasn't helping her breathing. She shook her head to rid it of the inane thought.

"I've been stabbed in my right thigh, Ambrose bandaged it. I've also been strangled and cut on the throat, and on my shoulder. And I'm covered in scratches. But I'm alright." Leda laid a hand on his arm, wrapping her fingers around his wrist and feeling the reassuring thud of his pulse. She knew that going by her blood-soaked and torn appearance he'd have a job figuring out exactly what was wrong with her.

Surprisingly she felt better than she should. The hibcus she took was a natural painkiller, and that mixed with the adrenaline coursing through her system was masking the worst of it. There was also the sheer relief of having him with her, safe and not a defeated rebel lying on the floor. It was a drug that rivalled any hibcus she'd ever taken.

Pyrrhus didn't seem to agree with her assessment, his hand moving to press over hers on her throat and his eyes closing briefly.

She was still learning to read him, but tonight his guilt was clear to see. She saw him swallow before sweeping her into his arms and standing. He was slow to right himself properly, a tiny grunt escaping him, and she saw the line of red on his shirt indicating a cut along his stomach. She bristled as he took her out into the corridor and hurried towards the staircase.

"Put me down this instant!" Leda insisted, though she was careful not to squirm to avoid injuring him further. "You're hurt!"

"I need to get you to the infirmary," he said, though his voice was hoarse with what she now knew was pain. Stupid, stubborn man.

"I can get there on my own," she lied indignantly. "How

bad is your injury?" She tried and failed to get a good look between them. Her voluminous skirts got in the way.

"It's a minor cut."

"Don't give me that!" she hissed as they reached the thankfully deserted fourth floor, his face now an alarming grey colour. "Don't you dare go spilling your intestines all over the floor because you decided to carry me like a stubborn idiot hero when you didn't need to!"

The word 'hero' made Pyrrhus stiffen, she'd clearly touched a nerve, and before she knew it she was being placed back on her feet. She threw an arm over his shoulders and they went the rest of the way to the infirmary much the same as she and Ambrose had, with a slow trudge. Leda tried to twist around to see Pyrrhus's stomach, but again she couldn't get a good view. What she did know was that his breathing had become laboured and shallow, and that it wasn't all from carrying her up those stairs.

Energy seemed to leave him with every step, to the point where she was supporting him more than he was her when she flung the doors to the infirmary open. Her leg screamed in protest, but she shoved the pain aside.

Most beds were full, the infirmary busier than she'd ever seen it before. It seemed a small army of healers who did not ordinarily work at the palace had been fetched. Every single one seemed to be taking the orders of Ambrose, who stood by one of the beds looking utterly harassed. Straining to get a good look, Leda saw Elina sitting on it and nursing a vicious cut on her arm, the heavy silk of her ballgown spilling out on to the floor in a puddle of midnight blue.

Her father was nowhere to be seen, and judging by Ambrose's presence here he would make a full and easy recovery. Leda could have cursed.

She felt a tug at her side as Pyrrhus lost consciousness, and lunged for his shoulders to prevent his head from hitting the floor. She succeeded in slowing his descent, but at great cost to herself judging by the pain now ripping through her leg, shoulder and throat. She whimpered, hands buried in the fabric of Pyrrhus's coat as he lay still on the ground.

Thankfully Ambrose had seen them enter and was already running up to them, enlisting the help of another physician to pick up Pyrrhus and place him on the nearest empty bed.

The sound of a shirt tearing pierced Leda's consciousness through the general cacophony. In absolute agony, but needing to see if Pyrrhus was alright, she dragged herself to her feet and over to where he lay.

Ambrose was slathering a thick, foul-smelling orange paste on to the long horizontal wound across Pyrrhus's torso. His shirt had been removed and the red of his blood was stark against his skin.

"Is he okay?" Leda choked out, one hand wrapped around the grille frame at the foot of Pyrrhus's bed as she lowered herself down on to her knees. The cold stone floor felt soft beneath her. The edges of her vision were turning hazy.

"He'll be fine, we got him in time," Ambrose said distractedly, his focus entirely on his friend as he pulled out a length of finely spun cotton and a needle.

"Good." It was all she needed to hear before sinking down on to the floor in a dead faint.

CHAPTER 19

*L*eda groaned a list of the most unacceptable curses she could think of, ones that would make even Azaria blink.

She was unable to comprehend a worse situation she could have ended up in. Someone had healed her injuries from the night before, for which she was grateful. Unfortunately, they had then chosen to dump her in a dungeon cell, for which she was very ungrateful indeed.

She woke up the morning after the rebels' failed incursion with her face pressed against a hard stone floor, pieces of hay stuck to her cheek. She'd been splayed out on her front like a starfish, and her muscles screamed in protest as she dragged herself on to her elbows and looked around.

It was certainly not the infirmary.

Her cell was small and spartan. There was no window to admit light, merely a few guttering candles in a candelabra that was mounted on the far wall. A small pallet with a clean white sheet stretched over it extended towards her, a few blankets tossed on top. A bucket and a chair stood in the opposite corner.

Good gods.

She was as clean as could be expected having slept on a stone floor that probably hadn't been swept since the palace had been built at the start of her father's reign. The unpleasantly familiar scratchy sensation told her she'd been put back in her brown wool Counterpart dress.

A glance up revealed that no less than three guards stood before her cell, including one she recognised. He was the only one without his back to her and was eyeing her warily, like he expected that she might explode.

"Atticus?"

Atticus was young to be one of the most senior guards, but her father had always liked to reward youthful ambition. It reminded him of himself, and if there was one thing he enjoyed, it was being surrounded by people who were as close to copies of him as he could get.

Atticus watched her drag herself up on to the pallet with something close to sympathy.

"Ambrose has prescribed you a number of medicines to take over the next few days, we'll bring them with your meals," he said gruffly. He had dark skin, a bushy black beard, and his form looked to be built with enough power to take down a horse.

"Why am I here?"

"You tried to escape, again."

That final word brought back a horrifying reminder. "Will I be punished?"

His eyes were kind. "No, the King needs you healthy for the ceremony."

Thank the gods for small mercies, she supposed.

"So you're going to keep me trapped in here like an animal ready for slaughter?"

"He said ... he said that if you were trying to run away like a panicked pig then you should be treated like one."

She couldn't tell if Atticus agreed with her father's sentiment or not, but there was something reluctant in the way he quoted the words.

Her father had compared her to a pig. Lovely.

At least Atticus seemed uncomfortable about it too. He'd always been fastidiously polite when she'd spoken to him in passing before. He'd been the head of Azaria's guard detail whenever she went outside of the palace with the royal family, and even her prickly sister had not taken an active dislike to him, so that was in his favour.

"Where's Eber? Is he alright?"

"He's fine. Well, his arm is bandaged up, but I was told he'd be fine. He's in a cell down at the end."

"Can I speak to him?"

"What do you think?"

She sulked for a good hour after that, refusing to speak with him until he said something that intrigued her. He was clearly bored, having to stand outside her cell all day to ensure she wouldn't transform herself into smoke and escape through the bars or something equally ludicrous. That led him to give away more information than he might have meant to.

"Leda, are you alright?"

"Shut up."

His eyebrows raised, though he didn't seem angry. "You're being just as obnoxious as your brothers and sisters, you know. My daughters could teach you all a thing or two about behaving properly, and they're half your age."

She didn't doubt that. "My brothers and sisters have always been obnoxious, it's a side effect of their circumstances."

He perked up at her response. Finally, some diversion. "Not like this. I've been here a long time, remember? Watching you all, it's like someone's been slipping madness into all your meals. Agon and Elias are snappy and disrespectful with the King, Azaria is doing the riskiest manoeuvres on hunts I've ever seen, like she's trying to get herself killed. Elina's in the gardens all day talking to herself, when she's not falling asleep on her feet in the temple. Caspari, Elov and Fessler are fighting each other like rabid cats. And you Counterparts ... well, you've all always been off your rockers, so that's not actually changed."

"Thanks," Leda said drily. She would have been far more cutting had she not heard the barely repressed sympathy in his voice. "I suppose your family's a dream compared to ours?"

"Most are, Leda," he said on a sigh, then seemed to remember where he was and straightened up. "I'm going to see when the shift change is, excuse me."

He was so polite. As if she could have done a thing to stop him leaving.

It was not pleasant to be left with her own thoughts, whirring in her mind. It had been much easier to contemplate the final days of her life when she had even a little freedom to move about the palace, maybe to see the people she cared about one more time before the ceremony. Now, she would be staring at oppressive stone walls until the end.

Maybe madness would take her before her time came, so at least she wouldn't know what was happening.

"You wouldn't allow that, would you?" She spoke up at the ceiling for the benefit of the gods, lounging around in whatever mystical plain they inhabited. "You want me experiencing every moment of my death, like they all did. Does it please you? Do you enjoy it?"

The only response she got was an awkwardly cleared throat outside her cell.

A new guard had arrived to replace Atticus, and he was now so afraid of her he refused to make eye contact.

Leda sighed and rolled over on her pallet to face the wall.

~

The guards who rotated outside Leda's cell were very professional and dedicated to ensuring that she did not escape, not that she was even remotely tempted to try. She had no skills that would get her through those iron bars. She'd taken a brief look at the lock to the door and snorted, knowing her hairpins would disappear inside it, never to be seen again.

Still, the guards were lax about one thing. Either they didn't realise, or didn't care, that when they gathered at the end of the long corridor that split the line of cells, the stone walls amplified their voices so that Leda could hear them as clearly as if they were in her cell with her.

They were gossipers, this lot, despite their stern and stoic expressions as they stood bolt upright outside her cell.

Their whispers revealed that the King was in a triumphant mood. He had put down the pathetic rebellion with barely any losses. The gods were still on his side, his way to keeping all of his power and influence was clear, and he'd celebrated it by getting the court drunk and keeping them that way for the whole of the previous day. Apparently some of the servants were fainting on their feet in the kitchen, working too hard to prep for feast after feast, not due to stop for the next week.

Leda's mouth was as dry as if her breakfast were comprised of raw wool when she heard the conversation turn to the preparations for the ceremony. They speculated that, despite his victory, some part of the King was rattled. He was still making his sacrifice to the gods sooner than planned, and therefore must be looking to appease them.

He wanted to add the strongest and most calculating of his brood, Azaria, to his ranks of gods-blessed children— whether to protect him or to pursue further conquering, they weren't quite sure.

Leda was relieved when their shift changed and the chattering stopped, and looked up with interest when she heard the sound of another prisoner being brought down into the bowels of the palace.

The usual protocol, as Leda understood it, was for a person to be forced bodily into their cell by at least one, if not two or three, of the burliest guards. For some reason, they had decided not to enact that strategy when they brought the next occupant down to their cell.

Because it was Azaria.

It was for that reason that Leda briefly entertained the wild idea that her sister had come down to visit her, before gawping in surprise as she walked into the cell opposite Leda's. A trembling guard waited several seconds before closing and locking the door behind her.

"Leda." Azaria sat on her pallet with an elegant sweep of skirts.

"What ... why are *you* here?"

Atticus appeared in the corridor with a pained expression. He looked dead on his feet with exhaustion and cast Azaria a frustrated look, reaching forward to pull on the bars of her door to ensure it was securely locked.

He decided to answer for her sister. "Princess Azaria decided today would be a good day to throw her parasol at the back of Prince Elias's head when the family was taking a walk in the gardens."

"Oh, well, that's not so terrible." For Azaria, anyway.

Atticus shook his head, leaning against the dank and dripping wall with a clank of armour on stone. "Tell her what you did next."

To Leda's surprise, Azaria obeyed.

"Elias started screeching, and you know how I hate noise. So I punched him in the throat. It stopped his cater-wauling promptly."

"And then?" Atticus said tiredly.

"Agon became involved."

"And what is he now missing?"

"A finger."

Leda sputtered. "I ... WHAT?"

Azaria had stopped, as though that were all of the story that was worth telling. That gave Leda time to drop her head into her hands and let out a groan at Azaria's stupidity. She was lucky Agon hadn't ripped her head off. He might still.

It was a while before Leda could look at, let alone speak to, her sister.

When she finally looked out between the bars of her cell she saw Azaria sat on her pallet with her back to the wall, her attention fixed on Leda with the focus of someone who'd not had much to look at over the past few minutes. She didn't appear too affected by the condition of her cell. Her knees were drawn up to her chest, hands linked loosely over the top.

"You are an absolute nightmare, but I still can't believe they put you in here," Leda said.

The King had always delighted in Azaria's violent streak, he thought it a gift from the gods that would allow her to conquer even those kingdoms he'd never been able to touch.

"Yes, well, he's been goading the royal children against one another recently. He didn't expect the ... magnitude of the response."

That was one way to put it.

"Are you alright?"

Azaria looked surprisingly unbruised for someone who

had emerged from a confrontation with two of the cruellest and most skilled fighters in the kingdom.

"As well as I can be, given the circumstances." Azaria's gaze fell to Leda's leg, but she said nothing.

Leda wasn't inclined to bring it up either. "Let's put aside the fact that you took a finger off Agon, quite frankly I don't know where to start with that one. But you breaking Eber's arm? That, I have a problem with."

Leda came to the abrupt and unwelcome realisation that her sister had a proclivity for maiming the arms and hands of their brothers.

"He touched me," Azaria said simply.

"So what? How does that give you the right to—"

Azaria continued as if she hadn't spoken. "He knew what would happen when he started it. He was anticipating that reaction. He is a brainless, loyal puppy. The only people he cares about at court are you, Ami, Markus and Mira. If one of you were planning to escape, he was bound to offer himself up as distraction. You were the only one desperate enough to make the attempt."

"How astute of you to figure this all out while you were snapping his bones apart," Leda said.

Azaria waved a hand. "He'll be fine. He was prepared to accept the consequences."

Leda's lips had pressed into a thin line. "You can be a real monster sometimes."

Azaria rolled her eyes. "Of course Eber gets all of the credit for helping your ill-fated escape attempt. And yet when I try to save you, I receive no praise whatsoever."

"I'm sorry," Leda scoffed, dusting hay off herself as she got to her feet. "When exactly have you tried to *save me*?" The phantom pain of her hairpin being dragged through her thigh felt almost real as the memory jerked to the fore-front of her mind.

"From the fire," Azaria said, as though Leda were being unbearably dim. Her head tipped back against the wall and she stared up at the dark ceiling.

"The fire?" Leda said as realisation slowly began to dawn. Surely not ...

"Yes. I set it."

"The ... you what?"

"When you were being whipped, I went to the ambassador's waiting room and set the curtains on fire."

Leda sat down on the rickety chair at the side of her cell. It creaked ominously beneath her weight, but was just about sturdy enough to hold her.

She took a deep breath. "Why would you do that?"

"I didn't want them to hurt you," Azaria said, drawing her knees up again so that her arms were braced on top of them.

"Why?"

"You're my sister."

"That doesn't answer my question. You didn't want them to hurt me but you'll still kill me as part of the ceremony next week?"

Azaria did not reply, as if the question hadn't been asked.

Leda could not for one second fathom how her sister's brain worked, though she supposed she should be pleased that Azaria's plans to do her harm were linked to their birthright and not genuine hatred.

"So you didn't want me hurt, and yet yesterday you tackled me in a river and attacked me with one of my own hairpins?"

That got Azaria's full attention. Her eyes snapped up to look Leda full in the face and she leaned forward as far as the bars of her cell would allow. "You're not to leave me. You promised that when we were children, you seemed to have forgotten."

Leda gaped at her. "If I'd known that the consequence of failing to uphold my end of the bargain would be YOU STABBING ME, I probably would have worded it differently."

"Don't be melodramatic, Leda." Azaria leaned back against the wall. "You're fine now. No lasting harm was done."

Leda would have liked to tell Azaria exactly how much harm she had done to her over the years, but held herself back. It would make no difference. Azaria was not capable of remorse. Besides, the final harm would occur the following week.

How kind it was of their father to ensure that she'd have to look into the eyes of her murderer every day until her death.

CHAPTER 20

*I*t was unlikely that the King had sensed Leda's increasingly panicked boredom as night slid into morning to herald the day before her ceremony. Perhaps the gods were smiling on her and had put the idea into his head to let her out of her cell for one last experience.

He had decided that evening was the perfect time to throw a masquerade ball, with his royal children as guests of honour, showing visiting diplomats and dignitaries from countries beyond the Five Kingdoms that they were formidable and united.

And that involved parading the Counterpart out so that she could be gawped at by those who were feeling morbid. She was the symbol of the gods' love for the King, after all.

They wanted to see their sacrificial lamb in the flesh, one last time.

When Atticus told Leda she and Azaria would be able to leave their cells that evening she hadn't been able to contain the leap of excitement in her stomach at the thought.

Leda had mere hours of life left, and there were things she needed to do, things she'd never contemplated before that had suddenly become critical.

She needed to eat one last plate of delicious food, drink a cup of her favourite mead, be in a crowd of people for a final ball.

And she needed to see Pyrrhus, one last time.

The good news was that Atticus appeared to suffer with a mixture of boredom from standing outside Leda's cell all day and sympathy for her situation.

Leda had wheedled him the day after Azaria's arrival into telling them about his family: his wife who lived down in Gemdark with their twin daughters. She helped run her father's tavern, and the girls were a few years into their schooling. He let slip that one of them reminded him of Leda, and she filed that piece of information away in her mind just in case it became useful.

He was also oddly charmed by the incessant bickering that went back and forth between Leda and Azaria's cells. Up to a certain point. His patience was not limitless; he was human after all.

So when Leda asked him to bring her a dress she had been working on from her room before she'd been imprisoned, with the rest of her sewing equipment to finish it off, he had hesitated.

She refused to attend this event meekly in her old, tired ballgown that no longer fit her. The new dress was something she'd struggled to allow herself to create, knowing it was so beautiful she'd never be allowed to wear it as a Counterpart. Now, however, she doubted anyone would care.

Atticus was still making unsure noises as Azaria rolled her eyes in the background.

Leda looked as pitiable as she could. "I've sat here, docile as a lamb, day after day. I haven't caused you any trouble. Please can you bring me the dress?"

"Leda—"

"I'm dying tomorrow," she said with all the subtlety of a rampaging herd of cattle. "Do this for me."

Atticus gave an incredibly long-suffering sigh, like she'd just asked him to give away his firstborn child, but eventually nodded, as she'd known he would.

"And bring my good needles, the copper ones, not the wood!"

His voice echoed along the walls back to her. "You'll be getting the first ones I find, brat."

She'd given the biggest smile she could muster when she saw him striding back down the corridor twenty minutes later with her dress balled up under one arm, an exasperated expression on his face.

The dress was a deep crimson, a colour Leda would ordinarily avoid at all costs for fear of drawing attention. Now, she found she didn't care. It had a bodice with a flattering heart-shaped neckline to which she had added dropped sleeves of soft silk, leaving her throat and shoulders bare. It drew in tightly at the waist and flared out in layer upon layer of floating tulle to swirl around her legs. Or it would, once she finished it.

She thanked him sincerely when he pushed it through the bars into her cell with a pot of her sewing supplies— including copper needles—then a hairbrush, a fistful of hairpins and three mismatching earrings. He'd clearly swept off whatever finery was lying on top of her dressing table, and it was such a sweet gesture that tears lined her eyes. Not that that was rare, this close to ceremony day. Everything was setting her off at the moment.

"Oh"—he pulled out a small velvet sack that she hadn't seen and pushed it through the bars too—"there're some extra supplies in there too, for your mask." He sighed when she looked at him in surprise. "My youngest wants to be a dressmaker, I know more about the subject than I ever thought I'd need to, alright? Take your fabric and be quiet."

She couldn't resist the small laugh that bubbled up. "Alright."

"Will that be all, then, Your Highness?" Atticus's words were sarcastic, but without any bite. Still, the use of that word on a Counterpart, it was dangerous and she had to repress the cringe that overtook her when she heard it.

"I'm not royal."

"The King's blood runs in you, girl, I'd say that makes you royal enough."

She eyed him speculatively, building up her courage.

He started to walk away.

"Wait, there's one more thing I need to ask you."

Leda dressed with difficulty in the tiny cell and made her best attempt at twisting her hair into an elaborate bun at the base of her neck with no mirror. She pulled out a few ringlets that would hopefully frame her face and looked sourly at Azaria, who somehow looked radiant having finished her own hair and makeup within her cell.

Leda went to put one of her favourite gold hair slides into her hair, remembered the feel of one being stabbed into her leg, and promptly dropped them all on to the pallet.

She could barely believe it when Atticus opened the door and led them through the corridor and up the steps into the entrance hall. While the dungeon corridor was dark and empty, she could hear the ever-increasing sounds of hundreds of people talking and drinking above, the decadent swell of music from a full orchestra reaching them.

Azaria marched up the steps, giving a very intimidating

look to the guard who dared to follow her. He stepped back a few paces, but continued to stick to her.

Leda moved to the centre of the entrance hall, staring up at the grand chandelier and feeling the light soak into her skin. She hadn't been in a properly lit room for days and the illumination was so strong it hurt her eyes. Why had she never appreciated light properly before now? So many things she hadn't even thought to be grateful for.

There was movement on the grand staircase, and she turned towards it, looking up and straight into Pyrrhus's eyes. He stood where the staircase split in two, framed by that hideous portrait of her family, one foot on a step and hand on a bannister. He was seemingly frozen mid-motion as he stared down at her, as though the idea that she might be there had not occurred to him.

He was immaculately outfitted in a black tailsuit and white silk cravat, blending in seamlessly with the nobles and courtiers mingling on the stairs behind and in front of him. His mask was an intricate and expensive silver filigree.

As Pyrrhus descended to meet her he rearranged his face into something courtly and bland. He nodded stiffly in greeting, noting the presence of Atticus over her shoulder.

"Ledazaria. You look ..." He lowered his voice. "You look lovely."

Leda flushed, taking in everything about him that she possibly could with her ravenous gaze. This was the last time she would ever see him this close. "Thank you."

"Can I get you anything?"

She didn't have an answer for that question and so shook her head, instead showing him the mask she'd made from leftover dress material Atticus had brought her. It was a mix of rich burgundy and gold, embellished with red feathers spilling down one side. "Would you mind?"

The idea of her face being covered made it much easier

to prepare for the evening. Even though everyone would still know who she was, the thin material still offered something of a barrier.

Once Pyrrhus had established that the people already in the entrance hall had little interest in them he took the mask and placed it against her face. She turned and felt him tying the ribbons at the back of her head with his usual care. He paused, and she looked over her shoulder to see that his attention was focused where the corset strings were woven tightly across her back. His eyes traced the dip between her shoulders as if searching for the scars of the whip. Fortunately there was only smooth skin, bisected by a criss-cross of the thinnest of white lines, only visible if one were to study it intensely.

When she turned to face him he reached out a hand to ensure the fabric of her mask sat straight on her face, his fingertips lingering for a moment on her cheekbone before he pulled back.

Something dark crossed his features. He nodded with something that looked like resolve.

"I'm needed upstairs," he said. "I'll see you later, Leda."

"No, wait—"

Desperation clutched at her. That couldn't be it, not their final conversation. She snatched back the hand that automatically tried to follow him as he broke away from her.

He couldn't do this to her, not now. That did not count as a proper goodbye.

But there was nothing she could do to slow his exit. He was up the stairs and around the corner before she could blink.

She took a shuddering breath, smoothing the feathers at the side of her mask, and squared her shoulders. Now was not the time to fall apart, now was the time for final experiences.

Filled with resolve of her own, Leda let herself get swept into the crowd of newcomers coming through the palace front doors as they trickled towards the ballroom. She enjoyed the shield of her mask, though by the way most eyes followed her as she passed she knew they weren't fooled in the slightest about her identity. And given how close Atticus and a slew of other guards stuck to her side she also didn't have a chance of sneaking out alongside any of the other finely dressed guests this evening.

Leda strode into the glittering ballroom, feeling the swirling music of the orchestra in her very bones. She stopped a passing servant with a hand on his sleeve.

"May I take that?"

He handed over the full tray of petit fours with a bemused expression, and nodded blankly as she thanked him.

Leda picked a delicious morsel from the tray and before she could get it to her mouth it had been knocked right out of her hand by Atticus.

"Excuse me? Am I not allowed to eat here?"

"Royal children and Counterparts are only to eat food tested by tasters, under your father's orders."

He lifted the tray off her and handed it to a passing servant.

Leda dusted off her hands irritably. "You could have just told me that, instead of ensuring someone spends the rest of the night with pastry stuck to their shoe."

Atticus wasn't listening, too busy telling the other guards next to them to scatter. They were a very obvious and telling sight, and a King who needed five guards stuck to the Counterpart at all times couldn't be counted as a confident one.

Thankfully, Atticus managed to convince them of this, and finally she could breathe. They dispersed and he was the only one who remained by her side.

"I've sent a tankard of mead to the tasters for you; they'll bring it to you once it's been tested."

He was far too kind to be in the job that he occupied. It was nice that he was the one with her as the end approached.

She looked over the heads of dancers on the main floor, seeing her brothers clustered over in the corner near the King's throne. They looked like they were having an unpleasant conversation, and Leda couldn't resist crossing the room until she was close enough to hear their words without being spotted in the crowd.

Elias had dispensed with his mask already and was wearing it draped around his neck. Agon, meanwhile, cradled his bandaged hand, looking as dangerous and unpredictable as a wounded animal. He was clearly still in pain.

"I've had two gods-blessed years away from you and now I can't turn a corner without you yammering in my face, Elias."

"Just listen to me! Something's wrong, I know it."

"You don't know anything about anything. You've never been in a real battle, you had Rivernesse handed to you on a silver platter. Leave the strategising to the people with actual experience, Elias."

Then two of the worst people she'd ever known proceeded to give Leda the best opportunity she could hope to stumble upon.

All eyes were drawn to them as Elias ripped Agon's mask off his face and threw it on the floor. "You don't get to treat me like that!"

Agon's face, now revealed to them all, was preternaturally calm. "I don't? Well, then you won't like this."

He struck with all of the grace and speed of a snake. Leda barely saw the blur of his uninjured fist before Elias was down on the ground, clutching his face. His movements were sluggish, disproportionate to the injury he'd received. And Agon hadn't pounced on him to rain down blows as he normally would. Odd.

Even so, it was a distraction, exactly the kind she needed.

Leda gave a meaningful look to Atticus as she turned on her heel and began to skirt the edge of the ballroom. He followed her, but at a discreet distance.

Pyrrhus had arrived in the ballroom minutes before and was watching her brothers fight with a frown. He let out a choked noise of surprise when Leda's arm dove out of the crush of bodies to seize him by the front of his shirt and yank him towards the doors at the back of the ballroom.

They staggered out into the rose garden and she gave him no opportunity to speak. The perfume of the blooms was intoxicating, thickly coating the night air. Their feet crunched noisily on the gravelled path as she pulled him away from the small groups of courtiers who had gathered, chatting and drinking between the manicured bushes. They descended the steps on to the lawn and veered off by the wall beneath the rose garden, hidden from the view of anyone who might happen to look out towards the river.

Atticus stayed out of sight, at the top of the stairs, as they'd agreed. He'd know as soon as she left the secluded spot in which they stood, but wasn't able to see them now. Thank the gods, she didn't want to do this in front of him.

Pyrrhus's hand encircled Leda's wrist as she looked around to check that they were alone. His face was half in shadow.

Leda stared down at his hand, so much larger than hers, the heat of him burning into her skin.

The brush of his fingers against the thin strip of her red sleeve felt more indecent than it probably should. When she turned back to face him, finally satisfied that they couldn't be seen, Pyrrhus dropped her arm as if she were the one who burned him.

"What's going on?" he said intently. "The dungeon—have they been bringing your medicine?"

"Yes, I'm fine." Leda shook a little. She needed to get herself under control. It was dark, there were flickering torches illuminating the grounds, time was ticking away and he was entirely too handsome to be standing that close to her with a look of concern on his face when she was this off-balance. "They gave me my medicine, I'm not about to keel over, I promise."

Pyrrhus continued to look troubled. He was staring at her as though trying to memorise all of the details of her face. After tomorrow, he'd never see it again.

She knew what she needed to do.

If this was her final act, the last thing that she did for herself, she could be content with it.

Throwing caution to the wind, she pressed herself up against his side. He was stiff and unrelenting for a moment before he let out a sigh and brought his arms around her, shielding her from the cold wind.

Then, something shifted.

She was reminded of the other time he had embraced her, when she had first gone to him for help, but this ... this was different.

This time Pyrrhus held her like a lifeline, as opposed to her taking comfort in his arms. He held her tight, like he had spent months restraining himself from doing so, burying the impulse somewhere deep inside of him where it had simmered and boiled and finally overpowered him.

Judging by the coiled strength of his arms around her, this time he had no intention of letting her go. Good, because she didn't want him to. One of his hands was flush against the small of her back, the other at the dip between her shoulders. He almost certainly felt the shiver that rippled down her spine.

Leda nearly lost the strength in her legs from something other than pain when his head turned infinitesimally, lips mere millimetres from her cheek. His breathing was rapid against her skin, like he'd just sprinted a great distance, and from what little of him she could see those dark eyes had ignited. He moved closer, but it was Leda who eradicated the space between them, curling her fingers into his pristine white collar. She couldn't allow a second for that sharp mind to whirr and instruct him to move away from her.

What the hell, she was dying tomorrow, wasn't she?

She pushed up on to her tiptoes and pressed her lips against his.

For a second it was like kissing a very nicely shaped marble statue. Panic streaked through her as she wondered if she'd read every single signal wrong.

She felt the exact moment his control snapped. Between one moment and the next Pyrrhus had wrapped his arms around her corseted waist and slammed her body flush against him.

They staggered up against the stone wall and Leda knew that she was the one who had pushed them there, a desire and desperation she couldn't control rocketing through her. She gasped, a sensation she'd never felt anything but the ghost of before roaring to life in her veins. It consumed her, consumed them both.

Pyrrhus was lost to the world, shedding the restrained royal tutor demeanour he wore like a mask. He kissed her like a starving man who had just been presented with a decadent feast.

It was terrifying, and ill advised, and if he stopped Leda was quite certain that she would cry. She shuddered, opening up fully to him, and then his hands were in her hair and hers had fisted in the fabric of his shirt. Oh gods, she was about to ruin another one.

With an abrupt groan of frustration Pyrrhus broke away from her, his eyes closed tight as though the mere sight of her would cause him to lose control all over again.

"Leda," he hissed from between gritted teeth. "You need to leave."

She brought her hands up to her flushed cheeks. "Excuse me?" she said, a dangerous edge to her voice.

"Go back to the palace and hide somewhere safe."

"Safe? I'm hardly being attacked by a wild animal."

Besides, she would be perfectly safe that night, not able to move a foot without running into a guard. She could not say the same for the following day.

He was ruining her last perfect experience, gods damn him. She knew that furious tears glittered in her eyes now and she blinked them away.

Pyrrhus took in her dishevelled form and she was gratified to see how much of a struggle it was for him to regain his composure. "No ... no, that's not what I'm talking about. It's what I ..." He ran a hand through his hair, rumpling it up even more than she had. "You need to get somewhere safe, stay away from the ballroom tonight."

He was being extremely disagreeable. Half her brain had shut down and the other half was soaked in lust, it was only polite for him to reciprocate. But he was rapidly pulling himself back under control.

"What are you talking about—"

A scream pierced the air, coming right from the ballroom. An echo so similar to the scream that had led to last week's pandemonium that Leda could barely comprehend it. She whirled around and jumped up the steps into the rose garden, Pyrrhus at her heels.

Atticus was gone.

There was another yell from inside and Leda started towards it, but Pyrrhus grabbed her shoulders and held her still, looking into the ballroom with assessing eyes.

"Where's Atticus? He's supposed to get you to safety."

His hands were warm on her skin and that was the only reason she didn't throw them off her. "From what? Will you, for once in your life, tell me what's actually going on?"

He was unnerved now, obviously so. There was a plan and it had gone wrong.

"Why were you expecting Atticus to take me to safety? How do you know him?"

"No time to discuss that now," Pyrrhus said tightly, arms wrapping around her waist and stepping back as if preparing to slingshot her back into the palace. "Come with me."

She was about to protest when the sounds of plates smashing and people screaming ripped through the air. On second thought, perhaps following the directions of one person who knew what was going on was the more sensible choice.

She allowed him to push her across the rose garden and through a set of doors into the deserted throne room.

"Where are the guards?" Leda asked as they broke into a run.

"In the battle." He rushed her up the staircase in the entrance hall as people ran pell-mell below them, sparkling in their finery.

With a jolt, she realised he was manhandling her towards his old study. Leda nearly tripped over her skirts and he held her up as if she weighed nothing, setting her back on her feet and picking up the pace once more. He seemed to be so single-mindedly focused that he couldn't find words to respond to her with any kind of detail.

"What battle?" she cried as their steps echoed through the deserted corridor towards his study. "The rebels were defeated!"

"This army is a little bigger than the last one," he muttered as he unlocked his door and ripped it open.

Leda's voice had grown increasingly desperate, and she clutched his sleeve as they descended the stairs and reached the centre of his study, coming to a stop by the chessboard. "What are we doing here?"

"You'll remain here until it's safe."

Could this army win? Could they depose her father? Her brain would scarcely allow her to comprehend the possibility.

Leda let go of his sleeve in surprise, taking a step back. "Pyrrhus ... I need you to tell me the truth. Am I ... is the ceremony still happening?"

There was that fire in his eyes again. "Not if I have anything to do with it."

And instantly she understood—why he'd been so strange and reticent recently, why he had point-blank refused to treat her like she was about to die, even tonight. Because he was intelligent and stubborn and magnificent and had decided that she wouldn't die, and he had been dedicating every moment of the past few weeks to ensure that would be the case.

Leda grabbed the back of the armchair to steady herself and whirled around to see him already running back up the staircase. "Pyrrhus!"

She knew she had to stay there, but the thought of him going into battle once more froze her limbs with terror. He'd survived the first fight, barely, and that was when he'd pretended to be on the King's side. What if he didn't survive the second?

This time she wouldn't be there to make sure he got to the infirmary.

Pyrrhus stopped at the top of the steps and braced both hands on the bannister, looking down at her with what she could only describe as desperation.

"You *will not* die," he ground out, as if it were an instruction. "We will tear down this whole palace if we have to, but the ceremonies stop now. The invasions and the starvation and the executions stop. It ends tonight. All of it."

A high-pitched scream and a boom issued from somewhere in the palace, rattling the window, and Pyrrhus recoiled.

Leda had been mid-stride to go back to the stairs to catch him, but stopped abruptly. "How?" Her voice had a trembling quality that annoyed her immensely.

"You'll find out soon enough. I need you to stay safe here. Do not open this door to anyone until I come and get you."

Leda took a step backwards into the centre of the room and could practically feel his relief.

"What about you?"

"I'll be fine."

She was rattled and her hands were shaking, so her tone was surlier than intended when she said, "You'd better be. Get back here as soon as it's done, I mean it. If I see a scratch on you I'm going to be really cross. *Do not* go near my brothers."

She couldn't voice the feelings for him that were making worry overtake her, they stuck in her throat. The fear and relief and confusion threatened to dissolve her into a sobbing mess.

Pyrrhus's smile was barely a twitch on his lips but Leda caught it, now practised in detecting the glimmers of emotion that crossed his face. Before she knew it, the door was closing with a snap behind him and she heard the key turning in the lock.

Leda couldn't just sit there and listen to the sounds of battle as the rebel army breached the palace. Determined to make herself useful, she went into Pyrrhus's old room and took fresh sheets from his wardrobe, proceeding to tear them into long strips that Ambrose's team could use for bandages.

Hopefully they'd be of some use to them, and if not, the process of ripping them up was at least cathartic.

Judging by the sounds she heard downstairs, this was no skirmish like last week. This was a full-scale assault.

An hour later Leda was surrounded by a pile of shredded fabric and heard a new sound that caused her head to snap up.

"Leda!" a voice screeched, just outside the door.

Leda dropped an armful of sheets; that was Olora's voice.

"Mother?" She hesitated.

"Leda, let me in, please! Help me!" A series of shouts and clangs echoed along the corridor, and that final cry convinced Leda to disentangle herself and run up the stairs to unlock the door. It opened to reveal her mother's tear-streaked face, surrounded by bedraggled chestnut hair. A red mark bloomed on her cheek as though she'd been struck, and her dress was torn at the shoulder. Leda opened the door wider to let her in, and reared back with a gasp when instead Olora reached forward and grabbed her wrist in a painful grip, nails digging into her skin.

Her mother made no move to enter the room.

Foreboding settling in her stomach, Leda glanced behind Olora to find one of the people she wanted to see least in the world. Her brother Elias's broad face emerged from the shadows, blood seeping from a wound to his forehead. He didn't seem to care much, wiping the blood out of his eyes as though it were a mere inconvenience.

All that fighting downstairs, and he'd thought to seek her out. Godsdamnit.

He looked at her with delight that Leda wasn't stupid enough to interpret as brotherly affection.

"Did you really think you could escape what you were born for, you little runt?"

Elias was only five years older than Leda, but had never shown the slightest interest in her, which she'd always been thankful for. He'd been a pampered brute who only wanted the admiration of his royal family. He had made her wary, so she had avoided him, especially after Azaria had taken his arm.

"No!" Leda tried to wrench her wrist from her mother's grip and return to the safety of Pyrrhus's study, but Elias had leapt forward and seized her by the shoulder. There was a clang; he'd dropped his knife to the floor to free up his arm.

Leda screamed and struggled as, with Olora's help, he lifted her into the air and slammed her down on his shoulder. All her breath left her as his collarbone dug into her stomach.

"Elias! Let me go!" Leda tried to sound authoritative but the fear bled into her voice. He tightened his grip painfully and ignored her. She would have hoped the injury from Azaria would have weakened him but, though he had gone slightly to seed since she last saw him, his strength still far outstripped her own. He'd clearly learned to compensate for his injury.

"Where is father?" Elias asked her mother gruffly. Leda tried to kick him and he batted her legs away like they were nothing.

"He's down in the throne room," Olora said, watching Elias's arm around Leda's waist as they began to walk down the corridor. "You won't hurt her, will you? We agreed ... you can have her for the ceremony, but she's not to be harmed now."

Leda stopped her squirming immediately, looking through the curtain of her hanging hair to stare at her mother. What was she on about? Why would she care about preserving her daughter for the few hours that she had left?

"Of course," Elias said, and Leda knew immediately that he was lying. She just couldn't figure out why her mother would believe him. Was she really so naive?

Leda slammed her fist on to Elias's back and he made no sound at all. It was like his skin was made of rhino hide. He'd always appeared close to indestructible, how Azaria had managed to get his arm off and how Agon had got him to the ground Leda would never understand. She'd always thought there must have been something potent in the mix of Queen Celandine and the King's blood, some evil element, as both Elias and Azaria were a special kind of horrifying.

The further they descended, the more carnage they saw. The rebel forces, startlingly huge in number, were battling those of her father and they seemed evenly matched, causing damage to the fragile palace. Statues fell to the ground and smashed, blood spattered the marble, tapestries were ripped by careless sword swipes. The screeching sound of battle was horrific, and Leda fought the urge to cover her ears.

All the blood had rushed to her head and she couldn't get her bearings, upside down as she was. She fell silent as they pushed through the smaller fights to reach the one raging in the throne room. Leda had a sickening sense of déjà vu.

The doors into the rose garden were hanging from their hinges and the fighting was spilling outside into the darkness. Elias swept Leda with him up on to the dais by the empty throne so he could get a better view out into the crowd, clearly seeking their father.

"I've got her, we'll do it now! Where is he?" he yelled. Olora had a hand wrapped around Leda's ankle and was now attempting to pull her off his shoulder. Elias responded by tightening his grip so much that Leda coughed, struggling to breathe.

"Just take her to the dungeons, please, get her out of here," Olora cried.

"Stop squirming, useless thing! Don't try and tell me you had nothing to do with this, you traitor, this close to the ceremony! Tell me why I shouldn't end you right now!" Elias snarled at Leda, dropping down the steps to the main floor and shoving her unceremoniously off him. She crashed to the ground with a yelp, pain slicing through her hands and knees where she had managed to catch herself.

"No!"

Leda looked up in time to see Elias draw a sword from his scabbard and smash the hilt of it against Olora's temple as she tried to reach Leda. She crumpled like her legs had been cut out from under her, unconscious before she hit the ground.

Leda's mouth was open but no sound would come out. She frantically scanned the fighters surrounding them but saw no one she recognised, and now her brother was advancing on her with his sword in hand, eyes flashing. She crawled backwards until her spine hit the wall.

Elias didn't seem too concerned about the prospect of her getting away. When he had her cornered he swung his sword towards her in a broad stroke that showed he didn't mean to do this elegantly. Oh, no. He planned on hacking at her. He might not kill her, to avoid displeasing their father, but she knew that he envisioned torture in her future tonight. He'd endured humiliation and frustration since returning to the palace, and here before him sat a nice target on whom he could take out his rage.

Leda swallowed heavily. She wouldn't be able to outrun him, but he was not going to mutilate her as she crouched on the floor. She braced trembling hands against the wall, pulling herself to her feet.

Elias looked down at her shaking leg, and she knew that he remembered.

"Sometimes I forget I wasn't the only one she maimed," he said, twirling his sword in his grip as if it were a baton. "If only she had spared my arm as she spared your leg, Leda."

He reared back.

Leda tensed, closing her eyes, as if that would help anything. It took her a few seconds to blink her eyes open when she heard a shuffle, a cry, and felt nothing in the way of impact.

A heavy weight knocked into her, and she staggered sideways, instinctively reaching out to catch the person who had fallen on to her by the shoulders.

Shiny black hair spilt over her hands, and she looked down in shock to see Azaria on her knees in front of her. Blood seeped from her arm where she had taken part of the blow to knock Leda aside, but the wound looked shallow.

Elias had frozen and was staring at Azaria as though he could think of nothing he wanted more than to see her there.

He was malice given human form, all thoughts of Leda wiped from his mind. The bloodied sword dangled from his arm, and Azaria looked at him with that infamous self-satisfied smirk.

"Elias."

"Azaria." Elias executed a short bow in a gross parody of the respect they were supposed to show one another. "We haven't had the chance to speak properly since I returned. And now here we are, in a battle." He looked around at the preoccupied fighters surrounding them. "What a shame that a rebel killed you. I tried to save you, of course, but was unable to. Father will be devastated. But he'll get over it."

There was an unbearable screech of metal across stone as a blood-soaked Princess Elina appeared at Elias's elbow, barely able to stand upright, flinging a sword across the ground to Azaria.

Azaria grabbed it by the hilt and got to her feet, rolling her shoulders as if she could shrug off the cut that had blood soaking through her sleeve.

Leda pushed herself back against the wall, making herself as small as possible so as not to interfere. The palace guards and members of the army they'd called in to protect them slowly began to notice Elias and Azaria.

They started to circle one another.

Everyone in the room would probably notice if Leda tried to make a run for it, so she stayed still.

"You remember the last time we met with blades, Elias?" Azaria said airily, twirling her sword by its handle just as he had earlier. As his face turned puce with rage, she regarded him with a smile that was nothing less than angelic. While he was hunched like a predator, she stood straight and relaxed, as though she were about to take a stroll through the gardens. "I seem to remember I was the victor then."

"You are a vicious little bitch and no one likes you," Elias spat.

"That makes two of us, I suppose."

At that moment, Leda knew that if they clashed blades, Azaria would win. She was playing with her food before she ate it, as she always did.

As he had every time when they were younger, Elias fell for it. His easily triggered temper was legendary.

His sword, pointing directly at Azaria's face, dropped a few inches. "I *loathe* you," he snarled.

Elias roared and attacked. Azaria neatly sidestepped him.

Leda felt hands grasping the side of her dress, and looked around to see Elina, with a rapidly swelling black eye, trying to claw her way upright.

"Elina. Oh, gods," Leda breathed, taking in her injuries in horror and grabbing her hands. She had no idea who Elina had been fighting, friend or foe, but imagined they would probably be in a worse state. "Hold on to me, let's get out of here."

Leda got to her feet and put an arm around Elina, not entirely sure who was supporting who.

She couldn't believe that Elina wasn't helping Elias; they were both gods-blessed children, and siblings at that. Then again, shared blood meant little between royal children who were raised apart and taught to compete with one another their whole lives.

Leda was brought back to reality by the clash of swords at their backs; Azaria had made her first move to distract Elias from their escape. A few more of her father's soldiers skidded into the room and ran towards Elias.

"No!" he yelled, sweat pouring down his brow as he shuddered under a relentless barrage of blows from Azaria. He was immensely skilled but she was a whirlwind, her sword moving so fast Leda could barely see it. And she had the advantage of a second arm. "Leda is ours! Elina, get her to father!"

Said father's soldiers paused at the edge of the circle of people who had abandoned their own fights to watch the royal children face one another.

Elina tugged her towards the door, but Leda brought them to a jarring halt when she heard one of Elias's soldiers mutter to another that Agon was outside with the royal tutor, and perhaps they would be more useful there. The other soldier nodded to the first and they made their way outside.

"Leda!" Elina called out, but Leda was already gone, easily breaking out of her grip and jumping over prone bodies to reach the broken doors that had spilt glittering glass out into the rose garden. Her feet crunched loudly on the gravel as she ran through the bushes and down the stairs on to the lawn. She could hear the thud of footsteps behind her, and glanced over her shoulder to see a number of rebel soldiers streaking into sight.

They overtook her with ease despite their heavy armour, catching up to a group of palace guards.

The battle cries began again.

CHAPTER 21

*L*eda spotted two lone figures engaged in a confrontation by the river and instantly recognised the gleam of Pyrrhus's dark hair in the moonlight. Bodies littered the space around them.

Pyrrhus was putting up a valiant effort and his form spoke of solid training, but he was nowhere close to the calibre of her eldest living brother as a fighter, even injured as he was.

Agon had been given his first sword at three years of age, had learned to hunt at seven, and had only grown in blood-thirst since then. Pain was not something he ever allowed to get to him when fighting. He was the most proficient of the royal children at combat in all forms, Leda doubted even Azaria would be able to take him.

Pyrrhus was starting to tire, she could tell by the way he kept giving ground to Agon, staggering back towards the water.

Leda had not stopped running, and felt her heart rise into her throat as she saw her brother rear back to deliver a killing blow that Pyrrhus was in no position to block.

"STOP!"

Leda's legs had never carried her so fast in her life. She sprinted down to the river's edge, balled her hand in the back of Agon's tunic, and yanked with all of her strength. He wasn't expecting her, too focused on his prey, and she knew it was the only reason she could get under his guard. He twisted around in surprise as he staggered backwards, and tripped over her outstretched leg, pulling her down with him.

In the gaps between Agon's whirling arms as he tried to get himself upright, Leda glimpsed Pyrrhus. He stood by the water's edge, his sword in his hand, a vicious cut across his arm. She'd clearly knocked her brother off course, preventing the lethal blow, but blood was spreading down Pyrrhus's arm at an alarming rate.

Pyrrhus was staring at Leda, expression stunned. His fast breaths came out in puffs of vapour in the cold air. As Agon extracted himself from her, Pyrrhus looked down at the blood on his arm and took a step backwards.

There wasn't any ground for him to land on, and Leda screamed as he fell back into the water. There was an almighty splash coupled with the horrific sound of Agon's laughter.

Her brother now stood tall and looked down at where she lay on the snow with a raised eyebrow. He didn't consider her any kind of threat. A figure in a flowing white and red dress was running towards them in the distance, but he spared it only the briefest glance before returning his attention to Leda.

"Little Ledazaria," Agon said mockingly, crouching down as though to see her better. He had bright green eyes set in a cruel face criss-crossed with scars. His mouth was twisted into a permanent sneer.

Agon grabbed a tendril of her hair, twisted it around his gloved fist, and tugged. "Don't tell me you *love* him? Did your big brother kill your *boyfriend*?" He released her hair as her eyes began to water, clearly annoyed that she hadn't cried out in pain. He liked it best when he could see the hurt.

"You needn't be so melodramatic," he snorted. "For the sake of the gods, why are you crying? You'll be joining him in death tomorrow anyway."

An arm reached to wrap around Agon's neck from behind and he let out a shout as he was once again slammed to the ground with a crunch of snow.

"Nice to see you again, Agon," Elina muttered into his ear, her smooth and beautiful face in stark contrast to his scarred one as he started to turn purple in her grip.

"Elina—" He didn't need to turn to recognise her.

Something like alarm had crept into his eyes.

"Do you remember the times you used to sneak into my rooms and beat me when you were twenty and I was nine? Because I do. I've always hoped you'd come back to the palace, but you've been too much of a *coward* before now, haven't you?"

Agon gurgled, frantically clutching at her arm, eyes bulging. He didn't seem disposed to defend himself with words. Leda knew that while Elina had the upper hand now due to the element of surprise, it would take Agon seconds to overpower her. Sure enough, there was a thud and a cry as he managed to twist around and knock Elina into one of the large rocks at the riverside. Snarling, she produced a dagger and ran at him.

Leda paid them no attention whatsoever, too busy yanking off her shoes and untying the heavy outer skirt around her dress. Without sparing them a glance, she sprang up from the snow to the river's edge, and threw herself in.

The frigid water hit her like a slap to every part of her

body and all the air left her lungs. Leda gasped for breath, pausing for a moment to acclimatise herself as the heavy fabric of her skirts whipped around her legs. Shaking her head, she sprang forward to follow the current. She couldn't afford to feel the cold, or be weighed down by her clothing. Pyrrhus was not a proficient swimmer, he was injured, and the current was fast. If she didn't get to him, she knew deep in her core that he would die.

She absolutely could not let that happen.

If the attack had occurred a few weeks ago he wouldn't have fallen in, the river would have been frozen. Leda cursed their luck that it had thawed.

She could see Pyrrhus's dark shape disappearing around a curve ten feet ahead of her, and paddled her feet frantically behind her, settling on a breaststroke to keep her head above water so she could keep him in sight. There was a dull clunk and a splash as he hit a rocky outcrop in the water and she saw him wrap his arms around it. His movements were sluggish, he must have been barely conscious. The current parted and flowed on either side of him.

Leda altered her course and the water smashed her into him, one arm around his shoulder, the other around the rock he held.

Pyrrhus looked at her in abject, bleary horror. "Leda?" Small cuts from his rough journey down the river littered his face. His arm bled into the water between them. Leda's leg hurt worse than it had in weeks, she'd put it through its paces to get to him tonight, and she gritted her teeth as she forced it out of her mind. It wasn't bleeding, he was. He was her priority at that moment. She could worry about everything else later.

They were both gasping at the cold.

"This is going to hurt," Leda said, wrapping a hand around the cut on his arm and putting firm pressure on it to stem the bleeding. He grunted in pain, his eyes screwing shut.

"Leda, leave me—"

"Don't be stupid," she said derisively, raising her voice to be heard over the rushing water. "We need to get you out of here before you freeze to death. Hold on to me and I'll swim us to shore."

Pyrrhus eyed the current doubtfully, but placed his hand on the wrist she offered without questioning her. She turned it so that he was facing upward, horizontal in the water. Pivoting so that she could use her legs to spring from the rock, Leda pushed with all her might.

It took a minute more than it should have for her to get them to the other side, but Pyrrhus was almost a dead weight as she towed him and the current was strong that night. The relief that consumed Leda when she felt mud under her fingers and they crawled on to the riverbank was palpable.

As soon as he was out of the water Pyrrhus fell on to the snow on his back, eyes closed and shivering.

Knowing she had to act quickly, Leda grabbed a knife from the strap he wore across his shoulders and ripped the bottom of her skirt until she held a thick piece of sopping wet fabric. It wasn't ideal, but it would have to do. They were too far down the river for anyone from the palace to easily spot them. As the battle raged on, she was almost grateful for that. She didn't want any enemy soldiers coming across them.

With quick movements modelled on what she'd seen Ambrose do in the infirmary, Leda wrapped the material around Pyrrhus's arm and tied it up tightly. He groaned quietly, but did not open his eyes. His body was convulsing in shivers, and Leda didn't think twice before climbing on top of him, stretching her legs along the length of his and wrapping her arms around his torso. She laid her head on his chest, heard the frantic thudding of his heartbeat, and could have cried with relief.

His good arm curled around her back, crushing her to him, and his shivers lessened as what little body heat she still had seeped into him.

"You were supposed to"—Pyrrhus paused to cough— "stay in the study." He didn't seem angry that she hadn't, though it was entirely possible he was too weary to feel any strong emotions at that moment.

"Elias found me. He decided to take the opportunity to torture me." She wondered if Pyrrhus knew his arm had tightened around her when she said that, or whether it was an unconscious action. "Azaria got in the way."

"And Agon?"

"He and Elina were fighting when I went after you. They have a history. I never knew …" Leda's hand clenched over the muscle of his shoulder. "Each of us is damaged by being the King's child, even the royal ones," she murmured.

It explained why Elina seemed to move through life with a ball of rage bubbling in her chest.

Pyrrhus ran a hand over the tangle of sopping wet hair down Leda's back. "We need to return to the palace."

Leda was freezing cold and in pain, yet strangely reluctant to leave their position.

She cleared her throat. "Of course." She got to her feet and hauled him up, staggering with the effort. Unlike the last time they had sought medical attention after a battle, so very recently, they didn't need to prop each other up.

Leda's leg was sore but still functional. They remained shoulder to shoulder as they trudged up the hill towards the palace.

"The palace soldiers were quickly overcome by ours, they weren't expecting the second attack," Pyrrhus said.

"I can't believe you're involved in this madness," Leda said dangerously. "Let's discuss that in a moment, we need to get to Elina first. It'll be a miracle if he hasn't killed her already."

They stopped short when they crested the small hill, seeing a huddle of dark shapes where Elina and Agon had been. There was a figure sprawled on the floor, no less than four different daggers and swords sticking out of its chest.

Leda was light-headed with relief as they drew closer and she recognised the body as Agon's.

Elina crouched beside him, expression triumphant, though her face was a mess of blood and rapidly swelling bruises. Ambrose was on his knees beside her, trying to get her to look at him so he could assess her injuries.

Eber stood staring down at Agon's body, arms crossed, and Leda was shocked to see their mother standing next to him, a violently trembling hand on his shoulder. It was a testament to his state of mind that he hadn't shaken her off.

None of them spoke as Leda and Pyrrhus joined them.

"How did you get out of the dungeons?" Leda asked Eber, her voice hoarse. She must have swallowed more river water than was advisable.

A smile cracked his expression. "The rebels are winning, they let me out."

Leda let out a sound somewhere between a sob and a cough. "They are?"

Pyrrhus seemed less convinced. "It's not over until the King is dead."

With that, he was running back up to the palace. The rest of their group followed him as if compelled, needing to see the evidence for themselves. They left Agon's body alone, one of the many silent figures on the snow.

The scene in the ballroom was one of utter horror, bodies and blood and discarded weapons everywhere, tripping up the fighters who attempted to move around them. The tables had been turned on their sides to be used as shields, the King's throne and table upside down and badly dented. A carpet of shimmering metal and glass made up of cutlery and crockery was strewn all over the floor.

Ambrose came to a stop as Pyrrhus pulled Leda away from the path of three fighters surging towards them, but her attention was engaged elsewhere.

Ten of the King's most elite guards had formed a protective circle around her father near his throne, and the rebel forces were throwing everything they had at them. One by one, his exhausted guards fell like dominoes beneath the sheer weight of numbers, revealing more and more of her terrified father as he cowered away from the fighting.

He was an aggressive and power-hungry man who enjoyed watching violence, but who knew that he didn't have any skill for inflicting it any more. He was a once-great swordsman who had gone to seed in his old age. Judging by his papery pale face he knew that if his guards were overpowered, it was over for him.

The bully who had trained up and sent his children to fight his battles for him was facing the consequences of his cowardice.

Leda's hands tightened around Pyrrhus's arm as the final guard was felled and her father was forced down on his knees by the rebels. One rebel, dressed more finely and with an expression more bloodthirsty than the others, held a sword to the King's throat.

"Your son Agon burned my village to the ground when he conquered Saint-Trevale," the rebel said, hatred etched on to every line of his face. "I escaped, but my mother and father didn't. It will give me great pleasure to cause Prince Agon that same pain."

He drew back the sword, ready to plunge it into the fine fabric covering the King's chest.

Leda's heart felt like it had stopped. She was about to watch her father die, and she planned to do nothing to stop it. Was she a monster?

Apparently, her sister was not of the same mindset.

"Don't kill him!"

The rebel paused, looking around for the source of the sound.

Ambrose groaned.

Elina stood in the shadowy corridor leading to the ambassador's waiting rooms, the jewelled axe she had been forced to use to behead Sofie clutched in one hand. It was so heavy it dragged on the floor as she stepped forward, but judging by Elina's expression, she was more than capable of using it to its fullest potential.

"I'm going to do it."

Leda sagged against Pyrrhus and he grunted with the effort required to hold her upright.

The rebel with the sword appeared too stunned and awed by the axe Elina wielded to debate her. At the cheers of the crowd around him, he moved reluctantly to the side.

Elina pushed her way through the crowd until she stood in front of the King.

Finally, he spoke. "Elina," he said, voice remarkably steady. Though there were a myriad of emotions on his face, Leda could discern affection. He really did love his royal children. The very thought of her betrayal was unthinkable to him. "Do not do this."

But Elina had a taste for revenge now, Leda could see it in her face. If she hadn't taken on Agon and won there was no way she'd have the courage to even contemplate what she was about to do.

Elina yanked the axe up so it rested on her shoulder, and the King's eyes followed it warily.

"Do you know that you once went two whole years without speaking to me, Father? You barely even looked at me. You didn't care what happened to me, what Agon was doing. I was nothing to you until you wanted to punish Azaria and skipped over her. You forced me to kill the sister I grew up with, the other half of me, who I loved more than anyone else in the world. And in return you gave me hollow treats and prizes, and your demands that I go out and bring you back more wealth. I hope that you *rot* in the netherworld."

Her voice was shaking, but her hand on the handle of the axe was steady.

Pyrrhus tensed beside Leda and she staggered.

There was an almighty thud followed by a horrendous squelching sound.

Eyes round with horror, Leda stared at her father as he slumped on to the floor, every sign of life extinguished. The axe was buried in his chest, blood gushing from either side of the wound. His last expression was one of mild surprise, as though even with the axe held against him he still couldn't believe that one of his children would dare defy him.

Leda noticed with a kind of detached horror that the jewels embedded in the axe matched those lining the King's heavily embroidered jacket.

It was over.

Ambrose was fussing over her then, taking her pulse as the adrenaline began to wear off and pain spread through every part of Leda's body. She slumped against him.

"Silly girl!" The rebel who had held his sword to their father's throat grabbed a frozen Elina by the arm. "The five families swore that I would have the honour of killing the King!"

In his rage he struck her, and Elina fell back with a cry. Blood gushed from her head, and she dodged the rebel's next blow and sprinted towards the door.

"Lina!" Ambrose strained momentarily as though fighting the instinct to drop Leda and run to her sister. He got himself under control in seconds, but Leda could also see the blood seeping into Elina's dark hair as she staggered towards the exit.

Slightly nonplussed after hearing the name he used for Elina, Leda made his decision for him, yanking herself away and steadying herself with one hand on Pyrrhus's shoulder and the other on a nearby table. She had to be careful not to step in the shattered shards of the vase that had once stood on it.

"Go!"

Ambrose didn't argue, sprinting out of the room without a second glance for them. He jumped over the body of the King to get to the corridor Elina had disappeared into, and Leda shuddered, barely maintaining her grip on the table.

Her father was sprawled half across the dais and half on the floor, now staring unseeingly up at the ceiling. His crown, the red jewels encrusted there shimmering like blood, lay by his hand.

Queen Celandine sprinted into the room with the pounding of heels on stone and let out a screech of fury and grief, sinking to her knees next to his body. She didn't succumb to tears, but lay a shuddering hand over the axe embedded in the King's heart.

She lowered her head, and Leda's vision began to blur. The fight continued around them, a horrible clanging of swords clashing, though the rebels seemed to be pulling ahead towards victory. Now that the King lay dead, his guards were faltering, moving towards the exits with panicked eyes.

She saw through a haze that Eber and Azaria had joined them, staring down at their father's body with equally unreadable expressions.

"Elias?" Pyrrhus asked Azaria.

"Dead." Azaria was somehow covered in more blood and fewer injuries than Elina. She carried Elias's ostentatiously jewelled sword in one hand, and didn't seem to notice it dripping crimson in a steady stream on to the ground. "I see that Agon and Father are too."

If she had an emotional reaction to that she did not show it.

She turned to Pyrrhus, who seemed to have nothing at all to say, and handed him the sword. He took it with his uninjured arm in a slack grip.

"The palace forces are all but destroyed, it seems you have won. I'll return to my cell now. Good evening."

Without further ado she turned and made her way out of the room, leaving everyone agape in her wake.

Eber shook his head. "She is the scariest person I've ever known."

And yet, on that night, Azaria saved Leda's life, and those of her brothers and sisters, before quietly going back to imprisonment. Leda would never understand that girl at any point in her life.

That, she was sure about.

CHAPTER 22

*L*eda woke with a pounding skull, groaning slightly at the bright light as she opened her eyes.

Thank the gods, this time she could not hear the rhythmic dripping of leaking water in a dungeon cell.

Squinting, she stretched her arms across the expanse of the huge bed she lay in. It was easily three times larger than her own bed and much softer. She was buried deep in white blankets, her head propped up on a thick silk pillow.

Where in the name of the gods was she?

She blinked at the ceiling. She remembered them all trudging up to the infirmary, Ambrose having his assistant see to her injuries and a very disgusting green concoction being forced down her throat. After that, everything was a blur.

There was no way this was an infirmary bed.

Leda felt the parts of her body that she'd battered on her journey through the river and found that they were tender, but not painful. Her hand caught on a soft collar and she discovered that someone had put her into a silk nightgown. She shifted her right leg tentatively and, though a flare of pain made her curse, it wasn't anywhere near as bad as it could have been.

She propped herself up on her elbows to find she was alone. The last time she'd woken so disoriented she'd been sprawled on the floor of the dungeon, so she was already feeling positive about what she was seeing. The room around her was lushly decorated in rose gold silks and white furs, a small fire burning in the ornate fireplace opposite her.

Leda's bed sat on a small platform slightly higher than the rest of the room, and a glance to her left revealed the source of the bright light. A huge, latticed window over-looked the glittering river as it rushed around the side of the palace. The cold winter sun streamed in from between a gap in the clouds.

Leda needed to get out of there before someone found her and she was punished for sleeping in a bed that wasn't hers. A wave of urgency rising in her, Leda threw off the blankets, crawled across the bed with a grunt at her sore muscles and staggered to her feet.

Her head spun and she was back on the mattress seconds after leaving it, holding on to her pounding temples with a whimper.

She looked around the room for clues about who it might belong to. It could only be a member of the royal family based on the luxuriousness of it all, but it was scrupulously clean and bare. The dressing table had no items on it. Perhaps it was a spare room. Or a guest room. She tried not to feel irritation at the idea of a lovely unin-habited room sitting here while she'd slept in a tiny room in the rafters all her life.

"Hello?" Leda's voice was hoarse from disuse. She could see the door at the other end of the room was open, she'd have to sneak out that way. Her head still pounded and her vision felt hazy around the edges.

The door creaked on its hinges and she dragged herself into a sitting position against the pillows.

Her insides turned over as Pyrrhus entered the room. The sight of him had the events of the previous night hitting her with all the subtlety of a sledgehammer.

Elias and Agon dead. Her father dead. Elina and Azaria allying themselves with the rebels, which precisely nobody had anticipated.

Leda's ceremony was supposed to be today.

She slumped back against the pillows.

Pyrrhus looked as sleek and put together as if he'd just walked out of giving a lecture to her siblings. No one looking at him then could have guessed that he'd nearly drowned less than a day ago.

His clothes were pristine, even more luxurious than usual.

She was happy to see that he didn't choose to preserve the formal distance he usually insisted on, instead coming to sit on the side of the bed next to her. He reached out to touch the bruises that still lingered on her neck, impeccably gentle, and her heart stuttered in her chest. He was alive, and her father was dead. She couldn't believe how lucky they'd both been.

"How are you feeling?" he asked. His voice was gravelly, as though he'd spent the whole night shouting. Something glittered behind him on a table next to an armchair in the corner of the room, but she was too busy looking at him to be distracted.

"Dizzier than I've ever been, but on the mend," Leda said, shaking off his concern. "And you?"

She fought the urge to rip his shirt open and check for

herself that his arm was healed. He caught the direction of her gaze and smiled wryly.

"Never better." He drew his hand back from her. She leaned forward slightly as though to follow it, but stopped herself.

"He's really gone?"

"He is. There will be no ceremony today."

Just as he had promised her last night. Relief hit her with such force that she barely knew what to do with herself, clapping her hands over her mouth to muffle the sob that she couldn't help but let loose.

"It's over?"

Something softened in that solemn expression. "It's over."

Just like that, a feeling utterly unlike relief flooded her body. It was like being drunk, the giddiness spreading through her in an alarming rush. She was free. Her whole life stretched before her. This man was here and he was incredible and he'd somehow saved her life.

He was also too far away from her and, if she wasn't mistaken, she was now free to do something about that.

He clearly wasn't expecting her to tackle him down to the mattress, a hand fisted in his shirt, coming to a stop with her lips hovering just above his. Though his eyes widened and burned with that fire she'd only seen once before, there was still conflict in his expression.

She leaned down, and then paused, her thoughts snagging on a sight that wasn't the achingly handsome man in front of her. It took her a few seconds to process it.

The smile was wiped from her face.

"Pyrrhus," she said quietly. "Why is the Crown of Coronation in this room?"

He closed his eyes, and it wasn't in anticipation of her kiss.

All of a sudden, their position shifted into something more dangerous, more like an interrogation. She lifted her upper body from him, keeping his hips pinned by hers, and her hand twisted in his shirt.

Leda had seen the crown only once before. It was such a monstrosity of rubies, diamonds and gold, tall and thick, that its image had been burned into her brain. It had been kept in the palace vault of treasures since her father's coronation, and she'd been equally repulsed and intrigued when she'd seen it while accompanying Azaria there to pick out some crown jewels to wear for a diplomatic reception.

"Pyrrhus?" Leda's fingers traced the elaborate patterns in gold thread on his shirt. He usually wore plain white. "Why are you dressed like this?"

He sighed, his eyes still closed.

Leda swallowed thickly. "I need you to tell me exactly what happened."

His eyes flew open as she shifted restlessly on his hips and he rolled her off him, hands firm on her shoulders. "You're exhausted, Leda, this conversation can wait until—"

He had risen from the bed but she had beaten him to it, scrambling off and planting herself between him and the door with her hands on her hips.

There was no way he was getting past her. Enough was enough; she would be getting the answers she needed today.

Pyrrhus's eyes traced her nightgown and he looked away to the window, jaw clenched.

"Talk."

He nodded stiffly. "Last night—"

"No," she cut him off, shaking her head. "No, further back. I'd like to know what you did to get involved in a *rebellion*?" she hissed.

"I wasn't involved. I was one of the ones who led it."

"What?"

"When I told you how my family died, I lied. They were high-ranking nobles in the Ariti court in Rivernesse, and were killed when Prince Fynn conquered it a decade ago. I was a teenager, and away studying as I told you. I returned as soon as I heard news of the attack, and I found their bodies rotting in our home. My parents had been tortured." His mouth twisted bitterly. "I thank the gods every day that my brother and sister appeared to have died quickly."

His devastation, carefully hidden for so long, was plain to see. Leda blinked away tears. "I'm so sorry, I had no idea."

"How could you have? I chose not to tell you."

"I understand why you didn't."

"I travelled all through the kingdoms as I continued my studies, and I saw first-hand the chaos that your father and brothers and sisters had wrought. The starvation in Slofray, the crime and squalor in Doviet. Saint-Trevale escaped the worst of it, but I suppose the King wanted to keep his favourite holiday destination as well cared for as possible." Bitterness laced every word.

"Then I met Ambrose, two years after the death of my family. He was living on the streets of Saint-Trevale. I bought him a loaf of bread and he told me his story. He had been a junior prince, low in the line of succession but nevertheless a Saint-Trevale royal. He had just finished studying to become a physician when his parents were killed and he was cast out. We were in a similar position and I pitied him. I brought him with me for my next period of study under a noted academic in Slofray, where he was able to find a job in a hospital."

"You engineered the coup together?" Leda asked. She should have noticed the connection between the two of them that transcended the friendship of colleagues brought together only by proximity. How could she have been so oblivious, so wrapped up in her own schemes?

"Yes, we wanted revenge. Desperately so. We worked together, and we managed to secure the backing of the five deposed royal families from the conquered kingdoms, in exchange for the promise of a fair chance at the crown once your father was gone. It was all for vengeance for our families at first, but over the years it became so much more than that. We saw the suffering of the people, and heard the stories of the ritual slaughter of the Counterparts. It sounded so barbaric we thought it must be an exaggeration. We used my travel between universities in the conquered kingdoms to build contacts with the five families and coordinate small factions of rebellion, until we had thousands of men and women who were loyal to the cause. Between my network and Ambrose's talent for politics and strategy we were able to create a plan to overthrow the King."

Leda started pacing, too much energy flooding her body. "So you infiltrated his palace."

Pyrrhus nodded. "It was easily done. He had heard of me, and had his chief advisor seek me out to join the palace as royal tutor for his oldest children. Six months later Ambrose joined as royal physician when the current one retired. He'd received a large windfall in a game of cards on the outskirts of the city, you see. We drew the armies closer and planned our attack."

There was a hollow feeling in Leda's stomach that had nothing to do with her injuries.

"And I was part of this master plan?" she said grimly, winding her hands together. "Your source of information on my father and brothers and sisters?"

He surprised her with his vehemence. "No. Never. You weren't supposed to have anything to do with this, something Ambrose saw fit to remind me every time he saw me over the past few months," Pyrrhus said, exasperation creeping into his tone. 'I saw you completely by chance from my office window. You were soaked through, yelling about the rules of swimming safety as you pulled Ami out of the water, and I couldn't believe I hadn't noticed you before. From that moment on I watched you become more and more withdrawn. I saw your spark die as your own ceremony approached. I couldn't ... I couldn't let you be alone, after I found you in my office."

The words were lovely, but Leda still felt ill. "Why didn't you tell me any of this sooner?"

"I couldn't," Pyrrhus said simply. "Hundreds of thousands of lives depend on this regime change. I could never risk it by telling someone who is linked so comprehensively to the royal family. You might have gone to your father with the information, and all would have been lost."

"I would never have done that," she said stiffly.

He nodded, "I know that now, and have done for a while. But I didn't want the knowledge to put you in more danger than you already were."

"So that's why you kept pulling away."

"Yes. The plan was faltering, your father's spies had begun to catch on to us. He increased the military presence in the palace and brought your brothers back to protect him. We had to change our strategy fast, take advantage of their weaknesses. We planned a small attack for the feast in honour of your brothers. We intended to fail."

"All those soldiers dying ... that was on purpose?" Leda remembered the sight of their bodies strewn across the floor and couldn't contain her horrified look.

His eyes were imploring, begging her to understand. "They knew it going in; they all volunteered."

She didn't know what to say to that.

"Your father and brothers were complacent after that— they put down the attack easily, and they hadn't lost a battle in decades. It restored their trust in myself and Ambrose.

They went straight to celebrating, as we knew they would, and they dropped their defences significantly. We'd planned to launch the real attack with our thousands of soldiers two weeks later, but ..."

"My ceremony had been moved up."

He ran a hand over his face, the stress evident in the tension of his shoulders. "It changed everything. I bargained with everyone in the rebel army leadership, convinced them that we needed to move our attack forward. We brought the forces we had already amassed in the city, and our spies in the kitchens contaminated the food at the masquerade with small amounts of sleeping solution to put everyone off balance. Ambrose called me a blinkered fool." His mouth curled wryly. "He said that I put our whole movement at risk for one woman."

Leda snorted. Next time she saw Ambrose he would be getting a slap to the face.

"I would make the same decision again," Pyrrhus said firmly, eyes fixed on hers with such intensity she couldn't look away. "You could not be allowed to die."

Leda took a deep breath and turned towards the window, overwhelmed by his words. She came to a stop with her hands clenched on the sill and stared down at the snow-covered grounds.

"So, what happens now? My father is dead, you all won. Which of the five families gets that?" She pointed behind her at the crown glimmering ostentatiously on the table in the corner. It was a hideously ugly thing and she did not want to share a room with it, even for a second.

"For the moment, none of them."

Foreboding crept up on her, and she kept her back to him. "Who gets it now, then?"

"Now ..." Pyrrhus took a deep breath, as though this was the part he was most dreading telling her. "I am king."

She whipped around with such speed her hair smacked her in the face. Awful suspicion had been growing in her from the moment she'd seen the crown, and yet rage surged up inside her as though it had been a complete surprise.

"You're ... you're WHAT?" she said, her voice coming out louder than she had intended.

A guard poked his helmeted head through the open door, and Pyrrhus waved him away. The guard followed the unspoken order with a swiftness that made Leda's mouth dry. She couldn't believe it.

"The five families all have a claim to the throne. Two families from Doviet, one from Saint-Trevale, one from Rivernesse and one from Slofray. It cannot just be given to one of them," Pyrrhus said briskly, as though the faster he talked the better she'd understand. "We needed to install a neutral head of state while a plan was made for the succession. Decisions must still be made in conjunction with other families about who should rule the Five Kingdoms. The representatives of the royal families in the rebellion chose me as their caretaker king until the successor has been chosen."

"Caretaker king," Leda hissed, striding towards him and then abruptly away. "That is the most ridiculous thing I've ever heard! Why would they choose you?"

He gave the crown a dismissive look. "I didn't want to be king, and never did," he said simply. "I was the only one they could trust to give that back."

"You don't want it?"

Underneath it all she was so deeply afraid that everything had been a lie, that he was as power-hungry as any one of her family.

"No," Pyrrhus said instantly and without thought. "When I was young I wanted a simpler life. Circumstances

268

have brought me here instead. It is my duty. I have no desire to be king, of here or anywhere else."

There was a lot Leda wanted to say to that, but she kept quiet. The idea that the man now sitting in front of had become her king, her ruler, that he held the position of her father, made her feel nauseous.

"This throne pollutes everything it touches, Pyrrhus. It's poison."

He did not disagree with her.

A thought slammed into her with all of the subtlety of a speeding carriage. "Wait ...," she said slowly. "If you're king, you have the power to release me. I can *leave* here."

That powerful, heady feeling was back, flooding through her veins once more. She could feel her hands trembling. No more ceremony, no more Azaria, no more oppressive prison of a palace. She could go and live her life on the beach of Saint-Trevale as she'd always dreamed of. She could freely travel to the home that Fayne had promised her.

Pyrrhus was watching her carefully, as if he'd known this was coming, and stood from his seat on the bed. "You'll be in danger if you leave now, there will be significant instability while the regime changes. If anyone recognises you ..."

"The risk is worth it, if I'll be free."

"I do not think so." He captured her hands in his and she stopped her pacing immediately. "Give me three months, Leda. Three months, and then you can go wherever you please."

Her hands clenched under his. "And why should I do that?"

"Give me that time, and I will come with you, wherever you want to go."

Her heart was in her throat. "Why?"

His hand had released hers and was curling around the

back of her neck then, unaware of the trail of fire his touch left in its wake. "You know why, Leda. You know that I can't spend a day without listening to you loudly point out mistakes in books or curse at your knitting or laugh when you lose at chess. And I know that you want me with you, too." His other hand joined his first and he was pulling their bodies together, resting her forehead against his. She let out a shaky breath. "Let me keep you safe, let me plan the trials to select the next monarch, and then I'll give up this throne and go with you. Anywhere."

His lips were so close. She only needed to tilt her face to seal them with hers, to accept his terms. It was so darkly tempting to do so.

Leda shook her head as she broke away from him. She couldn't think when he was that close to her. This was her future they were talking about, new and fresh and completely unmapped. It was important enough to require all of the focus she could gather.

"I can't condone any of this." She pointed at the crown and felt a strong desire to knock it to the ground. "I won't be with someone who is wearing that. Ever. It's an evil force."

That was to say nothing of the gods to whom he would now be beholden. Who was to say they wouldn't pressure him into a bargain even worse than the King's with his Counterparts to keep the kingdom together?

"These are my terms; I will stay here for three months while the kingdom settles and you finish this ... duty. At the end of those months, not one second later, we will leave here, and I will be with you. Until then, nothing will happen between us. I loathe the throne, I will not be remotely involved with it."

She wondered if restricting herself from him would help incentivise him to meet the deadline she'd set. Judging by the vexation in his expression, it might. How very flattering.

She realised she had started to sway towards him again and restrained herself.

He caught the gesture, as he always did, and a small smirk made its way on to his face.

"Very well," he said darkly, humouring her. "You don't want me to touch you for three months? Are you certain you'll be able to follow through with that?"

"Don't look at me like that. I have self-control," she said with more certainty than she felt.

He quirked an eyebrow in challenge. "I see. Well then, I agree to your terms. Three months, Leda. Then we leave."

She went to shake his hand, to seal their accord formally, but he stepped smoothly back from her. "No touching, remember? I hate to see you attempt to break your vow so soon."

He laughed as she glared at him.

Her biting response was cut off as a figure entered the room. A handsomely outfitted man with a large moustache bowed respectfully at Pyrrhus as he would have done for her father, and Leda fought the urge to retch.

"Ever so sorry to interrupt—Your Majesty, you're needed by the council. You'll have to be quick, I'm afraid."

Pyrrhus's sigh was barely audible as he went to pick up the crown and tuck it under one arm.

Leda followed him. "I have more questions!"

"I'm sorry, Leda," Pyrrhus said. "I need to leave."

She had never wanted to throw something at him so badly.

"I'll have them bring you up some food and your medicine. These are your rooms now. We'll speak very soon, I promise."

With that, he disappeared.

It turned out Pyrrhus's promise was not one that he was easily able to honour. Leda had received the food to what she couldn't quite believe were her new rooms and dutifully cleared her plate, barely aware of what she was eating. She could almost feel her freedom upon her, and yet she had just deferred it so casually, for him. She had no idea what was becoming of her.

Dazed by the changes that had come upon her so quickly, she set off into the palace and encountered uproar as workers fixed the damage to the rooms and corridors of the ground floor. Outside, a small army of gardeners attempted in vain to save the bulk of the rose garden. Leda paused in the corridor outside the throne room to watch a servant scrubbing blood from the marble floor and furiously stamped down on the urge to cry.

She had seen so much blood, it lingered behind her closed eyelids, she didn't need another memory to add to those.

CHAPTER 23

*I*t took only two weeks for Leda to begin to realise how wrong she and Pyrrhus had been.

This would not be a quick and easy transition. The crown could not be so easily passed on.

Most times Leda attempted to speak to Pyrrhus, guards blocked her way. His new head guard was Atticus, who knew her well enough by now not to fall for Leda's arguments.

When she saw him on that first day after the rebellion she remarked that he'd hidden the fact that he was a traitor well. He'd scowled at her, and then suppressed his laugh.

"I thought I was successfully manipulating you into being on my side," she'd said grumpily.

"You did very well, Leda. Trust me, if I hadn't already been part of the rebellion you would have won me over."

He was probably humouring her, but it was nice to hear all the same. She'd then embarked on making arguments that she should be let in to see Pyrrhus. He'd stared at her with an unimpressed face until she talked herself out, and told her to have a nice day without letting her anywhere near the door.

Pyrrhus was in council meetings until the evening, and then at a private dinner with the new army generals. The next day, he was in discussions with the five families to agree the design of a series of trials that would determine succession to the throne. Then, he was riding out into Gemdark to make speeches to the people.

He sat at dinner in the banquet hall one evening, surrounded by reams of paper and his economic advisors. He did not so much as glance at Leda when she entered and settled herself at one of the communal tables. There was a ring of empty seats around her, the nobles too wary and skittish to sit close by. They didn't know how to treat her now that she wasn't a Counterpart, doomed to death.

The fact that the ceremony was no longer looming made Leda feel like a ten-ton weight she'd carried for her entire life had been lifted. She was lighter and freer than she ever had been and yet was jittery and nervous. She almost didn't believe that something so good could have happened to her and her brothers and sisters, and spent days in continual worry that the other shoe was about to drop.

She almost groaned one night as one inhabitant of the palace braved the risk of sitting next to her.

Elina dropped herself into the seat beside her with her usual grace, tossing her sheet of thick, perfectly styled hair over one shoulder as she did so.

"I haven't seen you at the temple in weeks, sister," Elina said.

Leda struggled to keep her tone polite. "I've been busy."

"Too busy for the gods that have given you life and prosperity?"

"Yes, too busy for them."

"You should thank them for saving your life."

"I seem to remember you being one of the people who

274

saved my life, Elina. Oddly enough I didn't see any gods there," Leda remarked. "I should be thanking you instead."

Elina looked like she didn't quite know what to do with that, and waved a hand as though she could bat the words away. She'd clearly come here spoiling for a disagreement, and Leda being nice was no way to get there.

Elina watched Leda's gaze flick over to the high table and she harrumphed. "Of course, why spend time praying to honour your gods when you can salivate mutely over a man who pays you no attention?"

Leda wondered what the consequences might be if she stabbed her fork into Elina's hand.

It might just be worth it. She could brave a few nights back in the dungeons.

Instead, she held the delicate threads of her temper together.

"I can only admire your piety, Elina," said Leda sweetly. "One day I hope to live up to your example."

Elina did not believe a word of that. "Careful, Leda, the gods wield more power than you know. Our father was wrong about many things, it's why he had to die, but his goal to spread the worship of the gods out to the Five Kingdoms was a noble attempt to better millions of lives. Don't provoke the ire of the gods."

"I've had their ire my whole life, sister. If they want to curse me further they can go ahead, I'm used to it."

Elina turned to look out of the windows at the bruised purple of the sky and the rain beating against the glass like thousands of insistent fists.

"You are a fool, and you are tempting fate."

~

It did not take Leda long, faced with her newfound freedom to roam the palace and do what she wished, to realise she had no idea who she was. She'd had the identity of Counterpart stripped from her, and once the bone-deep relief had faded she'd been faced with the fact that it was a shield she'd strapped to herself for her entire life. What was her personality, beyond being the pitiable sacrifice who lived on borrowed time? What were her goals and dreams? Did she want a family, a settled life? Did she want to be alone? What occupation did she really want to pursue?

She posed those questions to herself again and again, and all her mind was filled with in response was chilling silence.

Being trapped in the palace certainly did not help, the walls bearing down on her no matter where she went. She felt suffocated, even when outside in the gardens and breathing the chilly air of early spring.

After a few days of Pyrrhus's avoidance, where Leda alternately sat across the room at pretended not to look at him or sulked in his deserted study, and further days filled with reading, sewing and stilted conversations with the other Counterparts, she finally cracked and decided to visit Azaria.

The dungeons beneath the palace were bleak and dreary as ever, the walls dripping with condensation.

Leda glowered as two guards who had taken to following her around everywhere for her protection shuffled noisily behind her as she made her way down the stairs.

The cells were full of guards, servants and nobles who had not accepted the new regime, and it took Leda a couple of minutes to locate Azaria in her new cell near the end of the long line in the dungeon. She'd certainly made it her own, adding an actual bed and a plush rug.

Leda paused as the guard at the door unlocked it for her, and stepped in a couple of paces, scanning the small room.

"Why are you still in here?" Leda asked. "Pyrrhus will let you out, you know, after what you did for them in the battle."

"I'd rather watch the dust settle from here," Azaria said, putting down the book she'd been reading and straightening up in the armchair she'd had brought in. "What happened to the others? Our family?"

"Pyrrhus sent the queens back to their homes, under guard to ensure they don't get themselves into trouble," Leda said. Pyrrhus hadn't had time to tell her this himself, of course. She'd heard it from Eber, whom Pyrrhus seemed to like. He'd certainly permitted her brother to speak to him with a frequency that she was apparently not allowed.

Leda tried not to burn up with jealousy about it, that would be petty.

"My mother?"

"Back to the temple in Lymialake."

Azaria nodded shortly.

"Our brothers and sisters?"

"Princess Elina is here still, she's not being punished for killing our father, though she spends most of her time in the temple now, doubtless praying for absolution." From gods who weren't listening to a word she said, in Leda's humble opinion.

"Princes Caspari, Elov and Fessler have been sent home, as well as Princesses Annagret and Gabriell. As for the Counterparts, Markus, Ami and Mira are still here, Eber is keeping an eye on them. Mistress Aina used the opportunity to escape during the fighting, not surprising given she was so heavily pregnant. No one's been able to find her since. No baby, no Counterpart creation ceremony. Gabriell will be the first of you with no Counterpart."

Azaria didn't seem particularly fazed by that. "The other mistresses?"

"Also dispersed to their homelands, with allowances to support them. My mother apparently insisted on staying, though. Pyrrhus is soft-hearted about evicting her."

She was looking forward to taking him to task about that one.

Just as Pyrrhus was avoiding Leda, she avoided Olora. Her mother had been seeking her out in increasingly desperate ways for days, but Leda had managed to evade her at every turn. Having guards on her side made the world of difference this time around, they were able to warn her when her mother was approaching and block the entrance to her rooms when she tried to enter.

"No doubt Olora wants to be near you for a reason. She likely anticipates the benefits of being mother to the next queen."

Leda looked sharply at her sister. "Excuse me?"

"Don't be evasive, Leda. I can hear the guards gossiping. It seems everyone has noticed the way the new king watches you when he thinks you aren't looking. They know that he's installed you in opulent rooms around the corner from his, and that you have a protective detail of guards hovering around you. I imagine he is not affording the same privileges to our siblings."

"He's only going to be king for three months," Leda said slowly. "He and I aren't ... we're ... nothing is going on." She refused to say 'yet', though it lingered on the tip of her tongue. "No one's going to be queen."

"You would say no if he asked?" Azaria asked idly. "That would be foolish, sister. You must secure your future. Your power would be absolute. And if you think he's only going to be here for three months, you're more fluff-headed than I thought."

Leda had some choice things to say about Azaria's words, but held her tongue.

"You're wrong," she said, and she disliked the way it felt like she was trying to convince herself. She and Pyrrhus had an equal need to leave this godsforsaken palace and live their lives, independent of the horror of the monarchy.

"Are you quite sure of that?"

All of a sudden, Leda was finished with the conversation. The thought that she was free to leave the cell whenever she wished was gratifying, and she stood up, albeit with difficulty. She didn't miss the way Azaria's eyes dropped to her injured leg, expression unchanging.

"It is still functional?"

"Yes. No thanks to you," Leda grumbled. She had recently learned it had taken Ambrose and a team of three other physicians to heal the nerve damage and get her back to a place where she was able to walk on it at all after her sister's attack.

"Good."

Knowing that was the closest thing to an apology she would ever get from Azaria, Leda nodded briskly. She turned to leave.

"You will visit me again?"

Leda paused. "Probably every day," she admitted. "Pyrrhus is avoiding me, Ambrose is busy with Elina, Eber appears to have been drawn into the new king's inner circle, the servants fear me and the courtiers watch me like I'm a circus performer. Talking to you is refreshingly normal. Leave the dungeons soon though, alright? You absolute lunatic." The last part she mumbled under her breath.

Azaria said nothing, watching Leda leave the cell with an unreadable expression on her face.

~

Leda watched from a distance as Pyrrhus set about his rule for the first month, ejecting most of the previous king's advisors and bringing his own in from around the lands. He seemed to be forming a new and complicated style of government that awed the newspapers with its ambition.

Leda's ambition was a little more limited. She'd decided to learn horse riding, and her instructor informed her that she'd taken twice as long to master the basics as anyone she'd ever taught, and on the most docile pony she'd ever known. Even so, Leda was pleased with her efforts once she overcame her abysmal balance, and trotting around the palace grounds on Willow felt so much more freeing than walking.

Meanwhile, Pyrrhus was convening frequent meetings of the representatives of the five families and mediating endless disputes about the trials. Diplomats streamed in and out of the palace at all hours to debate and sign treaties that would validate the process.

Leda wasn't sure how she felt about the candidates who had descended upon the palace and were now vying for the throne. All came with impeccable lineage from before their families' crowns had been stolen by her father, and all were slightly disconcerting to be around.

There were the three Ariti brothers from Rivernesse; young, intelligent and extraordinarily tall. They were charming and erudite and could always be found at the centre of a laughing crowd in the banquet hall.

There was Melia of the Red Mountains in Slofray, a renowned priestess of the Grand Temple who sent Elina into paroxysms of excitement whenever she appeared. She had beautiful cherry-red hair and wore fur shawls so enormous her silhouette was three times bigger than it would ordinarily have been. Leda could have sworn she'd seen her before, but couldn't for the life of her place where.

Linus Bolsh, a dour and enormous man of few words, represented South Doviet, while Thalia Bakirt, a thoughtful and unassuming woman, represented North Doviet. They both brought with them families who interacted with the court not at all, keen to keep to themselves.

And then there was Zephyr Bixel, who just so happened to be Ambrose's twin brother and heir to Saint-Trevale. Though they sported the same handsome face and waves of blonde hair, Zephyr's eyes were entirely black, and he moved in a twitchy, suspicious manner. Given Ambrose's descent into an even darker mood after his brother arrived at the palace and the fact that they did not sit together at mealtimes, Leda gathered their relationship was not a close one.

None of the candidates paid the remotest attention to Leda, and she was quite happy with that.

Despite feeling trapped in the palace by the deal she had struck, Leda had technically never had more freedom. She was able to roam the palace and grounds at will, and was even allowed into the palace library, from which she'd been forbidden her entire life.

It was a striking, cavernous and yet hushed room with black shelves bearing gold-bound books on every possible topic. Silver statues of the gods guarded each aisle and desks and settees lined the outer walls. It was more imposing and austere than Pyrrhus's library, and Leda spent days whiling away the time between the shelves with Eber and Ami, who had declared their intention to learn to read.

It had not escaped the palace's notice that Leda was suddenly being treated much better and was walking around the palace with new confidence. The courtiers, a generally spineless group, had quickly switched their allegiance to the new ruling order, and didn't seem to know how to treat her now that she was more than just a Counterpart.

She was royal but not royal. Free, but not yet able to go anywhere or be her own person, considering she had no idea who that was.

On one of Leda's visits to the dungeons Azaria told her that she'd heard from the guards that rumours were swirling about her relationship with Pyrrhus despite the fact that they had barely spoken in weeks. It seemed they were taking bets on whether he intended to court her, or if he had done so already and disposed of her. Leda's profanity-laden response had received an eyebrow raise from her sister, and the subject had been promptly dropped.

As mid-winter drew to a close, Leda reached the end of her tether with Pyrrhus. When he wasn't in council meetings or riding out to the nearby towns on progresses he was surrounded by people at all times of day and night. He didn't visit his old study, even to collect the belongings he'd left behind.

From what she could see from across whatever room they were in, he looked dead on his feet exhausted.

She'd thought that they would struggle to stay away from one another, that her resolve not to engage in anything remotely romantic with him would be viciously tested over the three-month period. She'd forgotten to account for the pure intellectualism with which this man attacked any task. He wanted to honour their deal and stay away from her until she would allow him to touch her, therefore he avoided her completely, and thus any temptation.

It was spectacularly well played.

Leda's frustration was in direct contrast to most of the palace. Everyone was calm, soothed in a way they had never been when her father strode the halls. Eber was bright and happy, as were her Counterpart brothers and sisters. Ambrose looked more relaxed than she'd ever seen him, and Elina was always near him in the infirmary as she used her botany skills to help him prepare remedies. Azaria continued to be oddly pleased to stay down in the dungeons, with no demands on her time, no need for socialisation, or expectations that she be polite.

Pyrrhus's decisions as ruler had led people to believe that he was firm but fair, and a suitable interim leader until the question of succession could be determined. Leda had even overheard one courtier saying to another that he wished Pyrrhus would stay in the long term, and she had frowned deeply as she passed them.

It was time to talk to Pyrrhus, if only because she missed him. She'd taken for granted all the time they'd had alone for the months before the coup—all those hours they had wasted sitting opposite each other in silence. Even when they managed to exchange a word or two in a corridor or after dinner he was stalked by advisors in his periphery, whispering in his ear.

One evening Leda left dinner early in a huff when her mother had arrived and attempted to engage her in conversation. She went up to her fancy new room and retrieved a basket, wanting to get as far away from the woman as possible. She was going to rip some hibcus flowers apart, that should make her feel better, and she needed to replenish her supply anyway. She spent an hour out in the freezing woodland trying to get a grip on herself and steadfastly ignoring the guards watching her from twenty feet away.

She'd collected so much hibcus she was debating giving some of it to Ambrose for his own remedies when she glanced up at the palace. The sky was an inky purple and there was little moonlight. She could see the flickering lights in various windows, though most appeared to be doused as the hour was so late. Her gaze caught on a particular window that she couldn't deny she'd been searching for on the third floor. To her surprise, light flickered there.

Unless she was much mistaken, that window sat behind the desk in Pyrrhus's study. He was in there. How strange, he had his own elaborate king's office now with room for all of the advisors who clung to him like shadows. She couldn't think why he'd revert to his old one.

With a stab of excitement she thought that probably meant he was alone.

Perhaps she should go and check on him, just to make sure he was alright. Leda carefully avoided the thought that he had a whole palace worth of servants and courtiers who would be only too happy to do the same.

With a sigh, she heaved up her basket, arranged her shawl tighter around herself, and made the journey up to his rooms. Thankfully the guards, her own ever-present shadows, peeled away as she entered the building. That removed the need for her to tell them to leave her alone.

The first thought Leda had, standing at the top of the steps leading down into Pyrrhus's study, was that he looked utterly exhausted. He was indeed alone, as she had expected. Every inch of his desk was covered in papers, a stack of books piled up on one side so high she was surprised it hadn't toppled over on to his head.

An ornate, slightly tarnished sword lay on top of a cabinet in the corner, and Leda realised she'd seen it before and had dismissed it as some artefact he must have been studying. How thoughtless she'd been; it was the sword he'd used in the battle against her father and brothers. He must have practised with it frequently and she hadn't paid the slightest attention to it moving.

He barely seemed to notice her entrance as she came

down the stairs, sparing her only a quick glance before turning back to his work.

She put down her basket of hibcus, not missing the nasty look Pyrrhus cast at it, and approached him. He was slumped to one side in his seat, face grey with fatigue. With a rustle of skirts, Leda crouched at his side.

"When was the last time you slept?" she asked softly. Judging by the dark circles under his eyes, the answer was certainly not 'last night'.

With all the time she'd spent pretending she wasn't looking at him, she had no idea how she hadn't caught his exhaustion.

Pyrrhus threw down his quill in frustration and rubbed his hands over his face. "There's too much to do. The Five Kingdoms are in turmoil, Leda. I need to arrange to sell off parts of your father's estate to fund the new ministries we're creating, which is fine, but ..." He shook his head at the paper before him, losing his thread completely. "Where in the world did he get *this much gold?*"

Leda opened her mouth to say something facetious but Pyrrhus was already muttering the answer to his own question, an academic through and through.

"Stripping all the valuable materials out of the Red Mountains of Slofray, no doubt. It's ridiculous, I ..." He looked down at Leda, properly, for the first time and the words died in his throat.

"What?"

He took so long to blink she fought the urge to wave a hand in front of his face.

"Nothing. What are you doing here? I thought you were staying away."

"I saw the light from the window, I came to see if you were alright. It's really late, Pyrrhus."

He didn't appear to be listening. Seemingly without

thought, he reached out and ran a hand over the soft material of the dress covering her shoulder. Even in this state, he was careful not to touch her skin. "You look beautiful in silk. Those dresses they used to make you wear ..."

Pyrrhus trailed off, and that coupled with the way he'd touched and spoken to her told Leda he was all kinds of sleep-deprived.

Her breathing a bit more laboured than it normally would be at the compliment, Leda stood to her full height, holding out her hand. He shot her a suspicious look.

"This is just me being a friend, it's not breaking any rules. Take my hand," she said in the most reassuring tone she could muster. "You're going to bed, right now." She pulled him out of his seat, glad that he appeared too weary to argue.

She pondered guiding him to the bedroom attached to his study, as it was only a few feet away, but was wary of him sneaking back to work as soon as she turned her back. Decision made, she led him through the corridors and to the palatial rooms that had been given to him as king. She was thankful they weren't her father's, that would have been too maudlin.

She had been surprised to discover a few weeks ago that Pyrrhus's new rooms were only a corridor away from her own, positioned almost protectively between her room and the rest of the palace.

It was just over a month until they could leave, and then perhaps they could share a room. Her blood went hot at the thought.

Pyrrhus was staggering by the time the guards pulled open the doors to his rooms and allowed them to enter. Leda had a hand wrapped firmly around his upper arm, and led him through the richly decorated sitting room and into his moonlit bedroom. He made his way towards the enormous bed and collapsed back on to the thick furs piled atop it, eyes closed and fully clothed.

How had he let himself get into this state? How had she not stepped in sooner? He'd been at this for nearly two months, had he had a full night's sleep for any of it?

Leda stood with her hands on her hips, torn between leaving and helping him. Pyrrhus certainly wouldn't leave her in that state, so that made her decision for her. With a sigh, she moved over him and began unbuttoning the ridiculous tiny buttons at the front of his tailcoat. He murmured when she did so, and sat up reluctantly when she jostled him so she could pull it off him.

Leda's face felt like it was on fire, but she pressed ahead with divesting him of his shirt. It was one that she'd made for him after the oil he'd used to heal her had stained one of his old ones beyond repair. She knew because the stitching on the cuffs was a little askew, a source of endless frustration for her while she was making it. Something in her stomach clenched when she saw it.

Leda kept her gaze firmly averted from Pyrrhus's muscled chest as she placed his clothes on top of the settee by the window. His trousers she wasn't stupid enough to attempt, she was keeping her vow after all, but she removed his shoes and socks with little trouble.

She coaxed his grumbling form to the top of his bed and his head on to a pillow. Kneeling on the soft mattress, she lifted the largest fur and wrapped it around him. As she made to move away, she felt a pair of hands wrap around her waist.

"Leda." His eyes were still closed, voice gravelly, and if he were half asleep she wouldn't have been surprised. She froze in his grip, all the air leaving her lungs. She hadn't been touched like this in months. "Stay," he mumbled into his pillow, hands still firm around her.

She waited a second and then tried to move off the bed, and his hands slid from the silk of her dress and on to the mattress.

"Stay with me," he sighed, voice barely above a whisper.

She looked down at his relaxed face, paralysed by her indecision. She shouldn't under any circumstances stay, she wanted nothing to do with a man who sat on the throne of the Five Kingdoms. But she knew deep down there wasn't a chance that she was leaving him when he'd asked her, at his most vulnerable.

Eber had told her at dinner that servants were whispering about the new king having nightmares, and that the guards reported that he sometimes called out her name. It pressed on her conscience. She wondered what he was remembering, whether it was the moment he'd seen Thorodin holding a knife to her throat. Or perhaps it was watching her be whipped at her father's orders, helpless to do anything about it.

If Leda was partially responsible for his torment, then she was going to do her best to help. Maybe if he knew she was next to him he wouldn't be afraid for her and it would do something to help with the nightmares.

Or maybe she was just desperately searching for an excuse to stay, she thought with a frustrated snort.

By the time she made her decision Pyrrhus was fast asleep, his breath coming slow and deep. She removed her heavy silk outer dress, leaving her in a plain white chemise that fell past her knees. She watched him, marvelling at his peaceful face, as she drew the pins from her hair and laid them on the table beside his bed.

She doused the final candle on the mantelpiece and crawled next to him, laying a respectable distance away. It was easy to do in such an unreasonably expansive bed.

She could do this, it would not break her rules.

Unfortunately, Pyrrhus chose that moment to utterly obliterate them, along with any remaining tatters of her self-control.

As if he sensed her presence, his arm snared around Leda's waist and pulled her flush against him, rolling her so that his chest was pressed against her back. She took a sharp inhale of breath as his knees pressed up behind hers. The feel of the lines of him against the length of her body was a shock to her senses, the heat of his skin burning against her through the thin material of her chemise.

Leda gulped, all of a sudden very overheated despite the cool air in the room.

With an incoherent mumble Pyrrhus dragged his fur over her to make sure she was covered, and something squeezed painfully tight in her chest.

She thought it would take her a while to get to sleep. She'd never slept so close to anyone before, but the soothing sound of Pyrrhus's rhythmic breathing and the feeling of sheer safety lulled her into unconsciousness.

When Leda awoke, she blinked blearily to see that it was still dark outside, perhaps very early morning. Pyrrhus was on his back, a deep frown on his face, and twitching. She lifted her head from where it had been placed on his chest and scooted back. She had not recalled draping herself across him like that. Clearly sleeping Leda didn't have the inhibitions that awake Leda did.

'Leda.' Pyrrhus was still dreaming, he had no idea she was there. Despite the dimness of the room, she could see that his face was crumpled. He sounded distressed, and she was instantly alert. "Leda!"

She went to him immediately, heart breaking at the sight of him. "Shh, it's alright."

She laid a soothing hand over his forehead and pressed her face into the crook of his neck. "You're alright. I'm safe," she whispered, stroking a hand through his dark hair, brushing her fingertips across the curve of his cheekbone. His face relaxed under her ministrations, and with a grumble he settled back down. The arm slung around her back tightened, bringing her head down on his chest.

Crisis averted, Leda closed her eyes and willed herself to sleep once more. This time, it was more difficult.

~

"*Leda.*"

The first thought she had was that this was different to the nightmares, this time the word was groaned into her ear.

Leda woke to the feeling of lips at the dip where her neck met her shoulder, surprising a soft gasp from her. She was warm and comfortable, her legs tangled in the bedclothes. Pyrrhus lay behind her as he had been when they'd first gone to sleep, but this time was different. There was the pressure of his hips pressed tightly against her, one hand flat on her stomach to anchor her to him as his lips brushed across her neck. She felt the muscles of his chest through the material of her chemise and shuddered.

"Pyrrhus," she said on a sigh, going from sleep to wakefulness faster than she ever had before. When she rolled to face him, fully intent on getting her hands on him herself, her eyes met his sleepy ones and they widened almost comically.

"Leda?!"

He was halfway across the bed between one second and the next, his breathing unnaturally fast.

Her arm was outstretched slightly as if she had half a mind to drag him back to her. She let it drop to the mattress with a thud.

"Leda, I ... I apologise." Pyrrhus dragged a hand through

his rumpled hair, mouth open as his eyes fell to the loose white fabric chemise she wore, leaving much less to the imagination than the dresses he normally saw her in. "I ... what are you doing here?" His gaze moved up to trace the unbound hair curling around her shoulders and he swallowed, standing up from the bed.

They absolutely could not have this conversation while he was shirtless, because how dare he sit at a desk for most of every day and still have muscles like that?

Leda hurried to explain, mortified by his surprise at finding her in his bed and stamping down on the urge to tell him how much she approved of the way he'd woken her up.

"You asked me to stay with you last night. You were half dead with exhaustion. You had a nightmare and I ... helped you through it." Well aware that she was blushing furiously and that he could easily see its progression from her cheeks to her neck to her chest, Leda kicked off the furs and scrambled out of the bed. "I'm really sorry, I thought you'd"—she cleared her throat as she searched for her discarded dress— "I thought you'd remember."

Pyrrhus still looked dumbfounded, and she couldn't tell if his dilated pupils were due to alarm or something else as his focus remained completely on her. She wanted to spring immediately from the room. What had she been thinking, staying here? *Of course* he wouldn't be happy to see her there when he woke up, he spent most of his days avoiding being alone with her as it was. That was what they had agreed. She was such an idiot.

She stepped quickly into her dress and pulled it up and over her shoulders, lacing it loosely behind her. She scraped her hairpins off the table into one fist, knowing that her hair would need proper tending to in her own room.

"I should go."

She couldn't remember ever being so mortified, and she

was furious with herself for how her eyes caught on his shoulders, his chest. Her mouth was dry as she stumbled gracelessly towards the door.

That seemed to bring him back to life. "No, Leda, wait—stay, please. I've missed you." He ran a hand through that deliciously dishevelled hair.

She softened. "Me too, but I shouldn't have done this, I'm sorry. One month left, and then we'll leave and we can ..." She'd never blushed so hard in her life, it was quite possible her head would explode with the pressure of it. His expression flickered and he dropped the hand that had reached out for her. "Anyway, I'll see you later."

Leda knocked once on the double doors, waited for the guards to open them, and swept out with as much dignity as she could muster. She knew the rumours about where she'd slept would be sweeping the palace in minutes, and chastised herself again for being so stupid. She'd been far too accustomed to existing in a bubble with Pyrrhus that no one else had noticed, or at least she had thought so.

That wasn't the case any more, she needed to remember that.

CHAPTER 24

*L*eda finished her chimney.

And she didn't quite know why.

Well, she suspected she did know, deep down. But she wouldn't let her mind take her there, wouldn't allow it to dissect her reasoning.

Still, carving in the final hold had given her a profound sense of satisfaction that had her quivering. It was the biggest, strangest accomplishment of her life. Her father was no longer a threat, but even so, if anyone wanted to stop her leaving, she had an option before her. Just having it there provided a level of comfort.

That was one of the few bright moments in her days as they ticked on and on with no sign of change in the palace. Pyrrhus was still remote, working himself to the bone. Her siblings were still fighting, unsure what to do with this new mix of freedom and lack of purpose. And the nobles continued to satisfy themselves with the delights of court life.

Rather irritatingly, the weather seemed to be mirroring Leda's increasingly morose mood as those weeks stretched to months and the final day of her three-month bargain with Pyrrhus came and went, unremarked on.

The sky, laden with ominously purple clouds, had taken on a sadistic streak, alternating between driving rain and howling wind that kept the court inside most days.

Leda also noticed the increased number of guards following her from when she left her room in the morning until bedtime, the rattling of their armour announcing her long before she stepped into a room. Sometimes there were so many they could barely fit across the corridors, and they had to troop in a long line behind her. Leda held her tongue and said nothing, biding her time until she could tell Pyrrhus off.

Eber found the whole situation uproariously funny.

Not that Leda had managed to get any time with Pyrrhus over the past week without his advisors staring at her, counting down the seconds until she would leave.

She could tell by the drawn, tired look on his face as she tracked him down on the final day of their agreement that he knew as well as she did what day it was.

Her father's crown had shone from his head and Leda was visited by the urge to seize it and smash it on the ground. He'd shaken his head minutely at her and she'd walked away with more than a little unsuppressed anger.

She knew she was unravelling by the way her body craved hibcus more than it had in months. She was still taking the medicine Ambrose provided her with, which perfectly counterbalanced the reduced dose of hibcus she was taking so she could wean herself off it. But the oblivion of a full dose called to her nonetheless.

Leda ruthlessly stuffed those thoughts into the back of her mind with great effort.

In a clear, but better-targeted, act of madness, Leda went

to spend the day after the end of the three-month bargain with her siblings.

They had gathered together on the floor of the empty banquet hall, the picnic they had planned ruined by snow during a season no snow belonged in. Elina was sitting elegantly on the floor, trying to teach the youngsters some of her favourite prayers to the gods, and Eber was making comical noises on his flute at the most sober parts.

Leda had the pleasure of watching Elina try and fail to control her temper as the children roared with mirth. The atmosphere soured when Elina loudly compared Eber's laugh to the barking of a golden retriever, and they dispersed shortly after.

Leda had hurried to catch up with Eber as he'd strode back towards his rooms, tapping his flute against his thigh.

"He's not abdicating any time soon, is he?"

Eber shortened his stride so she could keep pace with him, and she was struck by how quickly he'd shot up in height over the past few months.

"Why would we want him to? He's good for us, Leda. Good for everyone. Let's give the families time to battle it out. We've got all the time in the world now."

The nearby windowpane rattled with a boom of rolling thunder that nearly made Leda jump out of her skin.

"The throne corrupts, Eber," she said anxiously. "None of us should be anywhere near it."

"You worry too much," he said jovially. "Everything is fine, now, Leda. No more bowing and scraping in the temple every day, no more creeping around trying not to be noticed. Father is gone and the ceremonies are over and we can live!" A shadow, a glimmer of fear, crossed his face and was quickly replaced by his ever-present smile. "We have to actually figure out what we're good at now, what we want to do, but I'm sure it'll be easy. We'll work it out together."

"I might not be around for very long, Eber."

He looked around at her so fast he seemed to wince from cricking his neck. "I know you've said that before, but we need—"

Eber cut himself off mid-sentence, and then disappeared around a corner so fast Leda was left gaping at the empty spot he had occupied seconds before.

A rustling along the corridor told her what was coming, but she'd known before she looked up. With their father gone and Caspari away from the palace, there was only one person who could make her brother abandon whatever he was doing and sprint in the opposite direction.

Leda would have done so too, if she'd had more warning. She was not equipped to deal with this conversation when she was in such a toweringly bad mood.

Olora's skirts were a shock of shimmering silver. She looked bright-eyed and vivacious as she came to a stop in front of Leda, the new regime clearly suiting her. The pallor that had been on her skin all the time that Leda had known her had disappeared, which made sense given she was no longer confined to the basement for most of the day.

Lightning streaked across the sky through the window that framed her.

"Mother." Leda made to bow her head and move away, but was stopped by Olora's surprisingly strong grip around her forearm, yanking her back into place. Leda pulled her arm away, but remained standing there.

Damn, foiled so easily. There was no way she was getting out of this conversation.

"It has been difficult to seek you out when you've been prowling around in pursuit of the king at all hours," Olora said, following Leda's gaze back towards the throne room. "You're nothing if not predictable, Leda."

Leda scoffed. "You'd have to know something about me to predict my actions, mother."

"I know as much about you as it is possible to know, Leda," Olora said, her eyes lighting on Ami and Markus as they crossed the palace entrance hall ahead of them, tossing a ball back and forth between them and laughing. "And Eber and Ami. I kept my distance from all of you, to keep you safe. Mistresses were not allowed to socialise with their children."

"Those who cared found a way," Leda said dully.

Olora inclined her head in the smallest of nods. "Yes. The truth of the matter is that I did not know how to bond with you."

"You never tried."

"You're so wrapped up in your own misfortunes, Leda. Did you never consider it might have been difficult for me too?"

That got her attention. "What do you mean?"

"I was seventeen years old and still living with my parents in Slofray when the King noticed me during one of his visits. He was parading down the lime walk and stopped when he saw me in the crowd. I was young and beautiful and in love with another man. We were to be married the following week. I was happy."

Olora's eyes were glazed as she looked at the hustle and bustle of servants moving past them, lost in her memories.

"The King chose me as his next mistress. My betrothed tried to resist, but he was beheaded for his ... ungraciousness. Do you know the real reason he chose me?" Olora asked bitterly.

Leda floundered in response. "Your youth? Your looks?"

Olora shook her head with a bitter laugh. "While they undoubtedly helped, that wasn't the reason. He said the gods had given him a sign that I must be his next mistress.

You see I had inadvertently stood between two ancient oak trees, and on branches either side of me sat two crows. He always had an obsession with crows; harbingers of sorrow and joy, he called them," she said snidely. "And so the decision was made. He was compelled to have me."

"Mother—"

"I was brought to the palace, buried down there in the basement, and had to compete for his affection with his other wives and mistresses. Each year I did not produce a Counterpart for him, I was a disappointment. Eventually I had a child, a boy."

"You did?" Leda said, horror creeping over her. She had always thought herself to be the oldest. "When?"

"Two years before you. He would have been Princess Evia's Counterpart, but May was born just before him. You know, the King had no use for illegitimate children who were not needed as Counterparts. I named him Galen the day after he was born, and the following night they drowned him in the river, as they did to all children who did not fit the pattern," Olora said, her voice catching. "Galen was not *sacred*. For all that you, Eber and Ami had a terrible lot in life, your father did at least consider the three of you blessed, part of his great plan."

Leda had no idea what to say. It felt like someone had opened her chest, taken hold of her heart, and squeezed it viciously. "I'm so sorry."

It struck her then that if the King was killing off the spare illegitimate children, then it was unlikely he had a group of them he could use to replace an errant Counterpart. Instead he'd just used the threat to keep them all in line.

Olora waved a hand as though Leda's apologies were inconsequential. "I could not bond with a child who would grow up away from me only to be killed, let alone three," she said bluntly. "Your brother's death nearly finished me. I did not have the luxury of loving my children. I would have been like Elsbeth," she said, naming the mistress who had taken her own life after her Counterpart children had been killed.

Olora grabbed Leda's elbows roughly, pulling her forward so that they stood facing one another.

"I'm sorry for all that I have done, Leda," Olora said urgently. "Just know that it was never because I found anything lacking in any of my children. I simply don't have the capacity to care for you, it was burned out of me. Even now, when there is no danger, and the kingdoms are safe, I can't summon it back."

Leda dipped her chin in a nod. It hurt so much that she wanted to curl up on the floor in the corner, but she kept her head high.

"I understand, and I'm so sorry for what you went through. But please, please don't ever say this to Ami and Eber. It will break them."

Olora stared at her, tears glistening on that lovely face, and nodded.

Leda walked away.

A week later a few coins to one of Atticus's less morally upstanding colleagues revealed that the king would be staying late in the throne room. Apparently he and Ambrose were discussing measures to clear up the devastation from the uprisings against her father's forces in Rivernesse and Saint-Trevale. Knowing it was an important conversation for both of them, Leda generously allowed them an hour before she entered the throne room.

She dreaded what she was going to say; it was a pit in her stomach.

They didn't see her at first, and had thankfully moved on from their political discussion.

Pyrrhus seemed to have stopped listening to Ambrose and was now staring into the middle distance from his throne. A quill dangled from one of the his hands, but she couldn't see any paper around for him to write on. He looked seconds away from falling asleep.

"There are *eight* guards following me right now!" Leda's voice rang through the cavernous, empty space.

Pyrrhus sat bolt upright on the throne and Ambrose jumped a clear inch off the floor, rearing back at the sight of her as though a demon had swooped into the room.

One of Leda's guards attempted to enter behind her and she placed a hand on his metal breastplate, shoving him back out into the corridor with the others. She slammed the gold doors to the throne room in his face with two great booms of sound.

She could see the dark circles under Pyrrhus's eyes from all the way over there, and her stomach ached, but she had to remind herself that he had brought this on himself.

Pyrrhus looked at her with a kind of reluctant fascination, colour blooming in his deathly white face. It was unfair that he could be going through this amount of physical degradation and still look better than any other man in this damn court.

Ambrose had the exasperated look of a person who had wasted a good deal of the past hour arguing. He strode up to the dais on which Pyrrhus sat and dropped a very long scroll into his lap.

"Just consider it," he said gruffly, before pointing at Leda, who froze on the long walk up to them. "Not her though, for the love of the gods."

Something sparked in Pyrrhus's eyes. Even now, resplendent in his royal attire as he sat on the throne, Leda could see the changes in him. He sat at a slanted angle as he had that night she'd found him in his study and put him to bed. Holding himself upright was clearly a struggle.

Though the expression on his face was neutral as he scanned the scroll Ambrose had passed him, she knew enough of Pyrrhus by now to know that he was not at all happy.

"This conversation is over," he said icily.

"You need to provide stability for the Five Kingdoms, Pyrrhus!" Ambrose said, equally vexed. He ran a hand through his hair and, judging by its state, that had not been the first time he'd done so. It seemed Pyrrhus's intractability had the same impact on Ambrose's temper as it did on Leda's. Finally, something they could see eye to eye on.

"It was always the agreement that I would only be king for a matter of months. I am the caretaker," Pyrrhus said from between gritted teeth. Leda resisted the urge to remind him that it was in fact three months, and that they had passed.

Pyrrhus moved restlessly on the throne as though the seat were uncomfortable. "This is unnecessary—"

Ambrose threw his hands in the air, his exasperation evident. "Don't be naive. You think the Five Families will reach their decision on the trials within *months*? They can barely stand to be in the same room without drawing swords as it is!"

Ambrose followed Pyrrhus's gaze to Leda and failed to keep the frustration from his face. He looked at her like she was the source of every single one of his problems.

"Good evening, Leda," Ambrose said with a small bow that she knew cost him greatly. "I believe the king and I have reached the natural end to our conversation, so I will leave you to speak." He cast said king a dark look. "Pyrrhus, remember what I said. After all that we've done and sacrificed to get here, don't forget your duty to the people now. Don't be a fool." He was looking at Leda as he said that last part.

Leda barely noticed Ambrose leave the room, her attention fixed on Pyrrhus. She had to force herself not to feel sorry for him. He had brought this on himself. She eyed the scroll in his hand as she approached.

"What's that?"

"A list of names of eligible noble and royal ladies throughout the kingdoms. It was curated by the previous king's advisors for his sons' marriages." Pyrrhus looked down at the paper as though he dearly wished to set it on fire. "The council proposes that I choose a queen to rule by my side, to provide *stability*." His mouth twisted around the word. "Ambrose agrees."

Leda was visited by the immediate desire to call Ambrose back and deliver a kick to his shins.

"I see," she said. She had to crane her neck a little to see him, up on the dais as he was. "An interesting suggestion given how soon your abdication should be. Any tempting prospects on that list?"

He gave her a look she could only describe as sour. "Not at present."

"That's a shame," she said, ruthlessly stamping down on the relief that reared its head deep in her mind.

"What can I help you with, Leda?"

There were so many things she wanted to raise with him, and the topic of their escape from the palace hung uneasily in the air between them, but she settled on first airing the grievance that was causing her the most trouble.

"I want you to tell your guards to leave me alone, they've been stuck to my back, trailing me all over the palace."

Pyrrhus didn't look moved by her request as he dropped the list of potential wives on to the table next to him with a sigh. "They are there for your protection. They will remain."

"No." She stepped up on to his dais and she stood directly before the throne, no more than a foot from his knees. "You need to call off your henchmen. Two of them tried to follow me into the bathing room this morning."

"They're keeping you safe!"

"They're driving me insane!"

"Leda," Pyrrhus said, eyes closing. "I don't know what I would do if you—" He cut himself off again, and she could have roared with frustration. "If I die, Leda, whether it be through an uprising or assassination, you'll need to—"

Leda loomed over him. "*Assassination*?" she blurted. "Is someone trying to assassinate you!" She looked down at the fruit plate on the table beside him with wide eyes and then around at the empty room. "Tell me they're testing your food for poison! Where's your taster?"

"Yes, of course, and I'm fine," Pyrrhus said reassuringly, grabbing the white fist of her hand as she nearly knocked his apple clear off the plate. "I have a plan for you, if I'm killed, to keep you safe."

Oh no, they were not having this conversation. Leda shook her head. If he kept talking like that she was going to overturn his plate into his lap.

"I seem to remember once demanding that you stop trying to save me," Leda whispered, gently sliding her hand from his. "I'll be fine. Besides, you won't need to worry about it if you're still around, so make sure you don't die. Pass on that crown and we won't have a problem."

She did not like the guarded nature of his expression, not one bit.

"Your guards will remain, Leda."

She sighed. It was all moot anyway, she didn't know why she had even bothered to protest.

It was time to confront the ugly, unspoken truth that had been the force pushing him away from her over the past few weeks.

"For how long, Pyrrhus? Because I don't know about you, but I've noticed that three months have come and gone and you're still stuck to that throne as though glued to it. And it's taking its toll on you, as I said it would. I've heard of no new king or queen who will assume your responsibilities, and if an invitation to your abdication has been issued it must be lost in the post because I certainly haven't seen it."

He gave her a withering look.

Leda stepped closer, the skirts of her dress touching his knees, and took the ornate golden crown from the top of his head. The jewels embedded in it sparkled ostentatiously.

Maintaining eye contact with him, knowing no one else in the palace would dare to consider what she was about to do, Leda threw it clean over her shoulder.

It landed a few feet behind her with an almighty clang of metal on stone and bounced. Pyrrhus looked absolutely horrified.

"Leda!"

She leaned forward and took his face in her hands, smoothing her thumbs over those sharp cheekbones. He was a formidable leader, a king with power over millions, and he looked completely lost in her grip. "Pyrrhus."

"You're supposed to address me as Your Majesty," he said in a pale approximation of reprimand, but he seemed thoroughly engrossed in her as she leaned closer.

"I will not call you that."

A silent battle of wills played out as they stared at each

other. Her eyes fell to his parted lips and she ruthlessly forced them back upward.

"Come away with me," Leda said. She was pleading now, this was what she'd been reduced to. "This palace, this court, is wrong. Neither one of us can be happy here. We agreed. *Please*."

For a second Pyrrhus looked so tempted that she thought she might have convinced him.

His next sentence thoroughly deflated her. "I will, I promise, it's all I desire. But there is too much to do here first to ensure that people are safe and well. I just need three more months."

Leda's hands fell away from his face and she straightened up.

She saw her future in front of her as surely as if it had been set out in oils by the court painter. She would measure her captivity in this palace in years, not months, as she waited for him to make the kingdom safe enough to pass it on to the right person. He would approach it as methodically and meticulously as he did everything, and the fact that he was such a martyr would ensure that the circumstances would never be perfect enough.

On top of that, and worst of all in Leda's view, he was popular. The court liked him, his advisors tripped over themselves in praise of his intelligence and steady demeanour, and the people found him charming. They were in no hurry to be rid of him.

And Leda? She would give in to her explosive attraction to him in mere days and they would be together; she would be as close as it was possible to be to the corrupting influence of the throne that she hated, watching from an intimately close distance as it changed Pyrrhus and stripped away all of the good qualities that she loved so much about him.

He would suffer enormously, be in continuous danger, and she would be a spectator.

She would achieve nothing for herself, she would waste away in this place, never achieving anything. All her days would be filled with waiting, yearning to hear him say he was finally ready to abandon all this and go with her.

It would make her pathetic, and dependent. That was a person she could not be. She refused to even contemplate it. This was not what she had escaped her ceremony for.

Even if it was a selfish decision, it was the one she had to make.

"I won't trap myself here, even for you," she said quietly.

Leda went to move away, but Pyrrhus had anticipated her move and followed her. He snatched up her wrists, yanking her back down to him. His mouth crashed on to hers and she didn't know if it was him or her or just gravity that sent her slamming down on to his lap. She whimpered as he bent her over the arm of the throne, his hands plunging into her hair as he ravaged her mouth.

It was nothing Leda had ever experienced before, something hot and drugging burning through her veins like liquid fire. She grabbed his collar with desperate, shaking hands to pull him impossibly closer.

She knew exactly what he asked of her with his kiss. He wanted her to stay, he wanted her to be with him. He wanted her to drop their deal, to bet on the fact that the throne wouldn't change him, and that they could be safe and happy while he occupied it.

No.

Leda's eyes blinked open and the garish gold of the throne filled her vision, bright enough to blind her. It took more effort than she would ever admit to rip herself away from him and stagger to her feet.

Pyrrhus let her go, leaning against the back of the throne

and regarding her with heavy-lidded eyes. The view she had of him was almost indecent, he was the picture of desire and authority and power and Leda was quite sure it would be burned into her brain for the rest of her life.

He was fierce, panting heavily, fists curled on the arms of his throne.

Leda breathlessly tried to smooth her hair into some sort of order and pointed one of the hairpins he'd dislodged at him as she stepped down from the dais.

"That," she said glacially, "was against the rules."

"Well, I already broke one rule, so I thought it wouldn't matter if the rest were discarded." He was scanning her face intently, awaiting her response.

He'd asked her something with his kiss. She had to give him a resounding no. She had to save herself.

It nearly broke her to do it.

"I'm leaving."

Pyrrhus was as close to speechless as she'd ever seen him.

"Leda, don't. I just need more time."

"I'm so sorry, I can't."

She turned her back on him and withdrew from the room.

'You're leaving,' Azaria said flatly, arms entwined through the bars of her cell. Her hair was still thick and shiny, skin unblemished and dress pristinely clean. Her cell was decorated more lavishly than the first time Leda had seen it, with more rugs and throws, a bookshelf and a second armchair for when she presumably got bored of the first one. It could have been any lady's sitting room, aside from the bars stretching along one wall.

"This afternoon."

"You promised you wouldn't leave me."

"I know."

Azaria was silent for a moment.

"Where are you going?"

Leda pressed her lips together, staying silent. She cared for her sister, deep down, but would never make it possible for Azaria to find her again. Just as Leda had told Pyrrhus the palace was toxic for them, she and Azaria had the same issue with one another.

They were fiercely protective of each another, but hurt each other more than they helped most of the time. They needed to be apart.

Leda rested a hand on a bar of Azaria's cell. "Don't try and follow me."

"You don't have to worry about that. What you should worry about is a battalion of Pyrrhus's guards following you wherever you go, dragging you back to the palace the moment he thinks you're in danger."

Leda's heart caught in her throat. "He wouldn't do that."

"There seem to be a lot of things you thought he wouldn't do that he is currently occupied with. Ruling our father's lands, for one. And for significantly longer than anyone expected."

Azaria did not react to the stricken look on Leda's face.

Leda shook her head, though she couldn't dislodge the wariness that had flared to life within her. There was a distinct likelihood that she would be followed, if not by Pyrrhus then by his enemies who might use her against him. If there were a chance, however slim, that she would have her freedom taken away from her and be brought back here or imprisoned somewhere else? No. It couldn't happen. She was severing ties, no matter how much it hurt her heart to do it. They would need to be fully and completely cut.

She knew what she needed to do.

Did her sister?

"You need to decide what you want to do with your life next, Azaria. Though I'm sure the palace will have some sway over that."

Thankfully her sister was easily distracted from their previous topic of conversation. Something like amusement appeared on Azaria's face. "They're worried I won't resist the compulsion to conquer foreign lands? My birthright?"

Leda snorted. "They don't think you'll convert immediately to a pacifist lifestyle, Azaria, no. Despite the fact that you have incarcerated yourself here for no reason."

"You'd be surprised." Azaria tossed her head. "In a way, we're both free. Free of our parents, we can move on."

There it was, the confirmation of what Leda had always suspected. Azaria had loathed their father as much as she had. Being favoured made no difference to the abuse that Azaria had suffered for being his daughter, both at his hands and at those of his enemies.

"I care a lot about you," Leda said, pressing her cheek against one of the cold bars. "You know that, right?"

Azaria tipped her head in the barest of nods.

She wouldn't say it back. Leda wasn't even sure if she was capable of speaking the words. That part of her had been irreparably broken by her torture as a child.

Leda gave her a small smile before backing away from the cell, turning away from her sister for the last time.

That was the thing about Pyrrhus, he could always find her in a crowd, the only person who cared to. His head lifted as if Leda had called for him, his gaze moving unerringly to meet hers over the heads of hundreds of courtiers. She saw him take her in, standing framed in the ornate doorway to the banquet hall as everyone gathered for lunch, and the pull of his forehead into a frown as he took in her plain woollen travel dress. He tipped his head to the side, the rest of the room forgotten despite the fact that it clamoured for his attention.

The way he looked at her, the intensity and fire within his gaze. She couldn't take the risk that he'd be corrupted by the power that sat draped around his shoulders. Couldn't risk his enemies tracking her down like her father's enemies had once done to Azaria.

She couldn't walk out of the front doors as she'd hoped.

But she had one other option.

Time seemed to slow as she shook her head at him. She blinked furiously, refusing to allow any tears to escape. This was goodbye. She couldn't say it to him, not properly, or she wouldn't be able to go through with it.

He was halfway out of his seat by the time she turned around, a spike of adrenaline shooting through her. Lifting her skirts, she ran to the staircase and ascended, making her way to Azaria's rooms as fast as she possibly could, driven by the echoing sounds of the guards trailing her.

She slammed the door to her and Azaria's rooms neatly in their faces, grabbed her satchel from beneath the table, and hurried through to the cold, dusty room that had once been her sister's bedroom. On the far side stood the door to Azaria's expansive wardrobe, more than twice the size of Leda's own bedroom. It was filled with so many elaborate dresses that it had its own door leading to the servants' staircase, allowing them to move in and out without disturbing the princess.

Leda slipped through the door into the staircase and waited with bated breath. Silence surrounded her, both from the room she'd left and the stone steps above and below her. The guards would find her escape route, not that they could stop her if she wanted to, but she'd rather avoid the confrontation.

Leda padded down to the door to the fourth floor, across the corridor and back up towards the armoury.

She was choosing freedom. Her whole life stretched out ahead of her, everything she'd ever dreamed ready for her to grasp it. She couldn't wait for anyone else to allow her to do it. She'd never forgive herself if she did. She would not waste away in this godsforsaken palace even if the man she loved decided to.

It was time to use her chimney.

AFTERWORD

Thank you for reading Counterpart, I really hope you enjoyed it!

Reviews mean so much to authors, particularly those of the debut variety, so if you liked Counterpart please consider leaving a review.

Look out for Conspirator, book two in The Gemdark Dynasty series, set to release in spring 2023.

Can't get enough of Counterpart in the meantime?

Join the mailing list at www.EllaPyne.com for a free bonus chapter from Pyrrhus' perspective on the first time he saw Leda. You'll also get special access to sneak peaks, bonus content and information on upcoming releases!

Printed in Great Britain
by Amazon